The King of Ningxia

People change. So do countries.

By

Lanny Morgnanesi

To Lucy and Dante

Special thanks to Ellie Reader-Popjoy for copyediting this manuscript.

LANNY MORGNANESI *is a career journalist living in suburban Philadelphia. He has worked as a reporter and editor at newspapers in Pennsylvania and Florida. In the mid-80s, he served as an editor in Beijing at The New China News Agency. His short fiction has been published in The Fredericksburg Literary and Art Review, Ripples In Space, The Bangalore Review, Spire Light, and in anthologies such as Stories and Poems in the Song of Life, and Soulmate Syndrome. Nonfiction essays appear on his blog at NotebookM.com. Occasionally, he makes short documentary films.*

1. The Big Ask in The Big Apple

New York City, 2005

Duke Amici, a failed businessman, sat in a coffee shop at New York's Waldorf Astoria and shared nostalgic half-smiles with a woman wearing designer clothes and carrying a $43,000 Hermes red pink crocodile handbag. In just a few minutes, Duke would ask her for money. Lots of money. For now, both worked hard to control their expressions, exhibiting some past affection while maintaining distance and discretion. For more than a moment, while she talked of cabs and city traffic, he imagined her as she once was, not as one of the richest women on Earth, not as the person who recently bought the American landmark they sat in. No, he saw a young college student, an aspiring poet wearing the faded blue clothes of a worker and standing in a dank, dusty dormitory hallway lit by a single bulb.

It was a vivid mental picture, that dormitory at the Foreign Languages Institute in Beijing, China, a modest mess, considering the college's great prestige. At that time, in 1984, the Communist revolution was 35 years old; market reforms were beginning, Western investment was happening, production was up, modernization was evident. Even so, the dormitory looked like a third-world prison.

"I want you to meet my roommates," he recalled her saying.

He felt so foreign, so out of place, yet he was excited to be there, in a place few Americans had been. Seeing and learning. Getting the truth. Bridging the distance and the distortion between them and us. China's new cadre of leaders wanted this, and that's why he was there as a guest worker. If it also happened that he met a few women, well, that would be fine, too. And he had.

Her name was Song Mei. At the Waldorf, she went by Emily Song, the American name she had taken, with "Emily" a nod to her favorite American poet. At the dorm, he and Song Mei squeezed into a room no bigger than a tool shed. There was hardly a place to stand. On opposite sides of the room were triple-tier bunk beds made of unfinished wood. The mattresses were thin and shoddy. A fine dust covered everything. Freshly washed underwear hung on a line to dry. It dried quickly in Beijing, a city with almost no humidity. This little den of poverty was part of the reward for the top language students in a nation of 1 billion people. Who knew that one of them, maybe more, would conquer Manhattan.

In Beijing in the '80s, when guest workers like Duke wandered off into places they were not expected, they were treated like visitors from outside the galaxy. In the dorm, the other five women looked at him with intense curiosity and a degree of fear.

There were introductions, some very small talk, and then an exit by Duke and his poet friend into the concrete hallway and down eight flights of concrete steps. As they descended, with her leading the way, Duke wondered how she felt about him. He assumed any ambitious English major would be drawn to any American who could help with her English and be a gateway into an American university. Was there a secondary attraction? Did she like his looks, which weren't bad for a Caucasian? Did his personality translate? Chatty. A little jokey. A mix of upbeat and serious and – like her – an appreciation for literature, films, and art.

It was difficult to know. She had been his tour guide on a journey through the unknown and strange. He believed she had been honest and sincere with him, not a manipulative arm of something unseen. He felt she liked him, and, in an act of balance, he would try to make sure she didn't start liking him too much. When his two-year contract at the New China News Agency ended, he intended to go home, alone.

To her disappointment and tears, he did go home alone. Two decades later, here she is again, not a poet but a commanding force, a representative of something that had not existed when he first met her. In Beijing, he was the catch. No longer. Time and circumstance made him the supplicant. Once, she thought her future depended on him. His future now depended on her.

In the beginning, he called her Song Mei. Toward the end, he used the more affectionate Mei-Mei, but only for a short time.

Now what would he call her?

"You're Emily, right?" he asked.

"From Emily Dickenson," she said. "But I haven't written poetry in years. The name is the only poetic thing about me."

"You've been too busy accumulating a fortune," he said, moving the unmentioned to the forefront. "And you're drinking coffee, not tea." Emily Song also ordered a pork dumpling appetizer.

"I think it's better. Easy to get, with so many coffee shops, even in China."

"You're no longer a vegetarian?" he asked.

"No. How did you remember that?"

"I still feel bad about you wasting that Big Mac and going hungry at the embassy party. Well, how do I look?" he asked. He wore a striped dress shirt, gray wool slacks, and black shoes, which he shined. In China, he mostly wore sneakers, jeans, and khaki Banana Republic shirts. Clean and tidy now, back then his hair was long and shaggy and he had a beard.

With a cold stare, Emily Song focused on his eyes and the theatrics they were performing. She pulled back a few inches.

"You're older than I expected. Hair grayer than I expected. You're not as charming as you once were, and you carry the imprint of defeat. You looked better with a beard, more artistic."

"Brutal but accurate. You, however, look regal, a fixture in the heavens." He liked the way she smelled, a rich perfume of — what was it? — roses? In Beijing, sometimes — not always — Song Mei carried the unpleasant scent of cheap rapeseed oil commonly used for cooking. "What's that perfume you're wearing?"

"Jo Malone London, Rose and White Musk Absolu. I know you'll ask. It's $300 for 100 milliliters."

In between the rapeseed oil and the Jo Malone, there had been the rare letter and the even rarer phone call. Without letting on, they followed each other in the news and, more recently, online. Without his help or knowledge, Song Mei had come to the U.S. as a Ph.D candidate at the University of Pennsylvania, near his family's home. In a surprise phone call, she asked him to visit her in Philadelphia over a Labor Day weekend. It was the first Duke had heard from her since the goodbye at the airport. He was caught totally off guard by the call.

"But I'm in Florida now," he told her. "And … I'm engaged."

She ignored or didn't hear the last part.

"You have a car, don't you?"

"I'm eight hundred miles away."

"We have three days. That's enough time. You must be off for the holiday."

"I don't think you understand how far away you are," he said.

The call ended unpleasantly. He didn't even get her number.

In some respect, in the Waldorf, it was as if that phone call had just ended. Her English, always good, was now almost perfect. Her slight British accent, imparted by teachers who learned British English, remained, adding to her natural charm. The charm still came through, only with a hardness. Duke Amici sensed that hardness, and when he looked at her, he thought mostly of money, her money, and whether he could get some of it. In an unvisited mental recess, however, there was a faded, jaded, whimsical thought: Did I ever love her?

Probably not. But he liked her. The idea of an off-limits, exotic girlfriend had put him in a trance that did not break until the day he left.

Did she love him? Again, probably not. He was like some prince, a special person with intrinsic powers from a special place that was far away and beyond the reach of people like her. Her plan, thought through night after night in her crowded dorm room, was to have him rescue her, uplift her, open her world. Song Mei felt she needed him to secure her destiny, and that fate had supplied him. Time proved she didn't. Time proved that her strength, assisted by the rushing tide of history and the wild success of Chinese commerce and industry, would be enough to get her almost anything and take her almost anywhere.

And so, with everything on her side, the person who was arguably the third richest woman in China agreed to this coffee shop reunion. In old times, she would have written a poem – in English – about the anxiety and anticipation, about the expectations and the chance for either disappointment or exhilaration. But, as she admitted to Duke, she no longer wrote poetry, and the outcome of their meeting was not in the balance. It was strictly her decision, and that decision had been made.

Song Mei, as Emily Song, decided to give him the money needed to save his bankrupt company. Years ago, Duke had, for all practical purposes, saved her father's life. She was in his debt. This would make them even. In return, however, she would take a controlling interest in his company. If he didn't like the terms, she didn't care.

"How did you come to name your company ... your failed company?" she asked.

"Do you like the name?"

"I don't understand it. Why that name?"

The name of the business was Ningxia Enterprises. Ningxia was Song Mei's home province. Her family roots were there in that heavily Muslim, mostly backward desert province. As a young man, her father, working through a rigid meritocracy, fought his way out of Ningxia to cosmopolitan Shanghai, where Song Mei was raised and learned to speak Shanghai dialect. Then came a setback. During the Cultural Revolution, her father, a top surgeon, was deemed a counter-revolutionary and exiled back to Ningxia. Schools were closed and Song Mei, like millions of young city people, was sent to work on a farm, an attempt to reeducate and reignite revolutionary spirit. Because of her father, Song Mei held a low status on the farm.

"Maybe the company name was a way to remember you," he said. "Also, because of you and your sick father, I did some ridiculous things to help him out that in the end, unexpectedly, netted me the seed money for my company."

Song Mei swallowed hard, looked off to a far wall and said, "What you did was the most touching thing anyone has ever done for me."

In truth, the name for Ningxia Enterprises was directly related to Song Mei's plea on the day in 1986 when Duke left China. They went to the airport together and she begged him to stay, telling him that together they could have a great life in China. They could move back to Ningxia, where there are no foreigners. He would be unique, special, in demand, respected beyond all others, elevated to a status he could not imagine.

"I will make you the king of Ningxia," she said, in tears.

He never forgot that. As CEO of Ningxia Enterprises, he fancied himself its king. Song Mei's prophecy realized. If she invested, that would make her the queen.

Duke drank the last of his coffee. "The company name is to help remember you," he insisted.

"My impression is you don't remember enough," she said.

"I remember you looking good in the shabbiest of clothes. Your clothes didn't matter. It was the way you walked that caught my attention. In designer clothes, you're another person. Still, even today, the way you walk, you could stroll into Saks wearing peasant garb and they'd still sell you that purse."

"I never buy such things."

"And yet, there it is."

"This was a gift. I had three more just like it. Also gifts. I didn't need them, so I gave them to the wives of important officials whose approval was needed for my projects. In China, relationships are the key to success. Relationships are built on free dinners, lavish vacations, non-stop giving, and favors for favors. You haven't reached that point in America, or at least haven't acknowledged it. You keep it in the shadows."

"The smart ones understand," Duke said. "The dumb ones like me don't. We learn the hard way."

"May I hear your version of how you went broke?"

How to tell it without looking like a fool?

"You know I'm a journalist by trade," he said. "I knew nothing about business, what it requires. When I got home from China, I met an old friend, Jimmie. An odd fellow. He was a high school dropout, a former heroin addict. Mostly homeless. He slept on the street or on people's couches, did some jail time, joined a religious cult. He has the gift of an over-active, inventive mind. He has a natural understanding of mechanical engineering, heat transfer, and refrigeration. In effect, he is a genius. No one could guess this from his appearance. I was one of the few. As kids we'd play baseball. He'd explain the game in terms of physics and geometry. He was 12 years old."

"You feel quite comfortable among the lower classes, don't you?" she said.

"Right, a member of the Chinese Communist party insulting a working man. How fitting."

"This you misunderstand," Emily Song said. "The party is run by and for the elite. The ideology is a ruse."

"Anyway, I felt sorry for my old friend Jimmie. I was single then and let him work in my garage. After months of tinkering, he produced a remarkable machine. It takes in air and removes the moisture. Using minimal energy, it produces enough drinking water for an entire family. The machine is ideal for the developing world, for places in Africa where women trek three or four hours each day for drinking water they carry home on their heads."

"And someone stole your machine because you didn't have enough guan xi to protect it," Emily Song said, using the Chinese term for "connections." "You had a patent and felt safe, didn't you? People today, especially in high-tech, say patents are worthless. Things move too fast."

Duke had not expected this kind of conversation with this particular person. This particular person once spoke in images and metaphors, colors and shapes, of dream-like worlds that could never exist outside the mind. Her words now were too real. She had been a woman living apart from reality. This new specter was anchored in it.

"I'm going to take care of the 'guan xi' problem," he said, "after we are re-funded and fully operating again. I've got a connection that will work. For us, the patent probably was the proper move. What I didn't know then was that a patent must be successfully defended in court. We didn't have the money for that."

"Is it true you gave your machine to Menlo Industries?"

"We didn't give them the machine," Duke said, offended. "They stole it. One of their representatives saw it at a trade show and wanted to license the technology. Naturally, we loaned them our prototype … a prototype is a …"

"You no longer have to explain words to me," Emily Song said.

"Really. Out the wazoo. Do you know what 'out the wazoo' means?"

"No."

"Then I still have to explain."

Emily Song appeared impatient and unnerved, but interested in Duke. Her inconsequential gestures told him: I'm happy to be here, I'm happy to see you again. "Can you please continue?" she said.

"So, we lent Menlo the prototype. They were going to evaluate it and decide whether to license the technology and build their own machine, which would have been great for us. Then they returned the machine, said it lacked the proper sophistication, were unwilling to license it and built their own -- based, we claim, on our design. Menlo used its massive marketing and distribution networks to sell their machine cheaper than us. Then they buried us in lawsuits. Bankruptcy followed."

Emily Song put her hand up and requested the check.

"And what will it take to get you out of bankruptcy?"

Duke had his number, yet hesitated.

"Modestly, I think, after some changes, we could do it with 1.2 mill."

Emily Song's expression was blank. She rolled on.

"What is your plan for the 'guan xi?'"

The last thing he wanted was to get his wife involved in anything remotely related to Song Mei, but this was necessary.

"My wife," he said with an uncomfortable tone. "She has a very distant relative. She doesn't know him well, but we see him at least once a year at family gatherings. I've spoken with him. He's a nice guy. It's her mother's, brother's, ex-wife's second husband. The brother, fortunately, gets along well with the ex-wife and is friends with her new husband."

"Can you make this faster? I have to be somewhere." She didn't.

"Two years ago, this guy was elected as a United States senator from New York."

"That's promising. It's what you need. What does he get?"

"I'm assuming if you invest in Ningxia Enterprises, you'll require 51 percent ownership."

"You're not such a bad businessman after all," Emily Song said.

"Your 51 percent will come out of the 82 percent Jimmie and I own. That leaves us with 31 percent. From our share, we will give 11 percent to our friend in the U.S. Senate and put him on the board.

There are rules in the Senate about gifts and board positions, but we can finesse them and make it all work. He will be our protector, looking out for our interests and his own. With his help, we can win against Menlo in court and maybe even open up markets abroad. This is something I should have done two years ago."

Emily Song's minimal nod was taken as approval.

"You were smart to think of Africa," she said. "Generally, Americans have not been smart about Africa. My country has been heavily involved for decades. First with modest aid, university scholarships, goodwill, and friendship. Since then, we've constructed high-speed railroads, bridges, dams, highways, power plants, irrigation systems. We've pulled Africa up. We buy raw materials from them. Someday soon you are going to need African cobalt for the batteries in electric cars. You won't get it. We will have it all."

Duke Amici felt stupid for himself and his country.

"Sure, but when African countries make war, they kill each other with American weapons. I take it then that you're in, that you're my new partner," Duke said.

"I think I can convince the Chinese government to buy your – our – machines and distribute them in Africa as tokens of good will," she said. "I'll have my investment back in no time."

"One mill two?"

For the first time, Emily Song looked directly at Duke, seeing him as she saw him once before.

"My father is 91 years old," she said. "He lives because of you. Through your little intrigue with the Russians, you got him the heart medicine he needed. When you left China, my government, out of respect for your help against the Moscow crowd, awarded my father his medicine for life. Of course, now I could buy the company that makes it. Back then it saved him. A person who does what you did, risking your freedom and maybe your life, doesn't do it casually. I know that. I just wish I knew a little bit more about why you did it. No matter. I'll be putting in three million American dollars. That's how much my people say you need to turn things around."

A deep exhale. A huge grin. A string of humble thank yous. Even an apology for taking up her time. Duke softly grabbed her hands and shook them as a deal sealer. After five seconds she pulled away.

"No matter what you claim, the company's name is ironic," Emily Song said.

Duke was too happy to argue but said. "I didn't mean to imply anything about us with that name. It's just a good name. I like the x sound. It has a modern ring."

"The irony has nothing to do with our relationship. The name is ironic because this machine, designed to bring water to the thirsty, is named 'Ningxia' yet it won't work in Ningxia because Ningxia is too dry. A desert. That's all. That's the real irony."

The meeting was coming to an end. She was slow in getting up and clutched her bag.

"You own this place, the Waldorf. Right?" he said, smiling like a young man trying to impress a first date with a gag. "Do we have to pay for the coffee? Let's run out on the check and see if they stop us. Then tell them who you are."

"It's an investment group. I'm part of an investment group that owns the Waldorf."

Silence followed as Emily Song gathered up her things. Duke tried to reopen the conversation with something else.

"Do you remember when I first kissed you in the Friendship Hotel?" he said, then immediately wished he could take it back.

Emily Song reached into her $43,000 Hermes red pink crocodile handbag and placed $50 on the table. Paying cash was unusual for her, since a tech company she acquired had developed China's most successful pay-by-phone app.

"I'm an old woman now," she said. "I don't talk nonsense. My lawyers and my CFO will contact you in two weeks. They'll have all the details. I'll expect an office that is at least as nice as yours, hopefully better."

No longer poorly dressed, no longer without makeup, no longer a vegetarian, and no longer hopelessly infatuated with a young American, Emily Song walked through the hotel's grand golden lobby and out the opulent, art deco doors using the same engaging gait once displayed on the dirty, dusty streets of Beijing. In addition to the $50, she left behind the smell of roses. Duke took a deep breath, not leaving until she was in a cab and out of sight. The roses were now a new way to remember her.

Five blocks away, on 45th Street, the corners of Emily Song's lips turned slightly upward, in a way only she could perceive. By 35th Street, they had returned to a more business-like position.

2. The Trash Stealer

Beijing, China, 1984

Old Red looked at the much younger man, saw a bit of himself and said, "They hurt me, but they won't hurt you."

The younger man, in China now for about three months, hadn't been sleeping. His host nation of 1 billion people was just starting to develop, just starting to modernize, just starting to experiment with free markets. Yet it was still broken down, withered, dirty, backward, rigid, authoritarian, very communist and — for the foreigners living there --something to be at least a little frightened of. The young man took what Old Red said as a good sign. It was no guarantee he would go unpunished, but it counted for something. Just getting an audience with Old Red was a coup. A rough-edged former New Yorker, Old Red had lived in China since being stationed there in World War II. He was about as close as an American can get to being a Communist Party insider.

"You're a guest. They invited you here," he told Duke Amici, a 29-year-old journalist who had taken an editing job with a government-run news agency. "You work for them and get paid very little. Most important to them is that when you go home to the States, you'll tell everyone how special the experience was, that the Chinese are not a bunch of monsters, that they are real people, clever and ambitious, with a role in the future that will rival their pivotal role in the ancient world. No, they won't hurt you. It was different when they hurt me. Completely different."

Duke nodded while his mind drifted. He had hoped to avoid problems in China, to try to understand it and its government, to be liked and maybe even respected. Yet without even being fully acclimated, there was this poorly played error, this atrocious blunder. The old man had assured him nothing would come of it and in an hour or so he would know the truth. Following lunch, he was headed for a special meeting with his boss, where the topic surely would be his recent indiscretion.

Over lunch, after ordering, there was five or 10 minutes of small talk then the pointed directive, "Tell me about the girl. She's the real source of your problem. Right?"

Upon his departure for a country that once was his country's mortal enemy, Duke's friends had asked, "Suppose they don't let you out?" He never once thought that would happen, until now. The Chinese had been kind, but they also were kind to Old Red before they put him in jail.

Duke came to China, only recently opened, out of curiosity and the need for adventure. He was bored working as night editor at his old newspaper, and when he stumbled upon the opportunity to work in Asia – through a university connection -- he took it. Businessmen, visiting groups, scientists, educators, and entertainers were being welcomed in, but unconnected foreigners were still a novelty. It was a time when the country was poor and undeveloped but headed in a new direction, with many possibilities. For the average Chinese, any contact with the West and the English language was desirable because it was clear the East was turning toward the West and successful Western ways. One leader, signaling an opportunistic departure from communist dogma, explained, "It doesn't matter if a cat is black or white as long as it catches mice."

And so, foreigners were treated well. They were treated special.

Duke was mindful that the special treatment and regular flattery he received could compromise his judgment. He vowed to keep his wits and allegiances. Then came the lapse and confusion about whether he would ever see home again.

"You're pretty confident about me avoiding arrest or punishment," Duke said to Old Red while sitting in the worn yet glamorous Beijing Hotel. "Why?"

"Well, I have a sense for East-West conflict resolution," the older man said while digging heartily into his pork dish. After decades of practice, he still lacked finesse with chopsticks. "I've seen the harsh and the gentle. We're going through a gentle phase now. It'll be all right. Trust me."

"Yeah," said Duke, who ate very little. "Gentle smiles but iron fists. You can sense that."

"At the very most they'll kick you out," Old Red said. "No jail time for you."

Old Red was balding. Even when he had hair, when he first arrived in China in the '40s, it was not red. He was called Old Red – Lao Hong -- because he liked and accepted Chinese communism. He had liked it ever since World War II, when he served in the U.S. Army as ground support for the Flying Tigers, the famed airmen who fought the Japanese in occupied China. Old Red had been impressed with the resolve and sincerity of the Communist fighters and shocked by the corruption and ineffectiveness of the Nationalists, whom the U.S. backed.

When the war ended, he stayed. When the Communists took over in 1949, he was literally in their camp. People say his decision was influenced by a fiery romance with a dancer in Chairman Mao's revolutionary ballet troupe, but who's to say.

Old Red's real name was Josh Silberstein, a one-time sportswriter for the Brooklyn Eagle and a regular guy. He was not an ideologist or a philosopher or someone who cared much about politics. He just thought it was good for people to take care of each other, to share and to be on an equal footing. And this seemed to be what Mao Zedong wanted, and that's where he threw his support. And yes, there really was a dancer.

For years he worked with the government's propaganda arm and helped with western affairs, what little there was. With each year he grew more revered, except for those middle years during the Cultural Revolution, when all foreigners were considered spies and a group of radical youths called the Red Guard questioned everyone's loyalty. Old Red was locked up, but even then felt strongly about Mao's leadership.

While in captivity, he wrote a positive, book-length perspective on the revolution. China published it in five languages and, in effect, made the journeyman writer a best-selling author. When the Gang of Four, who in Mao's last years led the Cultural Revolution and brought the nation to near civil war, was deposed and a sense of sanity returned in the mid-'70s, freedom and honors were awarded to Josh Silberstein.

Old Red still had purpose, and for Duke Amici he was helping to make sense of the good, the bad, the bizarre, and the incomprehensible.

"This hotel has an old China feel," Duke told Silberstein, noting the red columns, the rosewood carvings, the Tang dynasty paintings, the calligraphy. "I've been in those new ones. There are, what, two Western hotels in the city now? None of them feels or looks like this. It would be a sin if they ever modernized it."

"There's a nice crowd in here now," Old Red said. "There's life and energy to the place. It feels good. But during the Cultural Revolution this palace of a building was deserted. People were afraid to go out. Before they locked me up, I'd sometimes wander over and eat alone. My voice would echo off the walls. It was spooky. Like something was dying. There was danger everywhere. You acted a little funny and your neighbor would rat you out, call you a reactionary. Sometimes I'd see Zhou Enlai, the sophisticated premier and the only sane leader at that time, eating here, alone, like me. He was a fan of their noodles. Can you imagine that? A leader of the largest country in the world sitting 10 feet away from a graduate of PS 137, in a room so empty we could hear each other chewing."

Duke had heard horror stories of the Cultural Revolution, and they frightened him. People were put in solitary for 10 years. They were paraded through the streets with dunce caps on their heads and cinder blocks hanging from their necks on piano wire. They were pushed out of upper story windows or beaten to death. Surely some of that lingers, he thought.

"Overall, China's been good to me," Silberstein said. "I think it will be good to you, too."

What Old Red didn't know (or did he?) was that Duke had a prior run-in with the Chinese authorities, that this new situation was a second strike. In his defense, the first wasn't exactly nefarious. It involved a small propane stove. But this rudimentary device, a gas can and two burners, was rare and prized in Beijing. If you had one, and most didn't, you'd be spared the soot and mess of cooking inside with coal briquettes.

With a Canadian friend named Larry Altman as an accomplice, Duke had stolen one. Relocated may be a better word. It was for his two-room apartment at the Friendship Hotel, a large, aging complex of residential buildings north of downtown in a district near several universities. Most foreign workers lived there. The Russians, once friends of the Chinese and now enemies, built the complex with Chinese architectural features, but it had a Stalinist feel to it. It may have been sturdy once, but no more. The ill-fitting windows allowed the ultra-fine sand from the Gobi Desert to drift in and thinly cover shelves, tables, and floors. The mattresses were saggy and the floors creaked. The electrical wiring looked frail and dangerous. But Duke kept his place neat and clean and he was comfortable there.

If only he could cook and host parties. With a stove he could, and the opportunity for getting one was there because the Friendship Hotel was being modernized to accommodate a new trickle of businesspeople. At this early stage they were mostly Japanese, and it was the Japanese who were getting the gas stoves.

Most of the people living at the Friendship Hotel worked for the Chinese government and were paid, by Western standards, a nominal salary. By Chinese standards, the pay was excellent. These guest workers were called "foreign experts." Some taught their native languages in schools and colleges, others worked for news organizations or publications by correcting and polishing the copy written in various languages for foreign consumption. Most were English speakers from the U.S., England, Canada, and Australia, but there also were Europeans from Germany, France and Spain and people from Japan, South America and a few from Africa, pretty much from all over.

As this scene slowly shifted, it was clear the new business class and their families would need more comforts than the foreign experts received. The businesspeople didn't need the free airfare to and from China, or the paid vacations and free tours around China, which were part of the packages for most foreigner experts. They might use the free minivans from the various workplaces that would come to the Friendship Hotel each morning to take the foreigners to work, and they might eat at the heavily subsidized dining hall. But the businesspeople, especially the Japanese, wanted newer and cleaner facilities, and they wanted the option of being able to cook for themselves. To placate them, a partial renovation of the massive Friendship Hotel complex began.

It was a gas stove from a refurbished unit that Duke tried moving to his less grand apartment. He had become friends with a Japanese businessman whose company had called him home. "Can I have your stove?" Duke asked during a good-bye party.

"I think it's supposed to stay with the apartment," the businessman said. "But go ahead and take it – if you can."

Before this particular stove became available, Duke had asked his boss at the New China News Agency – a government-run, international wire service known as Xinhua -- if she could convince the hotel to give him a stove. In China, your place of employment – your work unit -- basically managed your life. It assigned you a place to live and made many decisions on your behalf. It could punish you, but it also was paternal. In the summer, when there were beer shortages, the well-connected news agency got you beer.

Nothing became of the stove request, possibly because the stoves were so precious. Bolder action was necessary.

The stove transfer was planned for after dark. Duke showed up with Larry Altman, a short, stocky, good-natured person who had the skill of getting his point across using very few Chinese words. The apartment's occupant let them in, and the two carried the stove outside. They were walking toward Duke's apartment in another building when four young hotel workers came out of the shadows. These workers were called fu wu yuan. They did a wide assortment of manual chores but also kept their eyes open and acted as insidious spies. They closed in and expressed their anger in rapid-fire Chinese. Duke understood some of it and tried explaining himself with a combination of English and rudimentary Chinese.

With sarcasm and a nasty look, Larry simply said, "Gong an ma?" Are you the police?

One fu wu yuan, lean and baby-faced, paused and went silent, then took the stove.

Two days later at the New China News Agency, Duke was called in and told that what he did was wrong. When Xinhua spoke, you listened. It was a powerful force that not only put out the news in five languages and distributed it domestically and internationally, it also gathered intelligence and published daily eyes-only briefings for high party officials. Because Xinhua knew about the stove, Duke assumed that somewhere on some record a black mark appeared against his name, and that all government agencies would have access to it.

And now he had to deal with a second infraction that was far more egregious. It was not only criminal. It was espionage.

"When they locked me up," Old Red told Duke, "they said I was a spy. I wasn't a spy. In their minds, at that time, anyone from the West was a spy and every lame accusation was considered credible."

Duke Amici, unlike Old Red, was no victim of a lame accusation. He was guilty and without a defense.

"Tell me more about the girl," Silberstein insisted.

Song Mei was a 29-year-old poet and a graduate student at the Foreign Language Institute, just around the corner from the Friendship Hotel. She was about the size of an average Chinese woman, shorter and thinner than most American women her age, with medium-length black hair, sometimes in a ponytail, that didn't do much. There was nothing unusual about her facial features, which brightened sharply with a smile and dimmed darkly with a frown. Her best quality was her walk, which somehow spoke of desire and confidence. It drew you to her. Song Mei defined herself as a dreamer and romantic. She was a sometime loner who possessed superior social skills (she could charm and flatter) and used them when necessary to advance her position. During the Cultural Revolution, she and her family were considered "black" or counterrevolutionary, so such skills were essential. Song Mei was a consummate writer and penned an unpublished, hidden novel about growing up in a time of political chaos. Her encounters with Duke often inspired a poem.

"It's nothing really," Duke said of his relationship. "Very casual."

"When the two races overcome the cultural and political barriers between them, the results usually are not casual," Silberstein said. "You think I've been living alone all these years?"

"No, really," Duke said. "She was in the Friendship Hotel dining hall with a group of students and a visiting teacher, an American. On the table were several of those good Chinese-English dictionaries. You can't get them, so I walked over and offered to buy one."

"But you really just wanted to talk to the girl."

"Maybe. Anyway, the girl, the woman, a poet from Ningxia – that's in the northwest, a desert province."

"I know where it is."

"Out there, she lived among the Hui people, Muslims, probably a mixture of native Chinese and Silk Road traders from Arabia, Persia, and Anatolia. She adopted some of their practices."

"China has lots of minorities," Old Red noted. "Not always held in high regard. Not considered attractive, either."

"Well, she's not Hui. She's Han. She offered to give me one, a dictionary. I said I couldn't take it and she absolutely insisted. Forced it into my hands. Said she could easily get another. She told me China was honored to have a person like me help the country, that China can learn from people like me, that America was a strong, powerful, and important country, and that I, too, must be strong, powerful, and important."

"That's how it starts," Silberstein said.

"We chatted a little as the whole table watched and listened– maybe the rest of the room. I had to find a way to return the favor, so I asked her to go with me to the American Embassy for the Independence Day celebration. She agreed."

"Of course she did," Silberstein said. "She saw you not as a date but as a golden gate to the land of the free and the home of the rich."

"I don't think so," Duke said shyly. "She seemed sincere."

"Very sincere. Of that I'm sure."

On July 4, Duke picked up Song Mei in a taxi. They were hard to get, with the drivers, once they made their quotas, preferring to sit around and smoke rather than drive. Duke rarely used them, since he had a bike and noisy old buses went everywhere, but this was special. During the 30-minute ride he learned Song Mei had a good command of the English language, wrote massive amounts of poetry in both Chinese and English, and, as a graduate student, had special access to American books and films. Above all this, she told him she was fated for an extraordinary life, despite the incredibly limited opportunities afforded her.

When they arrived at the embassy, Song Mei did not get out of the cab. Duke exited on one side and shut the door, expecting his date to get out on the other. But she did not. He looked in at her with a questioning expression. She started to laugh.

"I don't know how to open the door," she said through the glass. "This is my first time in a car." Her host came around to assist, amazed that she had been so cool during what must have been an anxious or perhaps exciting ride.

Duke spoke a little Chinese but the two conversed mostly in English. Occasionally, he would ask Song Mei in Chinese if everything was all right. "Hao bu Hao?" he would say, literally "good or not good?"

She almost always answered "hen hao." Very good.

Overall, however, it was not very good for Song Mei. In fact, the embassy visit was an utter disappointment. "I thought it would be grander," she said. "I thought the building would be a palace. I thought it would be rich beyond my dreams. Out of a storybook, with statues made of gold and staircases almost to heaven. Isn't that America?"

Duke thought the embassy compound was castle-like and worthy of some awe, although, like Buckingham Palace, it was old and a little down at the heels. In 2008, the U.S. would replace it with a modern, eight-building compound, complete with an outdoor sculpture by Jeff Koons. It would be the second largest of all American embassies, but that's not what Song Mei saw. And the party was in the courtyard, so they didn't even go into the building. Duke had a sense for what Song Mei was saying. In so many ways, and especially to outsiders, the American promise had reached mythic proportions that did not reflect reality. Like the utopian future depicted at a world's fair, America could never be what so many wanted it to be. It was damn good, and offered hope to the skilled and the lucky, but it was not a living dream. There were tall buildings and stylish clothes, a powerful military, the Ivy League and Wall Street, gadgets and devices, plenty of food and endless consumer goods, but American cities were dirty and decaying and housed a large underclass of poor and disenfranchised people.

"America has always been a kind of fairy tale to those who want to come but can't," Duke told Song Mei. "When people do come, the freedom is intoxicating but it's still very hard for them. There's a story told by a comedian – do you know what a comedian is?"

"A joke teller."

"Yes, and one of his jokes is this: My grandfather came to America thinking the streets were paved with gold. When he got here, he learned the streets were not paved with gold. He learned the streets were not paved. And he learned he was the one who would have to pave them. Do you get it?"

"Get what?"

"Do you understand the joke? Is it funny?"

"Not really funny, but I understand, a little. Your country is actually poor."

"No, not poor. The joke is an exaggeration of a truth. For most people, life in the U.S. is comfortable and good," Duke said. "You can speak your mind and move about. You can act as you want and do what you want. But even the rich drive on roads with potholes."

"Potholes?"

"Holes in the street as deep as a pot."

"I see. America is a lie."

"No. Some streets are fine. I'm trying to explain that America is a real place and must operate like a real place. There's no magic to it. Can hundreds of thousands of immigrants suddenly show up one day and get rich? Some will. Most won't. But I guess they live better than in their home countries. Best of all, even among the obstacles they face they still have choices."

Duke hoped to thrill Song Mei. He was disappointed by her glumness and worried how this date was going to end.

"Let's eat," he said.

As a gesture of pure Americanism and the need for a taste of home, the embassy flew in an entire McDonald's kitchen from British-controlled Hong Kong. Authentic fast-food burgers and fries were served. At the time, there was nothing like this in China.

"I'll get you some food," Duke told Song Mei.

He brought back a tray of Big Macs, fries, and shakes.

She looked at the tray with sad eyes and said, "I'm a vegetarian."

"Bu hao," he said. Not good.

As they walked around, she picked at the hamburger roll and ate a few fries. Duke could see a poem of disappointment being written.

She's a great poet, he thought, but she's bound to overstate the negative and completely miss the heart, meaning and nuances of the event.

They didn't stay long at the picnic. Instead, they went back to Duke's apartment. He had some vegetables and eggs, and Song Mei cooked them Hui style on the gas stove his boss finally got for him. It was a reward for helping the higher-ups at the news agency understand why, to them, privately owned publications like Time and Newsweek read like government propaganda.

After eating, Duke gave Song Mei several English novels and a man's wool sweater that was too small for him. She was nearly overwhelmed by this simple gesture, and her reaction moved him to kiss her. He had his arms around her and could feel the thinness of her simple cotton dress. She acquiesced for a moment, then pulled away.

"They have cameras set up here," she said unconvincingly. "We shouldn't."

In the Friendship Hotel, Duke had never seen the slightest bit of technology. Custodial workers used handmade brooms of straw. Machinery of any kind was rare. Still, you could spy without technology, and Duke was certain the fu wu yuan reported almost everything of any consequence. They may have seen Song Mei go in, but they didn't see him kiss her. Even so, he took her home.

"Will she get in trouble for coming to my room?" Duke asked Old Red.

"She's an English major, right?" Silberstein said. "She's probably seeing you as a way to improve her English and later get into an American university. The authorities are quite aware that China is opening up and emerging and that people have to learn English. They'll look at this with some disdain, but actually think it is clever and necessary."

Duke was silent.

"Don't worry about it, kid. That's life. During my time here, I've had lots of girlfriends. I've got one now. She's 30 years younger than me. Right now, at this period, being from the West gives you a magnetism that is hard to understand. It's like being a movie star. If you're smart, you just go with it."

"I thought she liked me," Duke said.

"I'm sure she likes you. She probably likes you a lot. What did she ask you for?"

"She didn't," Duke said. "But she told me a lot about her life. Made me feel sorry for her. Her father is a doctor from Shanghai who had a rough time during the Cultural Revolution. He was exiled to Ningxia, which seems poor and isolated. It's sort of odd. He has a bad heart condition and even though he's a doctor he can't get the western medicine he needs."

"And you tried to get it for her," Old Red said. "That's the start of your trouble."

"I didn't just try. I got it."

The path to the medicine started at a poker game.

Even in this exotic land, day-to-day life at the Friendship Hotel could be routine, often uneventful, sometimes monotonous. The compound served as a zone of protection that shielded the foreigners from China and all that they couldn't understand. But it also protected China from the foreigners. Foreigners could leave their walled home anytime and go almost anywhere in the city. With the exception of going to work, organized trips and some shopping, most did not leave those walls. Occasionally, excitement could be found within them, like when visiting Western celebrities or sports figures stayed at the hotel, but otherwise breaking the boredom meant visiting Building No. 1.

Building No. 1 was at the compound entrance. Unlike the other buildings, it was for short-term stays. It had a formal restaurant with fancier food than the dining hall, an elaborate gift shop and a bar. You never knew whom you might see at the bar. It could be the conductor of the Philadelphia Orchestra or beat poet Alan Ginsberg. And the beer, the best Chinese brands that were not always available elsewhere, was cheap and sold in large bottles. Duke wandered by one evening when there was a poker game going on in the bar. At the table were two Englishmen, a Welshman, a Canadian, and a Russian from the Soviet Embassy.

"Hey," one of the Englishmen called to Duke. His name was Eric Davies and he worked with Duke at Xinhua. "You want in?"

Duke went over and was dealt a hand. The conversation was more interesting than the poker. The Welshman, James Maddy, a bookish coal miner before becoming a world traveler, said it may sound odd, but a miner feels safer the deeper he goes. The Canadian, Trevor Tremblay, said that in his far northern town, if you lose a glove you die. The Russian, known only as Yuri, said that in his consumer-deprived country, if you see a line in front of a store, you stand in it, no questions asked.

Eric drank more than his share. He groused madly about the current state of England, from Margaret Thatcher dismantling social programs to pubs being forced to close early. His anger and dissatisfaction with trends in western democracy clearly pleased the Russian, who calmly shook his head and chuckled at every complaint.

"I'm glad at least one of you can look at your country and see it for what it is," Yuri said. "I don't live in paradise, but neither do you."

"Three kings," the Canadian said.

The Russian beat him with a full house.

As the conversation moved around the table, Duke noticed Yuri had not made eye contact with him. When Duke asked him a direct question, it was ignored. The Cold War, apparently, had come to the Friendship Hotel. It reminded him of the time two English-speaking visitors from communist Eastern Europe ended a conversation with him before it began, telling Duke they could not understand him because he did not speak Oxford English. There was fear and dread in their eyes, and they just wanted to get away from him.

The poker table was filled with those large beer bottles and Duke picked up the cards around them to deal. To the Russian he said, "You're not getting any cards until you answer a simple question. Why won't you talk to me?"

The Russian was smoking an American cigarette and slowly put it out. He took a sip of his beer and answered, "These days, with your Ronald Reagan and his pronouncement of the Soviet Union as history's greatest Evil Empire, talking to an American means hearing lies and vile slanders. It means being the target of hate and getting treated like the devil himself. Who needs that?"

This man, this diplomat, was truly hurt and wounded.

"I've had too many arguments with Americans," Yuri said. "I've taken too much shit from Americans. I've found it best to simply avoid them. You will never understand us. You refuse to see us as people, as human beings. You abhor us. But I will tell you this. I don't hate you. Why do you hate me?"

The table was silent, and Amici searched for a response. Cold War rhetoric was just Cold War rhetoric, he thought. It was not to be taken personally. It was not intended to hurt an average Russian with three kids who goes to work each day. He couldn't imagine it hurting a Cold War professional, and yet it did. The Russian was crushed. His plea – "Why do you hate me?" – was genuine.

After a pause, Duke said, "I'm sorry. I apologize for my countrymen. I don't hate you. I have a different political outlook than most Americans. This whole Cold War is a ruse."

The Russian looked him in the eye for the first time, with one brow raised.

"The U.S. and the Soviet Union, as I see it, represent the most powerful alliance in the history of the world," Duke said. "Yes, an alliance. Basically, our two countries have gotten together and agreed to divide up the entire world between them. They cast big shadows with their nukes and everyone stands behind one or the other superpower for protection. No one questions the moral authority of these two empires, or why a divided world needs to exist. They just follow along."

Yuri lit another cigarette and threw in his hand, a pair of threes.

He cocked his head, smirked and half smiled. "You sound just like the fucking Chinese," he said, and the table erupted in laughter. Ice broken, crisis averted.

Duke took the pot with jacks over sevens.

"The beer here is pretty good, and cheap," Eric said. "But there is a lot I miss. I miss football."

'They have football in China," the other Englishman, Xavier Edward, said.

"I mean real football."

Several more months passed before Duke grew comfortable with everyone calling soccer "football."

"I miss blood pudding," said the Welshman.

"Wonderful name for a food," the Canadian said.

"I miss mayonnaise. I found ham and now I want to put mayonnaise on a ham sandwich."

"Christ, make your own. It's just eggs and oil."

"Not the same."

"You can get mayonnaise at the foreign store," Duke said. "It comes in a plastic squeeze bottle."

"Really!"

"I don't go there," Eric said. "They don't let in Chinese. It's off limits to them, so I don't go there. Fucking fascists. Treat their own people like dogs."

"They let them in if they're with a foreigner," Duke said.

"No they don't."

"They do. I took a woman in there with me last week. It was legit. Well, someone called her a whore, but otherwise it was fine."

"They called her a whore? In what language?"

"Street Chinese. Actually, they called her a broken shoe. That means whore. She told me."

"Broken shoe means whore?"

"Broken shoe means whore," Duke said. "A shoe breaks after it gets too much use."

"You know, I've seen you with that woman," Eric said. "Word is you brought her up to your room. That right?"

At the Friendship Hotel, all friendships were new and reasonably discreet, yet when a foreigner struck up a relationship with a native, deep, probing questions were common.

"Man, all people do around here is pry," Duke said. "At this key moment in history, all they care about is who's boffing who."

"Boffing. I like that," Eric said.

"Who said I took her to my room?" Duke asked.

The Welshman said, "You know, it's just the general report of the day that circulates by word of mouth, like: Starting today we'll get vegetables other than cabbage; the main roads are being spruced up for the 35th anniversary of Liberation; the Chinese national team won another international badminton competition; that tall German fellow from Building 4 got a leg over that small French woman from Building 3."

"Time to come clean," Eric said. "Did you get a leg over?"

"Now there's a phrase," Duke said. "Yet another clever Briticism. You Brits drive me crazy with the way you take an indirect approach to being so goddamn direct. A leg over. Well, I'm going to play the gentleman," Duke said. "Now bugger off."

"Hey! You're not allowed to say 'bugger off.' That's ours!" Eric said. "You steal all our good stuff. Your great sport of baseball is our rounder's, a girls' game. M&Ms, which you think you invented, are Smarties. Your entire culture is borrowed. You're still a damn colony and you don't realize it. The most popular band ever in the U.S. is English. Live with that."

In this international venue, conversation was like dueling. Lots of pressure to be bright and witty, characteristics the English seemed to have mastered and Americans were still learning.

"Without us you'd be speaking German," Duke said. "Sorry, any Germans here?"

Yuri corrected him. "Not true. You'd be speaking German if there hadn't been a second front in the east and 20 million dead Russians."

Duke looked at Eric and knew he'd steer the chatter back to Song Mei, a far superior topic than dead Russians.

"Seriously, she seemed like a nice girl," Eric said. "How did you meet her? Why'd she even talk to you? It obviously wasn't your looks."

Duke's looks were just fine, but they didn't have to be. The odd and ill-defined attracted certain Asians to certain Westerners, and Westerners to certain Asians. Going in both directions, you find the attractive with the homely. Looks don't always matter. It's probably the mystery of the foreign that brings people together, an opportunity to enter an unknown universe, or perhaps it's the inability to recognize what the other culture values as beauty.

From a western perspective, it could be argued that Duke and Song Mei were equals when it came to looks. Duke was slim, of average height, with thick, longish brown hair and healthy, olive skin and a strong Roman nose. Of Italian lineage, he could be taken for Greek. In a place like Beijing, with the beard he had grown, he could be taken for Arab.

Song Mei did not stand out among the women of Beijing. Like nearly every female, and every male, she normally dressed in worn, drab-colored, proletariat clothing, mostly blue, sometimes gray or green. She looked like a worker, not a student, one of the "blue ants." In winter, with heating fuel scarce, women (and men) wore three sets of long underwear beneath their clothes, one wool, two cotton, plus extra sweaters and shirts. This gave the unflattering appearance of someone 30 pounds heavier. In the summer, or when more formal attire was required, there were dresses, but to an American eye these looked like bargain basement fashions from the '50s. To gaze at a woman and see her appealing side, you had to look through this crippling couture. On occasion, you'd see a renegade, a strong-minded individualist who didn't fear the party, who wore make up, fixed her hair, and found the money and connections to purchase a tight pair of jeans on the black market. This was the avant-garde, the rebel element, and it indicated a shift was coming. Song Mei was an individualist, but not a wearer of jeans. Her clothes seemed older than most and her tied-back hair was often unwashed. There was never jewelry. Still, there was something to her, an enthusiasm, a light. Duke considered her pretty.

"Clean it up if you want, but tell us something," Eric said. "That's the code. You help unlock the conundrum that is China."

Duke went on to explain how he and Song Mei met, how they gave each other little treasures they couldn't get on their own, how their friendship developed, how she was truly a talented writer in English and must be exponentially better in Chinese, and that knowing her might just be the equivalent in America of having been buddies with Emily Dickinson.

"It's her mind you're after," the Welshman said.

"That's it," Duke said. There were grumbles all around.

"But do they do it the same way as us?" the Canadian asked. "That's really what we want to know. Someone said they like to squat over you."

Duke ignored this and told the table about her father in Ningxia.

"I took her to the foreign store because she thought there might be access to a pharmacy and special medicine. There wasn't."

"Oh, I see now," said Eric. "The idea is to save her father's life and let her repay you with a shag. Good plan."

It went downhill from there. As the night grew late and the beer too freely consumed, the discussion shifted to politics. There was some screaming and hand waving, some support for the Chinese system and some bombastic and foul-mouthed condemnation of it. With a sudden lapse into silence and last call, everyone decided to go home. Duke made 50 yuan from the game, about $6.50.

Back in his apartment, Duke realized how easy it is for westerners of various nations, surrounded by the East, to come together as friends. When that thought passed, Yuri came to mind. Duke decided Yuri was a Russian spy making contacts as part of his job. After all, half the people at the poker the table worked at Xinhua, a news agency that produced (without help from foreign workers) intelligence reports for high party officials. Yuri was not James Bond, but who was? Duke surmised that in real-life spying, simple contacts and conversations were good enough to enter into a spy ledger or a report or whatever a spy's superior required. Duke thought Yuri might even follow up with Eric, who clearly had a soft spot for socialism and a bad taste for his own government.

What Yuri did, however, was contact Duke, who, quite uncharacteristically, and with little effort or questioning, then became a Russian spy.

Duke considered the whole arrangement laughable, more comical than bad TV. But the facts were not in dispute: In exchange for heart medicine for Song Mei, he agreed to steal Xinhua trash. In Duke's view, he was not dealing in state secrets but rather crumpled pieces of tea-stained paper. Was this even espionage? Spies, he imagined, have their craft honed to a science, and part of it must be low-percentage plays that, during slow periods, show you are at least working. He bet spies even have a disparaging name for it, like chickenfeed or dredging the river. Adding to the casualness of it all was that the deal came together at a party attended by members of the U.S. diplomatic staff.

The location was a Friday afternoon happy hour at the Australian embassy. The English-speaking allies known as "friendlies" – the U.S., Britain, Canada, and Australia – rotated the weekly party among themselves. It was for embassy workers and expatriates of the sponsoring nations, but a European-looking Russian could walk in without being noticed. And Yuri, tall, blond, debonair, and always smoking, did. Duke watched him across the room and tightened up when the Russian walked toward him. Yuri, in his late 30s, was natural, charming, and convincing. In contrast, Duke was naïve and unfamiliar with the milieu he was entering. He was shorter than Yuri, not as cool, and comported himself in an undistinguished, pedestrian manner. With Yuri's skill, and with Duke's ready compliance, the business was done in 15 minutes. Song Mei's father would get the medicine he needed and once a week Duke would play janitor at Xinhua, filling a small canvas bag with discarded paper from waste cans. The drop points would change. The two would communicate with notes placed under a half-filled bottle of Five Star beer on a specific table at a specific time at the bar in Building No. 1. And so it went, smoothly and uneventfully.

Then from the mysterious world of China, at the normally placid Friendship Hotel, came a series of harmless, misunderstood events that, at least initially, induced fear. They were unrelated to the trash thefts, yet in the context of Duke's spying, of his duplicity and guilt, they unleashed a sense of heightened vulnerability and exposure. China was warm and welcoming to foreigners, but its mellowing attitude could not fully negate its past nor eliminate the possibility of a crackdown on liberalism, a fallout with the West and a return to Maoism. As an illogical means of protection, Duke took a razor-sharp hunting knife with him to China, in case the unexpected occurred.

And the unexpected did occur. In the late afternoon on a typical fall day, the Xinhua minibus returned workers to the Friendship Hotel and some notable changes in the scenery. The effect was as if the passengers had been transported into a new and hazardous world. Silence was the first reaction. Seconds later a few words of restrained panic were softly uttered. "What? How? Who did this?"

Unspoken was the question: Are we in danger?

Logic tried to overcome fear while the bus riders focused on the graffiti-style messages boldly painted in English and Chinese on several walls and buildings in the hotel compound. The graffiti had not been there that morning.

Mao is the brightest star in the sky.

The East is Red.

Kill the foreigners!

These were slogans from the Cultural Revolution. They were history. Seeing them now, in the midst of markets reforms and nascent capitalism, suggested a revolt, a burning Maoist anger that had seethed up in reaction to recent changes. The puzzle unraveled quickly and clearly as the minivan moved past a busy crew of construction workers and their noisy sandblasting apparatus. Everyone exhaled. Some laughed uncomfortably. A few shouted out the discernable explanation that the sandblasting had uncovered Red Guard activity from 20 years ago. There was no threat, yet these demonstrative messages enabled the foreigners to see the Chinese in a completely different light, to know beyond stories and books what they were capable of.

"I guess they're redoing the place," someone on the bus said.

For Duke, an agent of espionage, the time machine effect lingered and was unsettling. That night in bed, he thought he heard movement outside the compound walls. He thought he heard chanting and marching. It was soft, then it grew louder. He decided it was real, and it was. There was indeed an angry mob of hundreds outside the walls of the Friendship Hotel, the very walls advising that foreigners be killed. The mob spoke in Chinese and Duke could not understand the deep, forceful chants. He was terrified and went for his hunting knife. He braced a chair against the door. The only assumption he could make was the exposed graffiti inspired students at the nearby universities to take up against the foreigners in some kind of retro political movement. Everyone had been so friendly to him. Was that friendship a calculated act of misdirection? How could this happen? What should he do?

The boisterous, emphatic mob passed the hotel grounds and walked on, taking its protest elsewhere. Quiet returned. Eventually, Duke was able to sleep. But what was that? All was explained the next day by a senior Xinhua colleague called Lao Wang, with "lao" meaning old, a common honorific. The protest had no connection to the slogans, Lao Wang said. The protesters were university students upset because China, the rising giant for whom they had great hope, had lost a World Cup qualifying game to tiny Hong Kong.

"They cannot understand," the Chinese colleague said, "how a small island like Hong Kong could field a better soccer team than China. Something is wrong and they want it fixed. They no longer will accept being outdone by small countries, even the developed one. They want the government to know this, so they marched. But in truth, I will tell you it was about more than soccer. We Chinese almost always say one thing and mean another."

And he laughed.

"What was it about?" Duke asked.

"Japan."

Few countries have an enemy so mortal in mind and memory. The economic rise of Japan forced an uncomfortable relationship between the two former foes. They do business together. China welcomes the

Japanese while hating them. The atrocities of World War II, when the main body of the Japanese army occupied China, have not been forgotten and, in the Chinese view, have never been redressed. The Rape of Nanjing, for one, is seared in their psyche. It involved an excruciating variety of torture and mass executions, including death by fire, ice, and dogs. As many as 80,000 women were raped.

When the students marched, they were indeed upset that a smaller country had beaten them at soccer, but they were also upset that a smaller country and former enemy was beating them at everything else. The old Xinhua editor explained to Duke that the students wanted to send a warning to their leaders. Especially grating, he said, was a scheme where corrupt officials cheaply purchased defective Japanese TVs and sold them at full price to unsuspecting Chinese consumers.

"Do you see?" Lao Wang asked Duke. "Do you see how the outward dissatisfaction over soccer, accepted because it is not political, can suggest the inward and political?"

"I think so," Duke said.

"It was similar in intent to what people did after Mao died. They marched in the streets waving little bottles tied to sticks. You can't arrest someone for waving a little bottle, can you?"

"I guess not. What was the underlying meaning there?"

"In Chinese, the word for little bottle is xiao ping, and the person they wanted as the new leader was Deng Xiaoping. Deng's name does not mean little bottle, but it sounds just like it."

"Very clever."

"We never say exactly what we mean, yet everyone understands."

"How did you know about the student protest?"

"I work at Xinhua. We know everything."

Duke was becoming aware that you can't fully understand the Chinese unless you live among them. He realized this was probably true of any people, even some in his own country.

"Oh," Lao Wang said. "I was asked to tell you that your boss, Feng Yaohua, wants to speak with you after lunch on Friday."

"Did she say what it's about?" asked Duke, the reluctant Russian spy.

"She did not," and Wang sat down to edit a story on oil production reported out of Nigeria by a Chinese correspondent who filed it in his native language. It had been translated, but the English was clunky and odd. Wang, whose English was nearly perfect, polished it. Duke did the same kind of work. In addition, on his own initiative, he gave lessons in American journalism and tactfully told his Chinese colleagues they needed to assign and write more interesting stories, not just safe stories about oil production, that it wasn't 1950 anymore and that good journalists shouldn't scare easily.

On the day he met Feng Yaohua, known in the office at Lao Feng, Duke Amici was scared. It was chilly inside the Xinhua building, a barebones, basic concrete high rise. Nevertheless, Duke began to perspire. Did Lao Feng know about his deal with Yuri? Was Duke on his way to prison? Could he trust the assurance Old Red had given him just an hour ago at lunch?

The stereotype of the inscrutable Chinese Mandarin did not actually fit the Chinese. Lao Feng, cool and measured, was the exception. In her own way, however, she had always been pleasant to Duke. She was the one who picked him up at the airport and let him eat from a plate of food in the backseat of a chauffeured Xinhua car. She was the one who invited him to her home on his birthday for noodles, with the long strands representing long life. She was the one who gave him a beautiful and expensive gift of two handmade cloisonné vases. All Xinhua foreigners receive gifts on their birthdays, but few as nice as this.

Lao Feng sensed in Duke an honesty and a true affection for China. She could tell by the way he edited copy and the positive, useful advice he gave the Chinese writers and editors. She sought to reward this.

But now?

Duke didn't eat much lunch that afternoon with Old Red. When he walked into Lao Feng's office, he tried to avoid eye contact but noticed she appeared rather content.

"I want to thank you," she began, "for explaining to our journalists how important it is to write stories that interest people and reveal important facts. For many years, the practice here was to cover only the news that could not put a writer's politics in question. These were bland stories with little point or purpose. China is now finding its place in the world. We are competing or will compete on all levels and in all arenas, including news. This bad habit of avoiding controversy must be eliminated if we are to compete with your Associated Press, and Reuters and Agence France-Presse."

"I'm happy to help," Duke said.

"Yes, we know you are the kind of person who likes to help," Lao Feng said. "We see it in your daily work."

This was not what Duke expected and he fought off the instinct to relax.

"You also are kind outside of work," she said. "We are aware you have helped other Chinese people, giving small but important gifts."

Now his stomach tightened and his vision fogged. He rubbed his wrists as if they had cuffs on them. Lao Feng allowed the room to remain silent for a few seconds, then asked, "Is it true that you managed to get heart medicine for the father of a student at the Foreign Languages Institute? If you did, that would be considered a strong and valuable bond between you and the Chinese people. In some ways, it shows hope that, on a much larger scale, our two countries can assist one another and grow stronger together. It is a symbol of the future. Did you get her the medicine?"

Three questions crossed Duke's busy mind. First: Could Lao Feng have heard about the medicine but not the deal with the Russian agent? Second: Is admitting to the medicine a confession to espionage? Third: How preposterous would it be to say, "I refuse to answer until I speak with my lawyer."

"Yes," Duke said. "I got her the medicine. This woman has the talent to become one of China's most important poets. Clearly, she is very special. I wanted to make it easier for her to go on with her work. I wanted to eliminate the worry that might prevent her from writing. I had an opportunity to get her the medicine and I took it."

Lao Feng smiled the slightest of smiles and for the first time looked away.

"I can see you care very much about writing," she said. Then returning her gaze asked, "Do you also care about the woman, personally?"

"Of course."

"To what extent?"

"I'm not sure."

Lao Feng rose from her chair and walked from behind her desk while running a finger across its surface.

"My desk is so dusty," she said, with just a hint of a laugh. "You are aware we have no janitors at Xinhua. In an effort to eliminate lingering class difference between our employees, we require journalists to clean their offices. Most don't. . . . I don't. Not until I must. But they tell me you do, that you're neat and don't like the Beijing dust, that you frequently straighten up and clean. This is honorable, a strong lesson for your Chinese colleagues. If a representative from a class-ridden, capitalist society can do this, then certainly those in a classless society can."

All this praise. What is happening? Duke wanted her to come out with it. The suspense and misdirection were torturing him. He wondered whether he would sleep in jail that night or be shown mercy and put on a plane home. Will this become an international incident and a forever embarrassment?

Lao Feng made her way to a trash can.

"But we don't ask our journalists to take out the trash," she said. "There are special people doing this, just like there are drivers who take journalists to stories and cooks preparing food in the dining hall."

Duke exhaled then took a deep breath in.

"I understand you sometimes take out the trash as well," Lao Feng said. "Is that true?"

The end had come. Accept it, he told himself.

"Yes."

Lao Feng sat back down and again used silence to punctuate the discussion.

A senior editor entered the office and there was a five-minute exchange in Chinese. Duke understood a word or two and made out that there was a problem in the Hong Kong office.

The editor left.

"It is not necessary for you to take out the trash," Lao Feng said. "But we would like you to continue doing it."

Duke was trying to think quickly, to process information, analyze it and react. He was doing poorly, was panicky and indecisive. Was Lao Feng setting a trap? Did they need more evidence? They never need evidence. What does she want from me? he thought. What am I supposed to do? Why can't she just say it? Why all this hinting around? He thought about Old Red telling him they would not hurt him. OK, don't hurt me. Let's lay it all out and resolve this.

"Would you be willing to continue to put trash into your canvas bag and dispose of it as you have been?" she asked.

"I don't understand," Duke said.

"There is always a way to turn one situation into another. That's what we are going to do. If we continue in the proper way, our actions will be mutually beneficial. A few small changes are required, but no extra effort. Are you with us?"

Duke was inclined to repeat, "I don't understand." Instead, he asked, "What's the proper way?"

"You will tell your contact that you now have access to discarded papers from the office that produces reports for high party officials. Tell him you've made a friend in that office. Your contact will know this material is much more valuable than what he has been receiving. You will tell the contact that you appreciate receiving the medicine but there now must be a payment, let's say five thousand American dollars a month. No, let's say ten thousand. The less they have to spend on other projects the better. Yes, ask for ten thousand."

"A month?"

"That's correct. They will pay it. You can be assured of that. Don't settle for less. We will gather up the trash for you and put it in a place where you can find it. This will be easier for you and there will be no risk."

Duke had stopped rubbing his wrists and was now scratching the back of his neck. His vision remained foggy but there was a lightness in his head that brought him a degree of unquantified comfort. He was able to slowly but accurately analyze what was happening. In an instant, Duke had transitioned from a low-level, rookie Soviet agent into a double agent working with the Chinese Communist Party. He had been turned after a simple conversation that he did not even fully comprehend. Will the CIA be OK with this? If he told them – and should he? – would that make him a triple agent?

"How will I get the money to you?" Duke asked.

"You may keep the money," Lao Feng said. "This is a mutually beneficial arrangement. Your benefit is monetary. You need not worry about our benefit."

"Keep the money? All of it?"

"All of it."

Duke's mind was now fully functioning. He did the math. Twenty more months in China at ten thousand a month is two hundred thousand dollars – more if he extended his contract and stayed longer.

At this moment of clarity, he decided his days in journalism were over. Upon his return to the States, he would use his windfall as seed money for a new business. He would become an entrepreneur and use his knowledge of China and his contacts there to manufacture a product cheaply and bring it back home to sell. He sorted through a rush of ideas that flooded in until he realized he was dusting Lao Feng's desk with his hand.

I'll sleep well tonight, he said to himself. Or maybe I won't sleep at all.

By chance, this was the day Duke was to meet Song Mei to give her the medicine. It was around 5:30 p.m. when she approached the gates of the Friendship Hotel on her bike. Duke greeted her and they walked toward his building. Both were under the gaze of a skinny, snarling sentry, who looked around 19 years old. His uniform was too big for him and he shouldered a rifle that weighed him down.

"You look so happy," she said to Duke. "Are you glad to see me?"

"I'm always glad to see you, and yes, I am happy. It went well today at work."

In his apartment, he gave her the drugs and made tea. She expressed overwhelming gratitude. He told her it was nothing. They talked a bit and finished the tea.

"I'll ride home with you," he said.

She ignored him and asked about freedom and choice in America, what kind of life a writer or teacher can have, and if foreigners are accepted as equals.

"Don't you have to leave?" he said. "You must have studying to do."

"No," she answered, and she poured more tea.

The phone rang, a rarity when living in a country where you don't know many people. In China, the phone is answered by saying "wei," a word with no real meaning. Duke said "hello."

"Congratulations. You did good." It was Old Red.

"How did you know?" Duke asked.

"I'm a consultant," Old Red said. "I get consulted when problems arise. Well, you're free and clear. Got a license to kill. Now get on with your life. Go have fun, but from now on stay out of trouble."

"Believe me, I will." Duke thanked him for all his help, whatever that might have been.

Back with Song Mei, there was an uncomfortable moment as the situation called for a next step. He went to his desk, grabbed a tack from a drawer and a shirt off a chair.

"Recite one of your poems for me," he said.

"I wrote one last night, in English."

Song Mei was dramatic in her reading. The short poem was about Duke. It was overly romantic, with a degree of longing and the use of stock imagery. He had heard other poems of hers that were far better.

> *You remind me of the color blue, of the endless sky.*
> *Because of this, I will call you – in my language – Blue Dream.*
> *When I see the sky, even in rain, clouds and setting sun,*
> *I see you.*
> *I will always see you. As long as there is sky.*

"That's beautiful," he said.

Using the tack from the desk, he hung the shirt on a random section of wall.

"What are you doing?" she asked.

"The camera you mentioned on one of your visits. I found it. We can be more comfortable now. The lens is covered by the shirt. They have been blinded."

Song Mei looked away and grasped her blouse, a gesture of modesty by a woman who at this moment was unconcerned about modesty. Destiny was her preeminent thought. They were sitting together on a couch, each laughing a small, uneasy laugh.

When she said nothing, he asked her, "Hao bu hao?"

Song Mei looked at the shirt on the wall, looked down at the floor, looked up at him, and smiled.

"Hao," she said, adding a few more sentences of Chinese that Duke had no possible way of understanding.

She could see America in his eyes. In hers, he saw traces of the ancient and impenetrable but also the presence of deep and calculating motives. It frightened him a little. Only a little. Her plans were not his. Still, he didn't see any real obstacle. Someday soon he would be gone. Maybe she'd be gone, too. And maybe to the same place. He hoped they could remain friends and talk on the phone once or twice a year. If she wanted, Duke would help her get into an American college and pay some of her expenses. That was all. That was enough.

In China, there were a great many situations, circumstances, and people that Duke Amici had grossly underestimated or been shockingly surprised by. Song Mei, he would learn much later, was most certainly one of them. As China ascended and built untold wealth, so did she. Her poetry would diminish and die. It would be replaced by something shrewder, something harder, something with rhythm but no rhyme, something based on instinct and determination that simultaneously builds and destroys, something that makes for better and for worse.

And her influence and control over Duke would be greater and more complex than any other. At this moment, however, on the couch and in the Eastern world, there was nothing more unimaginable than the events that would unfold years later. There was just a man and a woman. Then there was a knock on the door. It was Ainsley Acker from next door, a rich New Yorker who enjoyed acting poor. She and Duke were friends.

"My TV stopped working," she said. "The damn electrical cord is frayed. Everything around here is so cheap. I have some black tape. I'm afraid to touch the cord. Do you mind coming over and fixing it for me?" When she saw Song Mei, she apologized. "Sorry. I didn't know you had company."

"No. It's fine" Song Mei said. "Please go and help," she told Duke.

It took him 15 minutes to get the TV working again. When he returned to his apartment, the poem was on a coffee table, but Song Mei was gone. At the bottom of the poem, she added the words, "Tomorrow, and every day after, the sky is sure to be blue."

3. In the Office, at the Ball

Jacksonville, Florida, 2005

"Can you please get her a better chair? This woman saved our company. Consider her the Queen of Ningxia. Whatever she wants, you give her. And nothing second-rate. Ever. Understand?"

"Understand," the office manager told Duke. "Did you know her?"

The desk was OK. The computer OK. The credenza, bookshelf, and curtains all OK. It was only the chair.

"Ningxia Enterprises is a failing company trying to make it back," Duke said. "We've got a lot more to focus on than who knew who, when and where. Get the damn chair."

When Madame Song — that's what they would call her, Madame Song— arrived at Ningxia's offices in Jacksonville, Florida, there was much to discuss. She wanted to hear about progress, and there was plenty.

"Did your senator agree to your arrangement?" she asked Duke, who before going full time with Ningxia Enterprises had moved from suburban Philadelphia to Jacksonville to take a newspaper editing job.

"He agreed. He enthusiastically agreed," Duke said. "We now have a guardian and protector, Senator Bruce Haywood from New York."

"That's step one," Song Mei said. "What's step two? By the way, I like this chair, but you're probably spending too much on furnishings. Keep an eye on that."

"Yes. Step two is – was -- to put our lawyers back on retainer and counterattack Menlo for copyright infringement," Duke said. "But guess what, the counterattack won't even be necessary. Our senator assured me our case would be reassigned to a sympathetic judge who favors small business. Once Menlo heard that, and once it realized Senator Haywood was on our board, they caved … that is, they backed off. They saw what was coming and will agree to our terms out of court. Bingo."

"Yes, bingo." Song Mei dropped her business face, at least briefly. "How does it sound when someone with my face says 'bingo'?"

"It sounds like when I surprised you at that new free market, when that peasant man charged me double for eggs and instead of giving me change for my five yuan note insisted on giving me more eggs. Remember your reaction when I said: Hu shuo (bullshit)?"

"You think I remember every minute I spent with you?" she said.

"I remember every minute I spent with you," Duke said.

"I won't say bingo. What are our terms?"

"Which reminds me," Duke said. "Why do the Chinese translate 'farmer' as 'peasant'? That's demeaning. Why not just 'farmer'?"

"I guess because farmers own land and peasants don't. What are our terms?"

"That egg man learned capitalism pretty fast, didn't he?"

"The terms."

"Our terms are that Menlo continues to manufacture its version of our machines, but must pay us a licensing fee, and that the fee is retroactive to every machine it has produced. They've produced at least 50,000 machines. With a $50 licensing fee for each machine, that's $2.5 million. You've almost got your investment back."

"You won't get rid of me that easily," Song Mei said. "Once maybe, but not twice."

Duke froze.

"That was a joke," she said. "What's next?"

"We get our lines up and running again in China and start producing new machines for a contract we'll get soon in the states."

"What contract?"

"The military recently closed a 1,100-acre naval air station near here. For decades, the toxic chemicals used to clean planes and such have been polluting the water supply to neighborhoods within 20 miles of the base. That's about 80,000 homes. People can't drink the water. The government's been giving them bottled water but …"

"Now your senator is going to give them your machines," Song Mei said without emotion. "Commendable. Next."

"No next," Duke said. "For now, from me, that's it. I was hoping you'd go to work on a Chinese government contract for distribution in Africa."

"You did well … partner. And, yes, I started on that. I have meetings scheduled. I leave for China in a week."

"Taking a crate of expensive handbags to pass around as gifts?" Duke asked. "What do you give to the men?"

"It used to be Rolex watches," she said. "Now they all have them." Song Mei gathered up her things and stood. "Let's go to lunch. I want to hear about your wealthy wife."

Francine Frick came from a long line of Fricks, who for a century or more had been accumulating profits from oil, steel, coke, and the occasional railroad. She believed, without really knowing it, that it was her right to have the world made in her vision, even if most of the world could not afford her vision. Those who, for this reason or that, departed from her vision, were looked upon with contempt, as victims of their own poor judgment, poor taste, atrocious style, substandard intelligence, and a calamity of woefully lacking genes. Francine Frick believed only a barbarian would wear polyester, or shop at malls, or watch sitcoms with laugh tracks. Yet she felt inferior to most people and readily acknowledged they were having much more fun than she ever would. This inferiority, never, ever exhibited, was rooted in her appearance. She had lifeless, un-coiffed, near-blonde hair and a complexion that needed sun. Her wardrobe, by design, never attracted attention. Francine never wore makeup and declined to fix her imperfect teeth. In school, she was not even the 10th best-looking girl in class. Luckily, something about her pulled you in, and it was not just the family fortune. It might have been her intelligence, her faux self-assuredness, or just the fact that people want to get in with those who don't like them. Duke saw her as a challenge. He knew what she was capable of – lots – and respected her refusal to conform to a society she found unenviable. Francine Frick liked Duke only because he – representing the world she rejected – showed an interest in her, calming her nagging inferiority and lack of place in a society she expected to command. They both had a fondness for words and stories, which could have been something. Overall, the attraction was fragile and indefinable. At times she loathed him.

When it looked like they would start dating, she gave Duke a litmus test, asking, "Do you and your parents contribute to PBS?"

He didn't, and his father, an assistant supermarket manager, did once. "Every year," he told her. His mother, a housewife who would iron the family's underwear after drying it outside on a line, read detective novels but never watched PBS.

How much of Francine should I reveal to Song Mei, Duke thought as he and his partner arrived at a diner not far from the offices of Ningxia Enterprises. As little as possible, he concluded.

"Nothing's great here but they have everything," Duke told his lunch companion.

"I'm just having a salad," she said. "What does your wife do?"

"Francine is in fundraising, for non-profit organizations. Right now she's the head of development for the Philadelphia Museum of Art. She spends most of her time up there."

"Why didn't she give you the money for your business?"

"She didn't give me the money because she wants me to fail," he said.

"What does she know about me?"

"She knows we were friends in China, that I helped you. She knows of your business success. She no doubt resents that you are new money. For her, old, crinkled, ancient money is the only good money. I don't think she's aware we dated. I'm sure she doesn't care."

Song Mei looked at the long, complex menu. "What's a Cobb salad?"

"It's got bacon, eggs, a good dressing. Get it. You'll like it."

She ordered the Cobb; he the California burger and fries.

"Your own rich wife wouldn't give you the money to save your company? How long have you been married?"

"Long enough for her not to care anymore," Duke said. "About 15 years. I knew her before I went to China. I thought we were serious.

She broke it off when a white-shoe lawyer, a friend of a friend, started showing interest."

"White shoe?" she said.

"Someone who works at an old, traditional law firm. An Ivy Leaguer. Someone who is not Jewish, Irish, Italian, black, certainly not someone Chinese," he said. "I went to China, partially but not completely, because it was over with her, and when I returned two years later the white-shoe lawyer was spending less time with her and more time with a topless Puerto Rican dancer. Francine and I, with reluctance, fell back in with each other. A mistake. Now, we mostly go our separate ways, you know, with exceptions for appearance's sake. Last year she moved to the guest room when I came down with the flu. She never came back. She may be considering divorce. It wouldn't surprise me. Under an agreement, I'll get virtually none of her family money, although I'll probably get our house."

"Do those lawyers actually wear white shoes?"

"No."

"I'd like to meet her," Song Mei said. "For business reasons. The senator is in her family, and we need to make sure that relationship doesn't fail. I want to meet her. In a social situation with other people. Can you arrange it?"

The food arrived. "That looks good," she said of the Cobb. "The dressing's warm. I like that."

"I'll never give you bad advice," Duke said. "I know exactly how you can meet my wife. Do you like ballroom dancing?"

"I've never done it. I don't know how."

"It doesn't matter," he said. "You don't have to dance. You can just eat and talk. This weekend, a Chinese couple we know – see, perfect, Chinese – is having a party. They've got a huge home, about 6,000 square feet, a giant basement with a hardwood floor that they use for ballroom dancing. They love dancing and hold these balls two or three times a year. Plus, the woman owns a Chinese restaurant and caters the party. Really good food. It's all very elegant. Wanna go?"

"What kind of Chinese woman holds balls in her basement?" Song Mei asked.

The kind of Chinese woman who holds balls in a 6,000-square-foot home is the kind of woman, actually is the woman, who in 1939, while trying to escape the invading Japanese army, with little food and little water and cloth shoes worn bare, walked 20 days from Shanghai to Wuhan, about 525 miles, with two small children in a wheelbarrow, then found passage by boat and went another 500-plus miles down the Yangtze River from Wuhan to Chong Qing, where China's central government was reforming, and where on May 3rd and 4th of that year she huddled with her children and hundreds of others, standing shoulder-to-shoulder in caves and tunnels, sometimes crushing each other, and withstood and survived a Japanese bomb attack that killed thousands.

That's the kind of woman who buys a 6,000-square-foot home with a huge, finished basement and leads her friends at least twice a year in an elegant example of grace and choreography. Now, if her shoes are worn, it's from dancing, not running from death.

"If I go, will you introduce me to your wife?" Song Mei asked.

"Yes," Duke said. "She'll be the one pretending to enjoy herself."

The stately home of Elizabeth Chu and her husband Samuel was in a freshly built, suburban neighborhood of modern, colonial-style homes, with stone or brick fronts, large windows, sometimes three garages, professionally landscaped lawns and sometimes a pool. Elizabeth and Samuel had a concrete pond with large goldfish. The home's interior was done in a combination of French provincial and classic Chinese, with paintings and porcelain throughout. The large basement looked nothing like a basement and had a chandelier, Greco-Roman columns, and hidden away, a full kitchen.

Duke introduced Song Mei in the same fashion separately to Elizabeth, Samuel, and Francine.

"This is Emily Song, my business partner," he said.

Francine smiled and shook Song Mei's hand.

"Thank you so much for helping my husband's business," she said. "Your trust brought him fresh hope and new enthusiasm. He'll see to it, I'm sure, that your investment pays off."

"He was very kind to me in China," Song Mei said. "I owed him as much and more. Do you know the story?"

"Most of it," Francine said.

"We couldn't have made the turnaround without the help of your uncle, the senator. He did us a huge favor," Song Mei said.

Francine smirked. "He's not really my uncle. Bruce Haywood is the second husband of my uncle's first wife. And believe me, it was you who did him the favor. A board seat and free stock in an upcoming company? Are you kidding? You don't know what it's like in the Senate. Aside from all that government and politics, there is a battle among the members for rivulets of power and prestige. They all try to outdo each other with board seats and business connections. It's a vanity battle, plus, the money's important and a measure of personal value."

"I was worried he might grow tired of us one day and quit, or that if he feuds with your family he'd cuts relations with us," Song Mei said.

"Believe me," Francine said, "you don't have to worry about that. He's with you for life."

After drinks, the food was put out, a wide assortment of dishes representing several regional cuisines, much more than this group of 50 – Chinese, Chinese-American and American -- would consume. After dinner, a state-of-the-art stereo system played a Strauss waltz. As was the custom, Elizabeth and Samuel had the first dance to themselves. They left the floor as the second number began, Glenn Miller's Begin the Beguine, and the other couples started dancing.

"Do you want to dance?" Duke asked Francine.

Nicely and with sincerity, she said, "Maybe you should ask your business partner. She's all alone."

"Maybe later," he said, feeling uncomfortable at the thought.

But Song Mei was not alone. Elizabeth Chu, who knew of Song Mei's business success and her status in China and the world, walked over to chat. "I'm honored to have you at my home," Elizabeth said in English. "Where are you from?"

"It was extremely kind of you to have me," Song Mei said. "My family is from Shanghai, but we've lived other places, although not by choice."

Elizabeth lightened, drop all formality, and began speaking the casual Shanghai dialect, like she would to a sister. "I'm from Shanghai, too." There was a rapid discussion about old neighborhoods and new, about the fantastic growth of the city and its expansion to the Pu Dong (east bank) section, its skyscrapers, subway system, fast trains, modern airport, and great influx of workers who were not Shanghainese (considered bad).

"Is it true you and your children went from Shanghai to Chong Qing to escape the Japanese?" Song Mei asked Elizabeth. A Chinese couple nearby looked on and listened but understood not a word of Shanghai dialect. "How did you survive such a journey?"

Elizabeth laughed. "It is true, and I don't know how I survived. I don't know how I was able to meet up again with my husband, who was a Nationalist soldier, in Taiwan. I don't know how we were able to bring our family to American, how he was able to get his Ph.D. from Yale and work 30 years with Hudson Pharmaceuticals and retire with a great pension. I don't know how my daughter was able to go to Harvard and become a news reporter for ABC in New York, how my son went out to California as an entertainment lawyer, how we are dancing in this castle. I was a flower dying in the desert, and then it rained."

"You must be a very clever, very determined, very resourceful woman."

"I had help," Elizabeth said, and she looked around cautiously at her guests. "I had treasure."

Elizabeth was trim and 86. She wore a black wig to hide her gray hair and had a young appearance. She comported herself like royalty, which, it could be argued, she was.

In 1949, a defeated Chiang Kai-shek and his Nationalists (the Kuomintang) fled China to Taiwan, conceding power to the Communist Party, which quickly announced that China had finally stood up. Under the new classless state, those with an education or the remotest ties to the west or western businesses were considered enemies. She had attended college and her father had worked for Bayer Aspirin in China, but she was in first-class jeopardy because in the civil war with the Communists her husband fought for the losing side. The chaos was no different during a prior revolution, when the once glorious, highly successful Ming Dynasty was overthrown in 1636 by the Qing Dynasty, whose rulers were not Han Chinese but foreign Manchu.

Relatives of the emperor and other high officials who escaped capture and death melted into the general population posing as simple people. The lucky ones were able to take palace riches with them, gold, gems, exquisite porcelain, and rare works of art. Hidden away for safekeeping, the treasure passed from generation to generation, up to the present day, up to Elizabeth Chu, who carries the blood of a princess.

"To get food, to get on that boat, to secure protection from every threat, every danger, I had gems, Ming gems," the dance host told Song Mei. "I used them sparingly, but I used them."

Song Mei, a woman of destiny, a woman who felt large and capable and with a life purpose unlike others, who had a longing for the romance that comes with a palace, said to Elizabeth Chu, "I think you are my cousin."

Duke sat down next to Song Mei with the intention, if not the courage, of suggesting they dance.

"How did you meet Elizabeth? she asked him first.

"Not long after I returned from China, I moved to Florida and was eating in her restaurant. My Chinese was never that good, very limited as you know, but I didn't want to lose it so when paying my bill I spoke to her in Chinese. I'd go there a lot, to speak, and we became friends."

Song Mei had noticed Duke had only danced once, and not with his wife.

"Then one day Elizabeth told me her niece was visiting from Taiwan and she asked if I'd like to go out with her. I said sure. She said she spoke no English. I said that was OK, that we'd get by. She was cute. Wore black leather pants and had a gold tooth. I think I took her to a museum. She was not my type, but it was fun. We only saw each other that one time."

"Yes, young Chinese women are for fun, aren't they?" Song Mei said. "By the way, I spoke with Francine and I'm comfortable the senator will stick with us. That was my main goal for the evening. Now, let's try and dance."

Duke choked. The wistful, nostalgic *A String of Pearls* was playing. He remembered it from the movie *Carnal Knowledge*, when Jack Nicholson, or was it Art Garfunkel, danced with Candice Bergen at a Harvard mixer. Without trying to seem off put, he held Song Mei with minimal contact.

"Do you know that man over there?" she asked. He didn't. "He's the marking director for a large company that makes recreational vehicles, the ones people drive across the country and camp out in. It would be nice if they had their own water supply. I'll have to suggest it."

Duke said, "That, partner, is what we call 'working the room.'"

4. The Moon Festival

Beijing, 1984

The play was a melodrama staged in a modest but crowded Beijing theater. A sad tale based on Bertolt Brecht's *Caucasian Chalk Garden*. Or was it the actual Chinese play, *The Chalk Garden*, on which Brecht based his play? In the play, a poor woman is running from soldiers. She carries a baby. They travel up a mountain, through snow and wind and cold. They come upon a bearded, evil-looking man living in a shed. Duke Amici, watching with Song Mei, understood virtually nothing of what was being said. But he could make out that the ragged, desperate woman was asking the mountain man for milk, for the baby. It was clear the man was refusing her. Some in the audience, even Duke, were near tears. Then, quite suddenly, the entire theater bursts into loud, hysterical, sustained laughter. The mood shift was cataclysmic, but the dramatic actors who got the laugh did not flinch or break character.

Duke Amici thought, "China sure is hard to figure out."

He tapped Song Mei on the shoulder.

"Why are they laughing? What happened?"

Whispering, she tried explaining.

"The woman needed milk for the baby," she said, putting down the sunflower seeds she had been eating. "She asked the man for goat's milk. He said no. She said she would pay. He said the price is 10 yuan. She said that was high. The man said, 'Well, it just went up.' Then everyone laughed."

"That's not funny," Duke said. "Do you think that's funny?"

Song Mei thought through her explanation, then said, "In real life, for a very long time, the government kept the price of milk low. Now we have free markets and inflation. Just yesterday, the government raised the price of milk."

Duke was astonished. In this capital city, the epicenter of strong, authoritative rule that required allegiance as well as respect and fealty, a bold, public, political joke – with no one shy about laughing. He had to wonder. Did the actor playing the old man recite the original line from the play, or did he ad-lib just for a laugh?

"In China, you could always criticize the emperor if you did it in a way that did not directly criticize him," Song Mei said as the poor woman on stage continued her climb up the mountain, with no milk for the baby. "Our language is structured so that you can always say one thing and mean another. In English you say, 'read between the lines.'"

"Like cross talk?" Duke asked.

"Not exactly cross talk. Something else."

Cross talk, which Duke had seen on stage, is a popular genre of Chinese comedy where two people talk and completely misunderstand each other due to the vagaries of the Chinese language. An American comparison would be Abbott and Costello's baseball routine, Who's On First.

"I remember one day in the office at Xinhua," Duke said. "One of the Chinese journalists was uncharacteristically glum."

"What's glum?"

"Sad. Depressed. I asked one of his colleagues what was wrong with him and was told he had a little bronchitis. Three Chinese guys overheard that and laughed. Laughed really loud. I said 'what's funny about being sick,' and one guy said that the Chinese word for bronchitis sounds exactly like the word for henpecked, and that everyone in the office knew the sad guy was having problems with his wife."

"Yes," Song Mei said. "That's how you criticize or make jokes about people. You say one thing and really mean another. The show was not like that, with wordplays, but it's the same idea."

Song Mei and Duke Amici were both busy people, she with her studies and he with his work and having little adventures and discoveries each day, like a visit to an underground ice cream parlor in a massive, repurposed bomb shelter. Although their time together was limited, it was meaningful. Duke took her frequent phone calls, and when they were together it was usually special, like this day.

With the play over, Duke Amici and Song Mei walk out of the theater, stepping on a wide carpet of discarded sunflower seed shells. They were to meet some of his friends for dinner at Beijing's premier roast duck restaurant. Crowds were expected on this particular day, a 3,000-year-old holiday known as the Moon Festival. Families gather while the harvest moon shines. It's the largest moon of the year. Round moon cakes made of sweet bean and other fillings are eaten. The holiday is similar to the American Thanksgiving.

After dinner, the group would spend the rest of the evening under a big, bright moon, celebrating with thousands of other young people out at the Summer Palace, which was not a palace at all but rather 860 acres of glorious ruins, a reminder of Britain's destructive power in the mid-19th Century. It took 4,000 soldiers three days to flatten the Qing dynasty's monumental suburban retreat. Tonight it would be a playground.

For the occasion, Song Mei had memorized Robert Browning's *Love Among the Ruins*. Standing on a shattered, Greek-style column, she would say to Duke:

> *That a boy with eager eyes and brown hair*
> *Waits me there*
> *In the turret whence the charioteers caught soul*
> *For the goal,*
> *When the king looked, where he looks now, breathless, dumb*
> *Till I come.*

Duke and Song Mei took a bus to the restaurant, arrived first, and waited outside on the crowded street. The other members of the party would be Larry and Shelly Altman, a Canadian couple working with Duke at Xinhua; Jennifer Bascomb, a Chicago journalist employed by the Chinese Communist Party to translate its documents into English; Hu Jing Ji, a reporter with the English-language China Daily; and his friend, introduced only as Ling, who, oddly, was from Taiwan, the independent island nation China claims as its own and insists it will one day rule. Taiwanese cannot freely travel to the mainland.

The Beijing Roast Duck Restaurant, known as Quanjude, is a bridge between old and new China. There was a little trouble during the Cultural Revolution, when Red Guards from several middle schools tore down the restaurant's sign as part of the "Smash the Four Olds" campaign (old ideas, old culture, old habits, old customs). Otherwise, Quanjude has operated continuously since 1864, specializing in a dish dating back a millennium and a half.

Within a few minutes, the other members of the party showed up. Mild chaos followed. People on the street, those waiting for a restaurant table and those just passing by, were inexplicably drawn into Duke's group, encircling it with smiles and greetings and signaling others to come. Duke had traveled to small, backwater Chinese villages where this happened to him. Those villagers had never seen foreigners. Beijing residents were more sophisticated than that.

Soon it became clear. The foreigners were not the attraction. Ling from Taiwan was the attraction. Duke turned to Song Mei for an explanation. "Is that guy a movie star?" he asked. Before she could speak, the restaurant manager came out to the sidewalk. With the same enthusiasm as the surrounding crowd, he ushered Duke's group inside the restaurant and to a private room. Several chefs and members of the wait staff joined and produced a bottle of mao tai, the most expensive, most precious, most potent of all Chinese drinks. With a punch equivalent to American moonshine, mao tai is usually reserved for high government officials and international dignitaries.

Drinks were served all around. There was a toast and pictures. Larry cobbled together some Chinese and asked Ling where he worked. "Right now," a grinning Ling answered, "nowhere." The restaurant owner declined to take orders, saying he would personally oversee preparations for a Whole Duck Banquet. When the group was alone again, Ling apologized.

"I'm so sorry," he said. "This happens all the time now."

Duke asked Hu Jing Ji, who organized the evening, "What the hell is going on?"

The China Daily reporter rose. With good English, he said, "I probably should have warned you. That's my fault. I just recently became friends with Ling after writing a story about him. His full name is Yang Ling. He's all over TV and the radio right now. Our leaders praise and exalt him."

"Why? Why? Why?" Larry asked impatiently, with a laugh.

"You know Ling is from Taiwan, which refused to agree to a unified China and remains our nemesis," Jing Ji said. "Ling was an air force pilot. Two weeks ago, he got into one of Taiwan's most sophisticated fighter planes. He took off, ignored his flight plan, headed straight for the mainland, signaled he was defecting, landed the jet and gave it to the Chinese authorities. He became our newest hero. The government rewarded him with thousands of yuan. He received thousands of marriage proposals. And, obviously, he can't walk the streets without drawing a crowd."

Duke looked at Song Mei for confirmation. She nodded. The foreigners, all working journalists, knew of Yang Ling. What they didn't know was that this Ling was that Ling. Everyone was afraid to speak, or simply didn't know what to say. Each had the urge to applaud, but that would have been a political statement, so they refrained.

"Well, I once got a cat out of a tree," Larry said. He hoped that translated. It did, and everyone laughed.

Then came an onslaught of questions from the group, and Yang Ling was gracious enough to answer.

The restaurant owner was back with more shots of mao tai, three of which can knock a sumo wrestler to the ground. "Gan bei," he said, using the traditional toast of "empty glass." With the exception of the owner, Yang Ling and Jing Ji, glasses were not actually emptied. That   was way too dangerous, especially for foreigners. Then came the food, a wide assortment of dishes, many created from the duck. There was also beef, pork, and vegetables. There was soup, salads, fried rice, duck's feet, duck's liver, and more. Endless. Then the main course. Actual duck. Thin layers of meat with crispy skin, placed on a steamed pancake-like bun and garnished with sweet sauce, scallion, radish, and cucumbers.

When it was over, Ling offered to pay but the owner wouldn't have it. Tipping wasn't a thing, but the group warmly thanked the owner and staff. Song Mei and Jing Ji spent five extra minutes chatting with the owner in Chinese.

Back on the street, Ling told everyone what a pleasure it was to meet them and hoped they could get together again soon. In Chinese, he said, "Due to the situation, I'm not going to join you at the Summer Palace. I wish you all a good time on this most festive of evenings." He walked off and the rest of the group made its way back to the Friendship Hotel, where they mounted bikes and, following Jing Ji's lead and direction, rode off to the Summer Palace.

They were not alone. A throng of other riders jammed the streets, making the trip both dangerous and exciting.

A few courageous foreign workers, Duke and Larry among them, occasionally rode bikes to work rather than take the company-provided minivans. On the wide streets of Beijing, the experience was like being in the center of stampeding cattle. At 8 in the morning, it was treacherous and required focused attention, quick reflexes, above average peripheral vision, and the ability to anticipate the movement of hundreds, maybe thousands, of people you did not know and who were nothing like you. In addition to the endless sea of bikes swarming around you, there were cars and trucks to worry about. But at 8 in the evening on a holiday, when the herd consisted of energetic young people looking to have a good time and get to the same place as you, when it's dark and the only guiding light is that of the moon, albeit an exceptionally big, bright harvest moon, the perilous jaunt was exhilarating.

The route to the Summer Palace that Jing Ji led the group down was like a wide, raging river fed by scores of fast-moving tributaries. The multitude grew. And grew. And grew. Hitting a bump, Duke went too far to his left and brushed against another. "Shi wo bu hao," he shouted, a standard apology, literally "my bad." Hearing colloquial Chinese from a foreigner, Duke's victim laughed and tipped his hat.

Bikes gave the foreigners a feeling of freedom, a chance to go where they wanted when they wanted, without having to learn bus schedules (written in Chinese) or wait and wait and wait for cabs, without having to rely on their work unit or the Friendship Hotel to organize excursions. Bikes were special and important to everyone. In the '50s and '60s, maybe even into the '70s, they were among the "four big items" wanted by every family: bike, watch, radio and sewing machine. In the '80s, the list probably included a TV set, washing machine and refrigerator, but a good bike was still a status symbol. You couldn't just walk into a store to buy a bike. There was a strange system of rationing/permission, and the bikes had to be registered, like cars in America. For convenience's sake, newly arrived foreigners mostly bought used bikes from foreigners who completed their work contracts and were leaving. If they needed repair, there were guys on the street who would fix them for very little money. Bikes were left outside in racks, with hundreds of others. They were all black, making it difficult to find yours. Duke, after jumping on his one cold night in January and feeling the jolt of the frigid plastic seat, added blue cloth padding for comfort but also to make it easier to locate the bike.

"Are we almost there?" Larry, the Canadian, yelled to Jing Ji.

"Just ahead."

Seeing the ruins of the Summer Palace for the first time shocked, thrilled, and embarrassed Duke, Larry, Shelly, and Jennifer. There was large-scale, unquestionable beauty. If something exquisite is assembled and then taken apart, it remains exquisite, only in a different way. To see all the downed pillars, the carved archways lying on their sides, the mountains of tossed stone walls, to see all this was both aesthetic and objectionable. There is awe and there is guilt, even though it was Europeans and not North Americans who did this. The root cause, after all, was white and western. The sense of responsibility cannot be shaken. It compromises the delight.

"Why didn't they clean this up, or build over it?" Duke asked Song Mei.

"We want to remember our shame so it will not be repeated," she said.

The shame occurred during the Opium Wars with Britain, which insisted – at gunpoint – that China continue buying Indian opium from them and, basically, addict its people. The Chinese economy under the Qing dynasty was soaring and Britain was buying more from China than China was buying from it. It was a balance of payments problem draining the British treasury. The British solution, basically, was to force its Indian opium on China, causing mass addiction and giving Britain enough Chinese money to buy coveted porcelain, silk, and tea. To end the wars, China gave in to the importation of opium, turned Hong Kong over to the British and opened Eastern China to a host of European countries, who carved up little fiefdoms for their own, including Shanghai.

"There's no shame tonight," Duke said. "Everyone is having such a great time."

Various student groups took up positions on various mounds of rubble. The students were joyful and intoxicated, although they drank mostly orange soda. Over here a group member sang. Over there one recited. Musical instruments were played. One person led others in the Charleston's optical illusional leg movement. Performers stood on rocks while the audience sat. Jing Ji and his group dismounted, parked their bikes, and set out on foot. They passed a Chinese guitar player mystifying his friends with a version – in English – of John Denver's *Take Me Home, Country Road*. Duke wondered where he heard it and how he learned it, since American popular culture was pretty much limited to *The Sound of Music* (which was anti-fascist) and authors Jack London and Mark Twain, who the Communist Party recognized (correctly) as harsh critics of the American way.

Yes, these young Chinese knew *The Sound of Music*. One yelled to the foreigners, "Sing Do, Re, Mi," and they did, with the Chinese students joining in:

> *DO - a deer, a female deer*
> *RE - a drop of golden sun*
> *MI - a name, I call myself*
> *FA - a long long way to run*

Afterward, Song Mei told Duke she had seen the movie at least 30 times.

Moon cakes and beer were passed around. Song Mei recited Love Among the Ruins, changing it from a man speaking about a woman to a woman speaking about a man. Larry, the funny one, asked Jing Ji to tell a joke, a Chinese joke.

"Let's see if we get it … if Chinese humor translates," he said.

Jing Ji thought for a bit, then said, "OK. Can it be a little … naughty?"

"Sure," Larry said.

"Very well," Jing Ji said. "There was a man with a pet duck. The man wanted to see a movie, and he wanted to take the duck with him, but ducks are not allowed in movie theaters so he stuck it in his pants."

"Wait a minute," Duke shouted. "I heard that joke in the sixth grade, in elementary school, in the United States. That's not a Chinese joke. How the hell did it get over here?"

"How do you know it's the same joke?" Jing Ji asked. "I didn't finish telling it."

"It's the same," Duke insisted. "The man sits in the theater and wants to give the duck some air, so he opens his zipper. The duck pops his head out and is seen by the woman in the next seat, who says to her friend, 'Look at this.'"

"It's not two women. It's a husband and wife."

"Doesn't matter. The first woman's friend looks and says, 'Honey, when you've seen one you've seen them all.' And the first woman answers, 'But this one is eating my popcorn.'"

"Not popcorn," Jing Ji said. "Sunflower seeds."

"A minor cultural difference," Duke said.

"In my joke the husband says to the wife, 'This man's cock just ate my sunflower seeds,' and the wife answers, 'That's no cock. That's a duck.'" And Jing Ji laughed.

"Considering we live ten thousand miles apart, it's the same joke," Duke said. "Still, I don't quite get your ending."

"I don't quite get yours," Jing Ji said.

"Enough of your jokes," Sherry said. "Let's share cultures." A native of Saskatchewan, she told a story about the Caribou Inuit people.

"The next time you are on the French Riviera, or in the Caribbean, or sunny Mexico, and the sun is strong and you are wearing $100 designer sunglasses, remember that 'sun glasses' were invented in the far north to prevent snow blindness. Credit the Caribou Inuit."

"Where did they get the glass?" asked Jung Ji.

"Not made out of glass. They were bone, ivory or wood, with two tiny slits for the eyes."

"Well, the Chinese invented the compass, the printing press, and the wheelbarrow long before you had them, and we burned coal for heat when you thought it was a useless rock," Jung Ji said.

Song Mei said to the Americans, "Can someone tell me something about America I don't know?"

"I can," Jennifer Bascomb said. "Ever hear of the Great Migration?"

No one had, not by that name anyway.

"One of the largest, peaceful migrations in history took place in the industrial cities of the north," she said, "with my city, Chicago, being one of the most affected. Beginning around 1916 and lasting several decades, six million people from the rural south, mostly impoverished people, left their homes and headed north. Wave after wave. This changed things in both the north and south. Cultures shifted. For one, the Great Migration brought a whole lot of good music to Chicago, music we never would have heard."

"Why did they leave?" Song Mei asked. "Was there a famine?"

"No," Jennifer said. "There were jobs up north. Good-paying jobs. But it's not that simple. The migrants were black, and, I guess, not as free in the South as in the North; not as much opportunity."

There was a discussion about freedom in America and whether it was real or an illusion, or, as Song Mei put it, just for one class. Jing Ji said, "We walk around Beijing late at night and never worry. There's no danger. Is it true you can't walk in New York's Central Park at night? Is that freedom?" The give-and-take ended when a band of students marched by loudly singing – with irony and nostalgia – revolutionary songs from their childhood. After a time, Jing Ji, worn from the mao tai and beer, said, "Should we be going back home soon?"

It was agreed they should, and the bikes were mounted for the return trip. As Duke pedaled back toward the college sector and the Friendship Hotel, he was stuck on the happiness displayed by all those students, nearly all sober, frolicking at the Summer Palace. In a country where a young person is lucky to have a one-room apartment and not live with his parents or in a company dorm, where after college you don't apply for a job because one is assigned, and that job could be hundreds or even thousands of miles from the woman you just married, a woman who can't move because of her job and because she doesn't have a kind of domestic passport that allows her to live in this or that city, with a government that still can find fault – serious fault – with the things you say or do if they are not the right things to say and do, with scarcity, with shoddy goods, with shoes made of cloth, with the air saturated with coal dust, with the inability to travel abroad at will, when your country's best friend is North Korea but you don't call it "north" Korea, and where your Asian culture is strong but you worship two white guys named Marx and Lenin and care little for God … with all this and more, how then can you be so absolutely content with sitting on a stone and bathing in a drenching cascade of vibrant moonlight? Americans, even the most prosperous ones, are not this happy at Christmas. Did the Chinese youth see, feel, and anticipate something coming, some reward for them, some place not under the moon but directly in the sun? Tonight, it seemed so.

Back at the Foreign Languages Institute, with a cloud now covering half of the giant moon, Duke walked Song Mei up the path to her dingy dorm. "Did you have fun?" he asked.

"It's fun being with you," she said.

"Thanks for the poem," he said. "The night was so magical. All that moonlight. All those bright souls. All that positive energy."

"Those students are simple-minded," Song Mei said, her mood now melancholy, a contrast to Duke's and all those people at the Summer Palace. "There's nothing deep or meaningful about them. They are the masses, and they are easily made content. Truth has no purpose in their lives. Fate is not for them."

A great flaw of Song Mei's outlook was her belief that fate was going to create a real-life storybook and put her at its center. She often talked about the fabled Xanadu as if her place were there. She would recite Coleridge's depiction of it and its lord and master Kublai Khan.

> *His flashing eyes, his floating hair!*
> *Weave a circle round him thrice,*
> *And close your eyes with holy dread,*
> *For he on honeydew hath fed,*
> *And drunk the milk of Paradise.*

"What did you think of Yang Ling?" Duke asked. "Wasn't that wild meeting him?"

"Wild?"

"Exciting."

She said nothing. "Thousands of women have proposed marriage to him," Duke said. "Do you think he's handsome? Would you marry him?"

"He committed a betrayal," Song Mei said. "He is not loyal to his own country. He is not for me. In my life, I hold loyalty as the most important quality. After meeting him and watching him smile and talk, and knowing what he did, I wondered if you will remain loyal to me? Or will you just go where you think life, and maybe love, is better?"

An unexpected and dangerous turn in the conversation.

"I'm not sure about your definition of loyalty, or how the word translates in Chinese," he said. "But, if I'm around, I will never let anyone hurt you. I will never sell you out."

"Sell me out? You mean bei pan?" she asked.

"I guess," he said.

How to explain oneself? How to be honest, to communicate properly, to not create expectations? It was hard enough at home. Here, it was nonsense to even bother. Knowing Song Mei was most comfortable with metaphors, Duke used a trite one, "Let's not forget, I'm just a passing ship."

Song Mei looked away. "I have three days when I'll be preparing for an examination," she said. "Can I call you after that?"

"Of course," Duke said. "You call, and we will try to see each other again."

From Duke's pocket he produced the heart medicine and placed it in Song Mei's hand.

"I hope you know how much I appreciate this," she said. "My father is much healthier. He can live and work and not worry. To get this medicine, you don't have to do anything bad, do you?"

"Not bad," he said. "A little silly, perhaps. The next time I see you I'll explain."

Their relationship was truly casual, partially because it was difficult contacting each other. Duke had a phone in his apartment, but students at the Foreign Languages Institute had access to only a few shared phones, and they were spread out and always in use. He couldn't really call her. Song Mei could call him, but if Duke wasn't home, they wouldn't connect. She often wrote him letters, sometimes with a poem expressing want, need, or hope, only occasionally joy.

Most times, they only got together monthly, when Duke would give Song Mei her father's medicine.

Duke said good night, kissed her lightly, then more firmly. He hoped it was enough while worrying it was too much. Back on his bike, it took him 15 minutes to leave the world of the East and reenter the cloistered world of the West. At the Friendship Hotel he went into Building No. 2 and the apartment of Xavier Edwards, a Xinhua employee and the dean of foreign experts. A world traveler originally from London, he had been in China six years. His Chinese was indistinguishable from a native's. Xavier, known as Exy, sometimes Sexy Exy, was short and balding and liked dressing up in ancient Chinese scholar robes. A frequent dinner party host, tonight he had prepared coq au vin, made, of course, with live chickens from the market that you bring home tied to the back of your bike. When Duke arrived, dinner was over. Brandy and Schnapps were being served.

"How was the Summer Palace?" Exy inquired.

"Beyond anything I've seen or done here," Duke said.

"You need to get out more," Exy said. "Sit down and have a drink."

Duke grabbed a new Australian wine the Chinese were importing. He cozied up to a French woman that everyone, behind her back, called Fifi. Fifi was leaving China at the end of the week to return to her editing job at a satirical magazine in Paris. She cozied back up to Duke for a minute or two, then rose to address the party. In a funny little monologue, she lampooned the speech of a French-Canadian who was not at the party.

"Her French is atrocious," Fifi said. "No one in France speaks like that. The Quebecois must spend all their time talking to reindeer. And when she speaks English, there are all these zees and zoes. 'I love zees cheese. I love zoes flowers.' It's comical, I mean like bad comedy."

Then she sat down and fell asleep. Duke finished his drink, had one more, and returned alone to Building No. 9 and his creaky, lumpy, weak-springed bed. The evening had helped him see his situation more clearly. Soon, he will know exactly what to do about Song Mei, he said to himself, thinking she is too valuable to lose and too dangerous to keep. His plan was for middle ground, assuming he could find it.

5. On the Farm, Marriage, and Divorce

Chongming Island and elsewhere, 1972-76

Song Mei, skinny, bookish, not terribly healthy, and 16 years old, needed to quickly learn how to survive in this new, hostile environment. On her first day at the farm, there was some pushing and shoving, some harsh words, and a horrible bunk assignment. Some, not all, reviled her. Others just avoided her. Most avoided eye contact. As a counter-measure, she wrote a poem glorifying Chairman Mao, the brightest star in the eastern sky. She read it aloud at dinner and everyone applauded. Song Mei, in this unusual and historic situation, would get along.

Not bad for a black girl. In dichotomous China, you were either black or red, with black being bad and red being good. The little girl from Shanghai who had been exiled with her parents to Ningxia province in the northwest was labeled black, or counterrevolutionary. After all, her father and mother were urbane intellectuals working as doctor and nurse. Worse, her father was a supporter of Liu Xiaoqi, a high official who had become Mao's rival, a man who would lose favor, be purged, and tortured to death. To avoid the sins of her parents, Song Mei would use her writing to show her redness, her revolutionary spirit, her changed heart.

Beginning around 1966, Mao closed all Chinese schools and authorized legions of young people to form Red Guard units that would travel the country for free on trains and make revolution. In Shanghai, before being "sent down" to the farm, revolution was made against Song Mei and her comparatively wealthy, highly educated parents. One day Red Guards entered their house and took the piano. On another they demanded gold and were given some. On another the family's cat was killed. Her father was placed under house arrest, and on special days paraded through the streets wearing a dunce cap. He was spat upon and ridiculed by the fervent throngs watching the spectacle.

To make the nation classless, to instill revolution in the upcoming generations, and to reeducate capitalist roaders, vast numbers of young people were assigned to work on farms. Song Mei was sent down to an island adjacent Shanghai, where she worked the rice patties and cotton fields and labored at scores of other agrarian chores. When not in the fields, there was political education and philosophy led by the more revolutionary-minded youths, the ones from proper backgrounds. The Reds.

The thoughts of Mao Zedong dominated China and were considered beyond wise and prophetic. Among them:

We should support whatever the enemy opposes and oppose whatever the enemy supports.

The weeds of socialism are better than the crops of capitalism.

Kindness in words creates confidence. Kindness in thinking creates profoundness. Kindness in giving creates love.

When the enemy advances, withdraw; when he stops, harass; when he tires, strike; when he retreats, pursue.

Enable every woman who can work to take her place on the labor front, under the principle of equal pay for equal work.

Not to have a correct political point of view is like having no soul.

...the evil system of colonialism and imperialism arose and throve with the enslavement of Negroes and the trade in Negroes, and it will surely come to its end with the complete emancipation of the Black people.

The first few weeks were exhausting. So much to learn. So much to do. All so unfamiliar. New smells. Getting up so early. Digging and picking and pulling and planting. Rice. Cotton. Hay. With time, the young city dwellers adapted. When politics didn't interfere, there was comradery. Like all young people, the new farm hands found ways to have fun and enjoy their independence and lack of parental supervision. For some, there were flirtations. For others, liaisons. With lots of boy-girl stuff going on, Song Mei sensed an odd attraction-aversion between herself and her group's teenage leader, Xu Gang. He only rarely spoke to her and would leave the room when she entered. As the son of a military officer, a general, in fact, Xu Gang wasn't expected to be friends with people of black parentage. It was acceptable, however, to have a working, civil relationship with her, but he didn't.

That was the aversion.

The attraction was indicated by the mysterious gifts that appeared on her bunk, one of six in her female-only dorm room. After a month on the farm, she found a book of poems by Lu Xun, a pre-revolutionary writer that Mao called the saint of modern China. It was known that Song Mei, on her own, was studying English, and after two months, under her pillow, there was a useful relic -- an English-language repair manual for an American World War II jeep. Sometimes she found extra food. There was always something. Song Mei tied these gifts to Xu Gang after another girl, exercising revolutionary fervor but also jealousy over the gifts, knocked her down and ripped her clothes. A week later, that girl was transferred.

The years went by, two, three, four, and Xu Gang grew more comfortable interacting with Song Mei. During the rice harvest, one of the toughest times of the year, an unsolicited sick note was written on Song Mei's behalf. For two weeks, she would sit comfortably in the farm's infirmary and study English while others strained, sweated, and tired.

"He secretly respects you," a friendly dorm-mate told her. "I can tell. He envies your book-learning and intelligence. He envies your father and what he has accomplished. He knows your grandfather worked for an English company. He knows your mother had the money to buy furs and fancy clothes. Xu Gang opened your chest and saw the photographs. He was taught to hate all that but can't. He loves it, wants it, and gets close to it through you."

"That's impossible," Song Mei said as the two of them shoveled dirt to strengthen an earthen dam.

"You're the poet," her friend said. "You should understand these things, the contradictions of life, the intense desire for all things beyond reach. Mao is Mao. Our heads may nod to him, but not every heart."

"Quiet. Don't say that. You'll go to struggle session."

Song Mei did understand. She had written about what her friend described. Still, for reasons of safety, she would never admit to it.

When the poet turned 20, the political scene was shifting. Mao was old and infirm, perhaps dying, and the Cultural Revolution, waged now mainly by his fourth wife, former actress Jiang Qing, and her notorious Gang of Four, was coming to an end. Clearer heads were preparing to take control of the chaotic nation. Schools were reopened. Xu Gang, sensing great change, sat next to Song Mei one night at dinner, saying nothing for 20 minutes. Then he asked, "If you could get off the farm and go to university, which would you go to?"

The unaccustomed familiarity was like a giant wave of water that refreshed her but also knocked her over. So personal, she thought. "They say the best foreign language school is in Beijing," Song Mei answered. "The Foreign Languages Institute. My dream would be to study English there."

Xu Gang, untouchable as the son of a Beijing-based general, finished eating and left. He left the dining hall, then left the farm, for a week, without permission. On the day of his return, Song Mei found some papers on her bunk. One set discharged her from the farm. Another set accepted her into a bachelor's program at the Foreign Languages Institute.

Not long after, Xu Gang and Song Mei were married. Elaborate celebrations were not common at this time, but the wedding of a general's son carried a few extras. It was held in the capital city, Beijing, where Xu Gang's family resided, and attended by many important people. Song Mei delighted in the attention while fighting off heady feelings that a great fate of prominence and acceptance awaited her. That night, the very night of her wedding, the beatings started. Beaten by her husband on her wedding night. It was as if the Cultural Revolution had reignited and targeted a single, defenseless victim – her.

In poetry and prose, Song Mei tried explaining this unexpected turn from thoughtful kindness to monstrous cruelty. There was this theory, then that theory. Ultimately, she concluded Xu Gang was not acting like some psychotic, dominant, authoritative male letting his property know it was property. He was acting politically. Fully indoctrinated but having capitulated to a capitalist roader wife, he was punishing not her but himself.

Divorce was rare in China at this time. It carried an unenviable stigma. Even so, Song Mei's bruises were enough to convince the authorities to make an exception. The divorce was granted. As Song Mei headed off to college and China entered a new era, her once-damaging classification as black became less important. Instead, she now contended with a new appellation of ridicule for divorced women, Living Widow. She would ignore it, as she had ignored so much else.

At college, she studied hard. Perfected her English. Read widely. Graduated and entered a master's program. All the time, she stayed in touch with her ex-husband and used his family for protection. At a distance, as long as she was not his wife, he was kind. And she dreamed the oddest of dreams. Dreams of palaces and princes, even riches. She dreamed of romance and watched – over and over – the one American movie readily accessible in revolutionary China, The Sound *of* Music. Oh, to be loved like that. As for Xu Gang, he continued to do favors for Song Mei and never struck her again.

6. Duke Arrives

New York-Beijing, 1984

In the mid-'80s, when Duke Amici left the U.S. for his two-year stay in China, there weren't many flights to Beijing. His was out of New York's JFK airport on a Chinese airline, CACC. With a Chinese crew and Chinese food, the flight provided a gradual entrance into his new world, even though the plane itself was a Boeing 747. Departure was 10 a.m. Including stopovers in San Francisco and Shanghai, he would be in the air for almost a day, arriving in Beijing around 11 p.m. local time.

On the day before his May departure, Duke got into a car with four old friends who drove him from suburban Philadelphia up to New York. The little group had dinner in Manhattan, talked about old times and times to come. There was a small going-away gift, a quartz alarm clock with a digital read out, something new.

"Don't forget when it's time to come home," he was told.

After dinner his friends dropped him off at the Radisson Hotel JFK. Kisses and hugs. As he walked up the path to the hotel entrance, he was unable to turn around for that one last wave, couldn't bear it, didn't want even one tear to be seen. He rationalized that two years wasn't long. He knew he'd return, but not as the same man. Something would be left behind on the JFK tarmac and it would be lost to the wind. If only he knew what.

The next morning a shuttle took him to his plane, which was not crowded. Duke had the option of stretching out over three seats. Onboard were both Chinese and Americans, with a fair number of Americans headed for "foreign expert" jobs like Duke. Well into the flight, groups of travelers would get up, stand, and chat. Duke joined one such group and mostly listened and watched. He had much to learn. Before departing, he read Chinese history and focused on the revolutionary period. He studied up on current politics, how the country was run and who was running it. He ate authentic Chinese food in Philadelphia's Chinatown and took Chinese lessons from a Taiwanese woman, learning the basics – the four tones, numbers, days of the week, where's the bathroom, how much is that.

On the plane, the central speaker in Duke's little chat group was a Chinese man in a well-tailored suit. He had a good haircut and spoke well. He had a modern, almost hip way about him as he explained why the Communist Party was so important to China. He stressed that China was not communist. "We are socialists. We operate on the edge of communism," he said. Regarding the leadership of Mao Zedong during The Great Leap Forward (where famine killed 30 million), and the civil war-like Cultural Revolution, he said, "Mao was able to start the car, but he could not drive it. In the future, people like me will drive."

This pretty cool guy wasn't the image Duke had of communism, and he was hearing things he didn't expect to hear, so Duke, the journalist, asked a question.

"You know," he said, "and I mean this as a compliment. You look like you could handle yourself on your own, in any situation, without a guiding, authoritative hand. Without communism."

Smoking was allowed on planes back then, and the Chinese man, named Xing, an engineer who used radio astronomy to make maps, took a long Hollywood drag off his British cigarette.

"You are right. I can stand alone. On my own. I'd make out fine anywhere, including the capitalist world, which I've just spent four weeks in. But I have a brother who is not like me. He's not as smart, very passive. While I act, he waits. And waits. He would be crushed in New York. Destroyed. Even in China, without the Communist Party to look after and protect him, his life would be feeble. He needs socialism to provide him with a job and a decent salary. This is why I support the party. It takes care of my brother and thousands like him. It will never cast people aside. I am willing to sacrifice so that people like my brother can have respectable lives."

There was a call for passengers to return to their seats and prepare to land. "That guy sounded biblical," Duke said to an American who had been in on the chat.

In a few minutes, Duke would see, feel, smell and touch communism firsthand, or at least the edge of communism. He left the U.S. for that very reason. Duke grew up during the Cold War, when students hid under desks preparing for a nuclear attack from the Soviet Union. Horrible things were said about the Russians, most notably that they would bury America. Later, as a reporter and then an editor at a suburban Philadelphia newspaper, Duke hesitated to believe anything he did not witness. When the opportunity arose to witness communism, he was working an unpleasant night shift, had just broken up with his girlfriend, was still single at 29 and losing friends to marriage.

The University of Missouri's School of Journalism, he learned, was looking for journalists to work in China. The school had a strong relationship with China that pre-dated the revolution. It helped China fill jobs at the many English-language publications it distributed around the world. Missouri also recruited for The New China News Agency (Xinhua) and Chinese radio and TV stations broadcasting to foreign markets. Duke was languishing in the suburbs and needed an adventure, a fact-finding mission. China was it. Not exactly Russia, but it would do. A different kind of communism, but communism nonetheless.

Prior to his plane landing, a customs declaration was given to passengers. It listed prohibited material that could not be taken into the country, including:

Manuscripts, printed matter, films, photographs, gramophone records, cinemagraphic films, loaded recording tapes and video tapes etc. detrimental to Chinese political, economic, cultural, and moral interests.

There it is, Duke thought, the heavy hand of communism. Still, something about the declaration made it seem old and out of date. After all, copies of the Asian Wall Street Journal and Time were on the plane. Either way, one of the friends who saw Duke off had slipped an assortment of pulpy pornography into his suitcase as a practical joke. In the end, nothing came of it, but Duke didn't think it funny.

All passengers were required to deplane in Shanghai, at a bleak airport in desperate need of modernization. There was no elevated tube connecting the plane to the terminal. Instead, people got off by descending a stair truck driven out to the plane. The Beijing Airport was much better, more like those in America. Waiting there for him with a sign bearing his name was Feng Yaohua, known as Lao Feng, or Old Feng, a respected honorific that implied wisdom more than age. She was past middle age, thin, of average height, with short hair, and wearing a set of drab, lived-in clothes common to all office workers and the masses in general. The two introduced themselves, briefly discussed the flight, the weather, spoke a little about Xinhua, Duke's new employer. Luggage was picked up. He was now with the powerful Xinhua, so customs was bypassed. Outside, Duke and Lao Feng met a waiting driver, a Xinhua employee, in a late-model Mercedes sedan. In China, driving was a profession. Unless you were a professional, you didn't drive.

At this time of night, airport traffic was light. Lao Feng handed Duke a warm orange soda as the car headed toward central Beijing and the Friendship Hotel, about 40 minutes away. In her role as head of the Xinhua's International Department, she attended to foreigners. Her attitude, at least around the foreigners, was cold and calm. She was matter-of-fact and expressionless, sometimes inquisitive. She had seen much at Xinhua, including the intense factionalism during the Cultural Revolution, when there was violence and even gun play between staff members, when the agency's chief was reassigned to the boiler room and the boiler room chief assigned to run the agency. In these calmer times, with memories still fresh, she remained ever cautious.

From the car window, on this warm spring night, Duke saw people on bikes, people outside playing cards, people walking, a peasant on a mule-drawn cart. One man read a book under a streetlight. Signs of construction were everywhere. Dust flew about.

Lao Feng handed Duke a plate of cold meat, sweet rolls, and pastries.

"My daughter goes to Dartmouth," she said. And they talked about that.

Duke's long journey into the mysterious unknown ended as the Mercedes pulled through the gate at the Friendship Hotel and up to Building No. 9. He was absolutely exhausted and living in a dreamlike state. He noticed the ornate pagoda-style roof on the main building, Building No. 1, but little else. His apartment was more than he expected. There were two rooms with hardwood floors, a living room and a bedroom with two single beds, an acceptable bathroom with a western- toilet (regular toilets were ground-level, requiring users to squat), and a small kitchen that had a sink but nothing else. The furnishings included a big, beautiful, wooden desk and a color TV.

Lao Feng was startled by the TV.

"How much would a place like this cost in the U.S.?" she asked.

Duke, thinking of an apartment and not a hotel – like this one -- where they clean and make your bed each day and bring you hot and cold water in thermos bottles (no one drank tap water), said around $350 a month in his town, probably $800 in New York City, plus utilities. At the Friendship Hotel, Duke paid neither rent nor utilities. The hotel was part of his compensation package.

"Rest for a few days," Lao Feng said. "We will call you when you are ready. After a tour of the city, we will take you to work." Then she handed Duke an envelope fat with bills.

"What's this? he asked.

"It's a month's pay," Lao Feng explained. "You will be needing it."

"But I haven't done anything yet," Duke said. "In America, you only get paid when the work is done."

"We are different. It's for work you will do."

Thinking like an American and trying out a bit of humor, he said with a smile, "Suppose I take the money and don't come back?"

Thinking like a Chinese bureaucrat and also smiling, Lao Feng said, "We don't expect you to do that."

Duke, freshly flush, decided that even a non-capitalist state had its good points. He put the envelope in a drawer. After Lao Feng left, he unpacked. When he placed a bottle of 300 multiple vitamins on a shelf, he had a sudden sense of being trapped in a potentially harmful place. Rationally or irrationally, he comforted himself with the notion that he'd be halfway through his tenure when the vitamin bottle was empty, and that he'd watch the pill level decline every day, which, after a week, he did not.

Duke inspected the tap water, washed up, turned the TV on and off, opened and closed the drawers of his new desk, looked out the window at the street below. Then the weary traveler set the alarm on his new quartz clock with a digital readout for 10 a.m. In a matter of minutes, on a bed covered with a spread of embroidered green silk, he fell asleep, for the first time ever, by the light of an unfamiliar, somewhat hazy, communist moon.

7. A Chinese Poet in America

Philadelphia, 1987-88

Prior to April 1971, Red China, as it was sometimes called, had virtually no ties or contacts with the United States of America. That changed when nine players from the U.S. Table Tennis team paid an official visit. A year later, President Richard M. Nixon became the first U.S. president to travel there. In 1979, diplomatic relations were established, and a mortal enemy became, if not a friend, at least an acquaintance.

Even with 25 years of isolation following the 1949 revolution, America was not unfamiliar with ethnic Chinese people. They began coming in the 19th century, first as part of the California Gold Rush, then to work in railroad construction. In 1870, there were 17,000 Chinese immigrants laboring just in American mines. By 1924, legislation was passed to keep them out. The flow began again during World War II.

But in 1987, when a woman who took the American name of Emily Song applied to the English doctoral program at the University of Pennsylvania, mainland Chinese from the Mao-era were rare in the U.S. Instead, the Chinese in America were mostly Taiwanese and Cantonese from British Hong Kong. As a mainlander, Emily Song, in addition to her academic credentials and her skill as a writer and poet, was an attractive applicant for an open-minded Ivy League institution founded in 1740 by Benjamin Franklin. With the approval of her own government, she was accepted and given a full scholarship.

Emily Song adapted quickly. She flourished amid free expression, creativity, and experimentation. Library resources were endless and exhaustive. There were American movies to watch, both old and new, and for the first time Emily Song began listening to American music and watching American TV. With money she earned working part-time in a restaurant, she bought clothes from Macy's and Bloomingdale's and looked just like all the other students.

It was a six-year program, and she planned a dissertation on a critical comparison between women poets of the Ming Dynasty and Britain's most famous male romantics. After arriving and settling into a graduate dormitory, Emily Song called Duke Amici, now living in Florida and unaware she was in the states.

"Do you know who this is?" she asked.

Duke recognized the voice. He was both happy and fearful.

"Of course I do. How are you? Where are you?"

"I'm at Penn. In Philadelphia. Isn't that your home?"

"It was. Congratulations. You should have told me you were coming."

"I wanted to surprise you," she said. "The Labor Day holiday is soon. Do you have three days off? Can you come see me?"

The happy faded and the fearful elevated. "You're 800 miles away," he said, stuttering and explaining geography and drive time. Jumping ahead way too fast, he added, "And you should know I'm engaged to the woman I dated before I left for China."

He didn't go, and that ended that. Duke expected more calls. He expected her to regularly vent her troubles and frustrations and seek his advice, like she did in China. But she didn't. Still, she thought about him, especially when walking the streets of West Philadelphia, where Penn was located. Emily Song recalled Duke's joke about the streets not being paved with gold, and some not being paved at all. These were paved, but in need of repair. When she saw the dilapidated homes in the poorest of neighborhoods, she wondered why the government hadn't fixed them up. The worst sight was in nearby Powelton Village, where rows of homes — en masse --had burned down. So close to Penn. This confused and perplexed her. It made no sense.

Next came the mugging.

"Give me that," said a young man who grabbed her handbag.

This never happened in China. She didn't know how to react. Would he shoot her? More than her personal safety, she thought about losing her passport, school ID and the only money she had. She fought back. She grabbed the strap of her bag and engaged in a tugging match. Emily Song pulled, screamed, and kicked. She actually hurt the young man, and he ran off, leaving her the bag. She was victorious, but shaken, unclear of what this meant, worried that this characterized American life. Her screaming had caught the attention of a policeman getting coffee nearby.

"What happened, Miss?" he asked. "Are you all right?"

"He tried to steal my money," she said, crying and pointing to where the young man had run. "Can you get him? Can you punish him?"

The policeman's name was Mike Boyle. He was 35, single, 6 foot 1, a Philadelphia native who had been on the force 10 years. His father was a retired cop. Not in the shape he once was, and with thinning blond hair, Officer Boyle was less prone than most to run down suspects. This one was too far gone and hadn't succeeded at his crime, so the effort was not worth it.

"He's halfway home now," Boyle said. "It's better that I take care of you. Let's sit and have coffee. Are you hungry?"

His voice was calming; his attention appreciated. Emily Song settled down.

"Does this happen a lot? she asked.

The policeman liked this woman's unusual appearance, simple but alluring. He liked how she exhibited both vulnerability and confidence, how she carried herself differently.

"It happens too much," he said. "That's why we're here. On some of these streets, you must learn to be careful and alert. You have to watch what neighborhoods you go into. How long have you been here? Are you a student?"

Emily Song answered all his questions. She noticed his service revolver and nightstick and felt safe with him.

"We don't have this in China," she said. Fifteen minutes into the conversation, she asked about the burned-out homes in Powelton Village.

"Oh, that," he said. "No one is proud of that."

In the early 70s, a Philadelphia man named Vincent Leaphart changed his name to John Africa and wrote a manifesto for a new way of life. He opposed technology and all forms of modernism, including medicine. He preached a back-to-nature philosophy that was anti-authoritarian, militant, Pan-African, Black nationalistic, and primitive. Followers came. They settled into a Victorian house in Powelton Village, all took the name Africa and, since they were starting a new life, changed their age to 1. Their group was called MOVE, but the letters didn't stand for anything. Members wore dreadlocks, frequently demonstrated, battled with police, and often were arrested. Their trash was dumped behind their home, bringing rats and pests of all sorts. Packs of dogs gathered. When the health department came, MOVE members erected barricades and resisted.

On May 13, 1985, with the intention of gaining access to the house, Philadelphia Police Department dropped two small military-grade bombs from a helicopter. Gasoline was stored in the MOVE house and a fire started. City officials decided not to risk the lives of firefighters, who could be shot. They let the home burn. The fire spread. In the end, 65 dwellings were destroyed and 11 people, including five children, died. Ramona Africa, the only surviving adult from MOVE, was arrested and convicted of rioting and conspiracy. She served seven years in prison.

Had Emily Song been at Penn on May 13, 1985, she would have seen the smoke from her dorm.

"Is this common in America?" she asked.

"No," the police officer said.

"Do similar things happen? Not as big but similar?"

"Maybe. I can't say."

"Were these people oppressed? Were they fighting to be free? Isn't America already free?"

Officer Boyle shifted in his chair and drank his coffee. "These are tough questions," he said. "It's hard to explain these things to people who don't really understand our country. The MOVE bombing was an unfortunate tragedy that everyone regrets. Can we leave it at that?"

"Okay," she said, asking herself: Would Duke have explained it better?

Officer Boyle took down Emily Song's contact information. He gave her his card and said to call if she had any more trouble or if she saw the purse-snatcher again. Boyle looked closely at her and recalled what a friend, a Vietnam veteran, had told him: "The best wives are Asian."

The incident taught Emily Song to stay close to campus and travel with friends. She loved campus life and was being recognized as a poet of some substance. Her mix of East and West was a sought-after novelty. Students and faculty gravitated toward her. She was asked to participate in an evening of poetry reading and eagerly agreed. Event fliers with her name and picture were posted around Penn and West Philadelphia.

About 200 people attended. Emily Song read a poem about the Cultural Revolution and then two about America. With five minutes left, she brought up the female poets of the Ming Dynasty.

"These were enlightened times," she said. "China was strong and the envy of the world. Later we grew so poor that few of you, I'm sure, ever think of China as once being great, but it was. Everyone wanted to trade with China. Everyone wanted what China had. We called our country, then and now, the Middle Kingdom, or Zhong Guo, not China, as you do. We were the center of everything. Maybe one day we will be again."

She laughed and so did the audience, which also applauded.

"During the Ming period, women held a firm place in society. There was a poet named Lui Rushi, who was born in 1618. She was especially strong and independent. On occasion, she would dress like a man. But she was also incredibly romantic."

The audience seemed attentive, wanting more.

"At a very young age, she was sold by her family to the prime minister. She became his concubine but displeased him. He sold her to a brothel when she was 13 years old. Can you imagine? There were many liaisons and affairs. When she was 25, Lui Rushi – who also was a painter -- married a great poet named Qian Qianyi. He was 61. When Qian Qianyi died, Lui Rushi committed suicide."

Emily Song then read her own translation of a work by Lui Rushi.

In the back of the room sat Officer Boyle, who was off duty. He had seen one of the promotional fliers and decided to go, although he had no particular interest in poetry. Still, he found Emily Song's presentation impressive. He approached her afterward and they walked the campus. They made a date for dinner and continued dating for three months. In June of 1988, they were married by a local judge. Their reception was held at a firehall in Northeast Philadelphia, where chicken was served and the music was provided by the groom's cousin's band. The best part came later, when Emily Song's temporary student visa was superseded by a Green Card, allowing her, if she wished, to stay forever in the United States of America.

About a month prior to this second marriage, Emily received a letter from her ex-husband Xu Gang, a well-connected officer in the Peoples Liberation Army, instructing her to be at JKF airport on a certain date, at a certain time, to meet a certain man, to take possession of a certain suitcase, and to use the contents of that suitcase -- $300,000 cash – to purchase a home as an investment property. He didn't care where.

Slowly but steadily, newly made fortunes were beginning to flow from China to America, and a Chinese poet who spoke excellent English and held a coveted Green Card would, without ever wanting to, become a bridge for much of this money.

8. Working and Vacationing with Xinhua

Beijing and elsewhere, 1984-86

For Duke Amici, the best part of working at The New China News Agency was quitting time, and not because the work was over. It was because at the end of a shift you grabbed your drinking cup, and whatever was left of the tea or boiled water in it, and threw it onto the concrete floor. You didn't just dump it. You threw it, using a swinging arm motion, as if you were bowling, to toss it out in front of you. The liquid evaporated quickly in the dry Beijing air and added humidity to the room. It also settled the dust. For Duke, and perhaps only him, this tossing of the tea was a satisfying, spiritual release, something defiant and rude that was not done in polite western society but was perfectly acceptable in this eastern workplace. For his Chinese coworkers, it was mindless and rote, like turning off the lights.

Xinhua editors didn't work hard, but they put in the time. Monday through Friday and a half day Saturday. Sundays were off. A minibus drove the foreign workers back to the Friendship Hotel each day for lunch, leaving at 11:30 and returning at 2. The day ended at 5 but went until 5:30 in the hot summer (no air conditioning) when the lunch break was extended. Once every two months or so, employees worked something called the da yei ban, or the Great Night Shift, from midnight to 6. It was a skeleton crew. The dining hall staff served only a limited menu, mostly fresh dumpling, which the day shift didn't get. When Duke thought of the da yei ban, he thought of dark hallways and dumplings.

The Xinhua compound was walled and guarded and required a company ID or pass to enter. There was an array of concrete buildings, and a new one was going up, with construction loud and messy. Duke's job title was "foreign expert." He worked in an unadorned 4th-floor office of a 10-story building. He and the other foreign experts considered themselves copy editors, with the task of improving news stories by making them accurate, more interesting, more readable, and with no begging questions for the reader. Xinhua, however, considered them "polishers," who sharpened the English and grammar of Chinese reporters, translators, and editors. The news agency was both a domestic and international service. Duke worked on the international side, the Guo Ji Bu, in the English section. He polished (or edited) stories written by Xinhua correspondents in 90 bureaus around the world.

For the homogenous city of Beijing, the Chinese crew in the Guo Ji Bu was fairly diverse. Its senior member was Lao Wang, or Old Wang. Highly educated, polite and selfless, Lao Wang had done 10 years in solitary confinement during the Cultural Revolution. He told his story to Duke Amici one night on the Great Night Shift, when they were alone and with only a few stories to polish. Lao Wang teared up in the telling and said his biggest fear in solitary was forgetting English. As a remedy, he had English conversations with himself for at least one hour a day, sometimes more. After being rehabilitated and put back to work, Lao Wang was the model employee. He never broke or bent the rules, always volunteered to work the holidays, and set an example by cleaning the office.

A contrast to Lao Wang was the young Xiao Wang, or Little Wang, who resented the "Xiao" title and hoped one day to be the more respectable "Lao." Xiao Wang, unrelated to the older man, was an unusual case. He didn't carry himself like the Mandarin Lao Wang, and although his English was good, he didn't come off as cultured. He was a bit tough and took less care with his hair and clothes. Xiao Wang began his working career in the Xinhua boiler room. During the chaotic insanity of the Cultural Revolution, he was one of many boiler room employees promoted to journalist. At the end of the Cultural

Revolution, when the former boiler room workers went back to the boiler room, Xiao Wang – miraculously -- stayed in the Guo Ji Bu.

Then there was Wu Jiahui, a small, middle-aged wife and mother who often complained about the double duty of career and home – being responsible for shopping, cooking, and looking after her 6-year-old child. She was effective at borrowing work time to get her domestic chores done and would come late to the office carrying bags of food she purchased for that night's dinner. Of course, she took advantage of the three days off each month during her period and had more funeral leave than anyone in the office, with some coworkers saying her father had died three times in the last two years. Wu Jiahui was funny, engaging, and a straight talker who didn't fear authority. Mao said women hold up half the sky, but Wu Jiahui would tell you her half was especially heavy.

In the Beijing office, Chan Yatching was about as foreign as you can get while still being Chinese. Tall, thin, and dressed like he was in the tropics, Chan was from Canton (correct name Guangzhou), Southeastern China, a place of distinctive culture, with a separate language that differed dramatically from standard Mandarin. When he spoke on the office phone to a friend back home, Wu Jiahui jokingly held her ears, grimaced, and shrieked. "That Cantonese language is the worst in the world. I can't stand hearing it." After that opening salvo, Xiao Wang followed up with his own insult. "The Cantonese will eat anything with four legs," he said. "The one exception is the table." It was like a group from Brooklyn making fun of a guy from Mississippi.

Like in any office, there was a crazy sort of fellow, a suspected backstabber who was not to be trusted. Everyone, Chinese and foreign, leaned away from him. He was Zhou Wen, a nervous type who smiled and laughed uncomfortably through his many worries. When his son was studying for the university entrance examinations, called the gao kao, Zhou Wen was a wreck. The rapidity of his hair loss increased. The gao kao is a harsh, intense, make it or break it exam. Teenage suicide rates jump after the results are released. When Zhou Wen's son passed and was accepted to Beijing University, the father was light as a feather and a little goofy, explaining to everyone in the office, "To celebrate, my son and I ate a whole chicken." And he laughed. "Can you imagine? A whole chicken! And nothing else."

These and others worked with a pod of foreign experts, primarily from the U.S., Canada, and Britain. With two-year contracts, they rotated in and out. The foreigners, at least the decent ones, carried an underlying guilt about doing the same work as the Chinese but getting paid 10 times as much, about $70 a month (500 yuan), which went far. The younger Chinese frequently asked about salaries in the states. One of them, Liu Chao, lived in the Xinhua dorm and used cheap, pre-paid meal tickets to eat in the cavernous Xinhua dining hall. It was not unusual for him to take his pay on the first of the month and spend it on a single item, say, a stereo deck. For the rest of the month, because of the protections and subsidies under communism, he could get by being penniless. He could walk the streets for 30 days with an empty wallet and survive.

"You can't do that in the U.S." Duke told him. "You wouldn't last the month. Americans make more money than you, but I'm guessing you have more disposable income. What we pay for coffee you pay for rent. Our utility bills are high. We have mortgages. We have loans and car payments, credit card payments. There are insurance payments on our cars, our homes, our lives. College tuition and day care, plus taxes, taxes, taxes – local tax, state tax, federal tax, sales tax. It goes on and on. Gym membership. Pool membership. You have none of this. For many people, at the end of the month there's nothing left, nothing to save. We usually get paid by the week, not the month, but no one can take a month's pay and spend it on something frivolous."

"Do they make you join a gym and pool?" Lui Chao asked.

"No," Duke said.

"But they make you pay taxes."

"It's inescapable."

"But what is your salary?" Lui Chao asked.

Duke was shy about this. "In 1984, at the small newspaper where I worked, before deductions, about $35,000 a year."

"That all?" Lui Chao didn't believe him. "Tell us the truth. What do you really make?"

Trust and understanding grew with time as the foreign experts and their Chinese colleagues worked together side-by-side and on equal terms. The operation was simple. Someone from another office, an editor or a translator or rewrite person or someone, would enter and drop a story in a basket. Then either a foreign expert or a native would pick it out, fix it up, and deposit it in another basket. The office tools were pencils and a few typewriters. The English was supposed to be corrected, but editorial changes were not encouraged. Still, for some of these western journalists, old habits were fixed. Lead paragraphs were rewritten and important information was brought to the top of stories. For the most part, British English was used, which the American polishers sometimes changed. (A big argument ensued over the correctness of either "Election heats up" or "Election hots up," with the latter being British.). Unlike news organizations such as the Associated Press, Xinhua lacked a detailed "stylebook" to explain accepted usage to foreign editors. The one point of style Xinhua did stress was that North Korea and South Korea would always be north Korea and south Korea (lower case adjective), suggesting the division of the Chinese ally was unofficial and temporary.

The first story Duke edited was written by a Xinhua correspondent in London. It was about a television workers strike. More frequently, stories would be from Third World countries with datelines of cities most Americans had never heard of. Duke found himself checking the spelling of places like Antananarivo (Madagascar) and Lilongwe (Malawi) and Kigali (Rwanda). As a supplier of international news to the world, Xinhua knew it could not compete with the Associated Press, Reuters, and Agence France-Presse. Instead, it positioned itself as the sole news organization that cared about the developing world and reported on it with objectivity. Its subscribers were mainly developing nations.

Too often, the news was about agricultural or industrial production, or complaints by groups of small countries – such the Association of Southeastern Asian Nations -- of being barred from trading with the West. Visitations of national leaders were covered, as well as stories from the United Nations, especially when a vote equated Zionism with apartheid. The main fare was safe stories with no chance of getting reporters in political trouble back home. Safe but also boring. As China refocused on its position in the world, Xinhua sought improvement, encouraging enterprise reporting and good writing. However, correspondents and editors, like those who served 10 years in solitary, were not apt to listen.

There was near paralysis at Xinhua when Indira Gandhi was assassinated by her Sikh bodyguard. China and India were considered enemies, with constant struggles over border disputes. Xinhua editors didn't want a story written until it learned the new government's position on China. When the delay exceeded professional limits, a writer was told, "Do the story, but don't make the Sikh look too bad and don't make Gandhi look too good."

Change was slow. Another problem was journalism training. Most at Xinhua had none.

"How did you manage to get this job?" Larry Altman, a Canadian college professor asked a young woman as she walked into the office and dropped off a story. Young, pretty, and extroverted, Li Li wore close-fitting tops and tight jeans, which were very hard to get. As such, she stood out. She was a billboard for the changing times. Her walk was like a dance and her conversation like flirting.

Li Li laughed at Larry. "I got this job because I speak Portuguese." And she turned and danced out of the office. Indeed, a Xinhua requirement in the international section was not journalism but language, and Xinhua employees were plucked out of language schools (they had no say in the matter) without ever knowing anything about journalism.

"What do you think of Miss Portugal?" Larry asked Duke. From that day on, Li Li was known to the two men as "The Portuguese."

On infrequent occasions, for part of the day, the foreign workers were alone in the office. This meant there was a Communist party meeting somewhere. Since most Xinhua employees were members, they had to attend, leaving their work for the foreigners. When the Chinese coworkers returned, the foreigners would ask about the meeting and what policy changes were imminent.

"What did they say?" Renee Mitchell, a Canadian journalist, asked the returning group. "What's going to happen?"

"That was a long meeting," Wu Jaihui said, relieved it was over. "They told us who the likely candidates are for party secretary, president and premiere, and some of the people who will be promoted to the Central Committee."

"Did anyone object or suggest someone else?" Renee asked.

"No," Wu Jaihui said. "They were good choices. The only complaint came when they said the xiu xi might end. No one wants that."

In all Xinhua offices and in offices all over China, there are old but comfortable armchairs near workstations. These are for the xiu xi, a sacred and almost universally observed noon siesta. When there aren't enough chairs, workers sleep on desktops or tables. In Beijing, you can't go to the bank or do business between 12 and 1:30 because everyone is resting. Party leaders, more attuned now to business, decided the xiu xi is bad for business. No more xiu xi, they decided. Xiao Wang, the former boiler room worker, smirked and predicted that any edict banning the xiu xi would be roundly ignored, suggesting that even authoritarianism has its limits.

In China, the place of employment is called your work unit, and it has significant control over your life, for both good and bad, to help but sometimes to hinder. Xinhua, acting as a surrogate family, was tasked with making the foreigners feel at home. It would invite them to various functions and formal occasions. Each year in Beijing, there was a big thank-you event for all foreign experts, whom top leaders would commend for helping to "build socialism."

"I don't actually build socialism," Larry told the person next to him at the event. "I correct bad grammar."

Some foreign workers hated everything about the Chinese. Some loved it all, from the ridiculous to the splendid. Most had mixed feelings. A scant few got into big trouble. In one case, the actions of two adventurous Americans had a collateral effect. They inadvertently took down the distinguished Lao Wang. It put a bitter end to a bitter life that struggled for happiness in the simple pursuit of knowledge.

Lao Wang was his father's son. The father cherished books and learned Spanish just to read *Don Quixote*, Italian to read Dante, Greek to read Homer. He was fastidious about his personal library, which filled three rooms of their pre-revolutionary house. The books were left behind and lost forever when the Japanese invaded. After the war, the father rebuilt the library, again filling three rooms. During the Cultural Revolution, he was told those rooms were needed as living space for other families, and that the books must be sold, which they were, not as literature but for scrap. When normalcy returned, the old man, with the help of Lao Wang, saw the library rise again for the third time.

Scholarship was everything to Lao Wang. As China modernized, he expected to achieve his life's apex and visit the United States. A quiet man, he was ecstatic on the inside when Yale offered him a position as a visiting professor. But Xinhua, and perhaps China's major intelligence officials, would not let him go. For this slight, credit the Americans Jessie and Amy Murdock, a young married couple who wanted to go to Tibet almost as much as Lao Wang wanted to go to Yale. At the time, travel to Tibet by foreigners was restricted. Lao Wang argued on behalf of Jessie and Amy, taking their case to the top Xinhua bureaucrats. Denied. Jessie and Amy's solution was to forge their documents and go anyway. They were caught, and Lao Wang, with no evidence, was considered an accomplice. His punishment: You will never see the shores of America.

That was Xinhua the tough parent. Xinhua the engaging parent, at least for the foreign workers, encouraged involvement in China's affairs, at least the approved kind. It often organized events for them, scheduling transportation and giving them time off. The first such event Duke attended was a commemoration of the 200th anniversary of trade between China and the United States. The American ambassador was there. It was widely covered by Chinese media, with TV reporters and camera crews rudely pushing in and intruding to get the best shot or the best interview, no different than the states. A speaker explained that in the year 1784, the ship Empress of China arrived home after a visit to America and trading began. As commercial ties grew, Americans wanted more and more Chinese goods, especially tea, but the Chinese wanted little from America, beginning a trade imbalance that would perplex and frustrate the West until the present day, but that wasn't mentioned.

There was food, drink, and entertainment at the celebration. With the official government line urging peasants to use private enterprise to get rich, a woman sang the popular message song, *Living on the Field of Hope*; a musician played *Old Susanna* on a two-string instrument called an er hu; and Duke Amici was introduced to Josh Silberstein, who had been in China for decades, longer than any American. The handful of high-profile people who visited closed-off China either sought out Josh Silberstein or the government hooked them up with him. Josh, known as Old Red or Lao Hong, tended to be standoffish and suspect of westerners but took a liking to Duke because, in conversation, he mentioned and knew about Yanan, Mao's revolutionary base of operations.

"Shirley MacLaine, the actress, came to China," Silberstein told Duke. "She didn't much care for me. Thought a lot of herself. Was writing a book on the sex lives of Chinese women. Stupid. Like it's any different."

Duke wanted to learn everything Josh knew.

"Candace Bergen visited. She was sweet. She thought about making a movie here. Kissed me on the head when she said goodbye. Then there was the time I got drunk on mao tai with two violin players from the Philadelphia Orchestra. I convinced them to play country fiddle at the Beijing Hotel bar. What a scene that was."

Duke, the curious journalist, asked more and more questions.

Finally, Silberstein, after failing to provide acceptable answers, said in frustration, "Listen, any silly son-of-a-bitch who says he's a China expert is full of shit. No one knows anything. There's really nothing I can tell you."

To the foreign experts, Xinhua – in addition to news gathering – appeared to be tasked with serving as an advanced guard for change. It was out front once new policies and practices were floated, helping to test and perfect them for national consumption. One area, for certain, was travel and tourism. In this matter, Xinhua foreign experts were the willing guinea pigs.

As part of their employment package, Xinhua's guest workers received five weeks paid vacation. To help them enjoy the time off, the news agency organized twice-a-year, 14-day, train-boat-plane excursions all over China, and covered the expense. In the mid-'80s, China was, for the most part, without a tourist industry. Yes, Chinese people came to Beijing to visit Mao's preserved corpse and the Great Hall of the People, to walk through Tiananmen Square (the largest in the world, able to hold a half million people) and tour the vast imperial palace known as The Forbidden City. Chinese tourists, in small numbers, also visited revered sites in the interior – Buddhist temples and mammoth carvings of The Enlightened One, the exquisite and unusual green limestone mountains of Guilin, the Stone Forest at Kunming. Overall, however, on any significant scale, in the mid-'80s

China – still closed off -- did not have a tourist industry. Outside the major cities of Beijing, Shanghai, and the new special economic zone of Shenzhen (capitalism allowed), people were unaccustomed to seeing foreigners, didn't understand their ways and didn't know how to treat them. In the smaller cities, if a foreigner wandered in, he or she would quickly be surrounded by a playful, curious mob. If tourism was to be a thing – and China had incredible potential for it – tourism workers had to be trained. In exchange for free vacations, Xinhua's traveling foreign experts were practiced upon.

For Duke and the others, the experience was rough but priceless. They stayed in spartan hotels that would be demolished later and replaced with 5-star accommodations. Chinese colleagues and bosses from Xinhua came along, serving as guides, problem solvers, interpreters, and chaperones. They'd get complaints like:

"The pipes make noise and the water is rusty."

"I can't sleep on that hard bed."

"There's no air conditioning?"

"Can I get a lock on the door?"

"The towels are so thin."

"How can they not have toast for breakfast?"

Shortly after a traveling Xinhua group settled into a town, the local Communist Party hosted a banquet in its honor, thanking them (once again) for building socialism and stressing the importance of developing a strong relationship with the West. These banquets were costly and excessive. When travel arrangements caused the group to be in, say, three different cities on three consecutive days, the gastronomic pleasure was more than some could handle. This caused a few weight-conscious travelers to skip consecutive banquets and opt for simple, smaller-portioned street food. At the banquets, one dish followed another and another and another. In front of each diner were three full glasses: a large one with beer, a smaller one with wine, and a shot glass of mao tai. If a mere sip was taken from a glass, it would be refilled. The hosts made repeated toasts, downing the powerful and dangerous mao tai, imploring gan bei, or empty glass. The idea was to get the westerners drunk and in bed before they caused unsupervised havoc with the local population.

The travel and the meals together gave the foreign workers better insight into their Chinese colleagues, who delighted in sharing the VIP treatment and gourmet cuisine. One dish the foreigners did not like was Sea Cucumbers, actually sea slugs, a delicacy reserved for the elite. Being ultra-polite, the Chinese journalists would take the Sea Cucumbers from the serving dish and put them on the plate of the Westerners, who didn't want them. When it became obvious the slugs were going uneaten, the Chinese, who felt undeserving, mustered enough courage to take some for themselves.

In each town, the foreigners were entertained by local performers and shown the local sites. They also receive tours of factories, where manual labor exceeded any machine processing. Renee, the Canadian, put in an order at a rug factory after witnessing the artistic but time-consuming handmade process. The rug workers, mostly women, sat before their work and followed an existing pattern, grabbing a piece of wool thread of the proper color, inserting it into the rug, then lopping off the excess with the blade of a sharp and deadly looking knife. Over and over and over. In some factories, it was clear that more workers than needed were employed, that greater efficiencies could be built in. It was also clear that these products – not seen in the homes of the average Chinese -- could be bought at an excellent price and sold in the U.S. at a considerable profit. Duke made a mental note of this.

One vacation took the Xinhua group to southwest China to look in on the many minority groups – called min zou – that comprise 7 percent of the population. In the southwest, members of tribes like the Bai, Dai, and Miao resemble the Vietnamese people more than the Chinese. The women wear traditional clothing, elaborate, colorful garb, with handmade jewelry, beads, and exotic head pieces. These women were princess-like and carried themselves royally (not so the rather shabby-looking men). Duke thought them beautiful and asked Lui Chao what he thought.

"Not for me," he said.

"Why not?" Duke asked.

"I don't like their looks. They are primitive, not Chinese. Not fully developed people."

"But they're beautiful."

"Not to me."

In one area, the group stayed in tropical huts, on stilts with thatched roofs and no running water. In the morning, in their rooms, the westerners washed up using only a bar of soap, a pitcher of water, a ceramic basin, and a small towel. Later, on an excursion, some swam in the Mekong River.

Particularly memorable was a Xinhua-sponsored three-day cruise down the Yangtze River, from Chongqing to Wuhan. "Sign up for this one," Eric Davies, a Brit, told Duke. "You're going to see something that in a few years no one will ever see again."

The planned journey would take a tired-looking ship and its passengers down river to the breathtaking Three Gorges, a path through the mountains and the future location of a monumental dam and the world's largest hydroelectric plant.

"The entire valley will be flooded for miles," Eric said. "Totally underwater. Acres and acres. Thousands and thousands of people will be forced to relocate. Their towns will cease to exist."

The idea for a Three Gorges dam was envisioned in 1919 by Sun Yat-sen, the first president of the Republic of China. But he did nothing. In 1931, the Yangtze flooded and killed 4 million people. A year later, Chiang Kai-shek, the Nationalist president, began work on plans for the dam, as did Mao after him, and so on. Now the reality of the dam was approaching.

According to the origin story of China, water management played a key role in the unification and formation of this ancient nation. The short version of the story is that the person who solved China's massively destructive flood problem with a series of canals constructed over 13 years was chosen to lead all the little kingdoms and give birth to a country of power and wealth. The 4,000-year-old engineering marvel that saved lives and crops was the beginning of China's great reverence for meritocracy. Engineers, they say, now run China, and those engineers are going to build one hell of a dam.

"Take lots of pictures of those gorges," Eric advised. In addition to the pictures, the foreigners did lots of gawking, imprinting in their brains what would soon vanish. They saw it as a loss. China, of course, saw it as a gain, an accomplishment for the ages.

During the boat trip, time was a commodity in search of purpose. The hours stretched out. The scenery only held the attention for so long. This ship was designed strictly for transportation, not entertainment. Passengers read, napped, chatted, walked about, waited for mealtime. Duke met and befriended a Xinhua editor that he had never seen at work, a fellow who tended to stay in his office. Huang

Defu and Duke Amici were about the same age. Huang was married without children, cautious and pleasant, chubby, with a head and body that resembled rectangles. In a room for gathering, Duke saw him playing Chinese chess and stopped to observe.

"Do you want to play?" Defu asked.

"I don't know how. I barely understand western chess," Duke said.

"I'll teach you."

Defu's partner quit, saying, "You've got me beat." To Duke he said, "Watch out. He's tricky."

Duke sat down. "In your chess, you have a king," Defu said. "We have a general. The game has two armies at war. On the board are squares, and a river and two palaces – which you don't have in your game. Other pieces are the advisor, the elephant, the horse, the chariot, the cannon, and the soldier. If you capture the general, you win."

They played slowly as Defu walked Duke through the various moves and explained strategy. The American did poorly.

As they played, Defu related a story often repeated by western chess masters: "A wise immortal once told a lowly human, 'In playing chess, there is no infallible way of winning, but there is an infallible way of not losing.' The human asked what that was. The immortal replied, 'It is not to play chess.'"

That evening the two men dined together.

"Tell me about America," Defu said. "Mr. Churchill claims the Americans will always do the right thing, once they have exhausted every other alternative."

"Mr. Churchill was angry we were too long in coming to England's aid during World War II," Duke said.

"But what of America?" Defu said. "You know the Chinese name for the United States is Mei Guo, which means beautiful country?"

"I thought that odd, considering all those years when we were mortal enemies. I thought you'd change the name."

"We weren't always so kind," Defu said. "Do you know what we called John F. Kennedy?" Duke shook his head. "We called him Ken Ni Di, which sounds like Kennedy but means The Dirt Eater."

Duke laughed. "Anyway, I love America," he said. "But it's misunderstood. Lui Chao thinks everyone makes $100,000 a year. A graduate student I met thinks every building must be a palace. Your propaganda doesn't seem to be working. You're supposed to tear us down not build us up. There's a joke that goes, 'Democracy is the worst system in the world, except for all others.' That should give foreigners a more realistic perspective of America."

"What do you like most about your country?" Defu asked.

Duke answered quickly. "For the most part, no one bothers you," he said. "Your system is based on making the individual do what's good for the masses and not what's good for the individual – like the dam that's going in. Sacrifice is the thing. My system is based on government leaving you alone, letting you do what you want and finding happiness on your own. The other great thing, for all its dastardly faults and its ability to crush people, is capitalism and the free market. If you want something or need something and are willing to pay for it, this intricate system will miraculously bring it to you, no matter where you are. And it will do so efficiently. If the lead used to make 10-cent pencils is produced cheaply in central Africa, some American businessman will find it, buy it, ship it, and make a profit off it. School kids will use those pencils and never think about that. If I brought you to an American supermarket and walked you up and down the aisles, you'd be in awe of what we can buy and the varieties everything comes in. I had a teacher in high school who said we could end communism and cause an uprising in Russia simply by flying over Moscow and dropping Sears catalogues."

"Sears?"

"A chain of big stores that sells nearly everything. Every year it publishes, for free, a four-inch-thick catalog listing all its products, which you can order by mail or buy in the store. Everything from a woman's dress to a TV to a set of quality wrenches. That catalog and Sears is a core piece of America."

In the ship's mess hall, Duke ate heartily. A mix of so-so food in both western and Chinese styles. Huang Defu didn't appear hungry. He'd rather talk than eat.

"Americans just do what they want. I like that," Defu said. "If they want to sing, they sing. If they want to dance, they dance. If they want to sit on the sand and do nothing, they sit on the sand and do nothing. Everyone has choices and your society respects those choices, right? And if you are really unusual, you move to California."

"That's funny," Duke said.

"I wasn't trying to be funny."

"It's funny because it's true."

"Have you eaten in the dining hall at Xinhua?" Defu asked.

"Mostly they take us back to the Friendship Hotel for lunch, but I have eaten there, yes."

"People bring their own bowls and eating utensils. After eating, there's a room with a long line of sinks and people wash their bowls and utensils there. Then, each and every person fills a bowl with water and rinses their mouth three times. Not once, not twice, but three times. We all do it the same way. In winter, in Beijing, we all wear three pairs of long underwear and on a set day in early spring, we all take them off – on the very same day. The Chinese like convention. Sameness. There is no nonconformity. I've always longed to step outside our conventions, like wanting to touch wet paint, but I lack the courage. And I wouldn't want my family to lose face. You know, my father is a true patriot. A hero. His name is known throughout China. I must follow his example."

Huang Defu's father, Huang Ming, was a senior technology specialist at Xinhua, what they call a gao gan, meaning a high official. In 1937, when Japan invaded China, Huang Ming was with Mao's Red Army. The Red Army and the Nationalists under Chiang Kai-shek were involved in civil war but called an uneasy truce to unite against the Japanese. Both sides headquartered in Chongqing and kept a close eye on each other. Huang Ming, a radio man, got the idea to use a Communist Party facility – which had been inspected and visited by the Nationalists – to build a hidden listening post in the attic. From there, he monitored Nationalist communications, allowing the Red Army to keep one step ahead of their rivals and to better position themselves for the expected post-war battle. On several occasions, Huang Ming learned of planned U.S. arm shipments to the Nationalists. Using that intelligence, the Red Army intercepted the weapons and built up its arsenal. The Nationalists never discovered the listening post, and the story of how they were outsmarted is told and retold. It's become folklore. The building with the hidden attic is a national museum.

"Hey," someone yelled. "The first gorge is coming up." Everyone rushed out on the open deck to view the sheer cliffs towering above them, making them and their small ship feel even smaller.

Two weeks after the Three Gorges trip, Duke Amici and Huang Defu agreed to have lunch in the Xinhua dining hall. They ordered chicken, pork, and fish, and like everyone else left the bones on the table. Duke and Defu lingered after hundreds of others rushed back to the office for xiu xi, the afternoon rest.

"I decided," Defu said, "to apply for a master's degree in journalism at the University of Missouri. Perhaps you can write me a letter of recommendation."

"Most certainly," Duke said. "It's my alma mater."

"I'm going to wait another year or two, studying and preparing and getting things in order, then I'll apply." Defu said. "I'm going to give it all I have. I'm going to learn and also experience America. I'll get a driver's license. On one of the breaks, I'm going to rent a car and drive to your house. Together, we will go to Disney World. How does that sound?"

"It sounds great," Duke said. "I'll be waiting for you."

Both men got up, washed their bowls, and once, twice, three times, rinsed out their mouths and, with great gusto, spit.

9. Duke Writes Home

Beijing, 1984

Dear Joey,

This is your long-lost brother writing from a far-off land. Well, maybe not so long lost. It's only been three months. But it sure as hell is a far-off land. Take these letters, for example. Very frustrating. I write one, mail it, and it takes two weeks to get to you. You wait a week, write back, and I get your letter four weeks after I mailed mine. In between, other stuff has happened, and I've written you about that after the first letter, and when I get your letter answering the first one, I'm expecting you to know what I wrote in the second, but you don't. It's like being trapped in some broken time machine. There's a phone here in my apartment. I guess I could call you, but I really don't know how that's done and haven't asked anyone. I guess I'm trying to do this the old fashion way and see if I can handle it, the isolation, the being cut off. Even if I did use the phone, it's really bad. The connection is horrible. You have to yell. When the Chinese answer the phone they say – scream – the word "wei." It's like hello, but hello is actually "ni hao." No one ever answers the phone with ni hao and no one ever says wei when they are not on the phone. Someone said it has no meaning. It's like a test pattern to find out if the other person can hear you. It's often shouted several times by people on both ends of the line. So I won't be using the phone, at least for the time being. Maybe one day they'll get that fixed, but technology doesn't seem to be their strong point.

Anyway, I'm fine and I hope everyone there is fine. Life here, while always different and unexpected, can be routine and mundane at times. Other times, it is wildly interesting and often bizarre. Let me tell you about last Friday night, which falls into the category of wildly interesting and bizarre. It's a fairly long story so brace yourself.

Me and some friends at the Xinhua News Agency were scheduled to work the night shift, which runs to midnight. But on this night, a rare evening event was scheduled at the Friendship Hotel, so us foreigners conspired to leave work at 11. The event? Well, miraculously, a band of western musicians (mostly young) had formed among the ex-pats here. They play rock, blues, reggae, and are pretty good. I guess they got their instruments and equipment from home, or maybe from Hong Kong. They even have a van to haul everything around. Maybe that belongs to an embassy kid. The sax player is an older adult, an English teacher, an American who brought his instrument with him to China. A band member saw that sax and grabbed him. With all the Chinese being told to work hard and get rich, the manager at the hotel's Foreign Experts Club – where not much ever happens – decided to book the band (for free) and double the price of the beer. Word got around in the foreign community, and it was expected to be a hell of an affair. There are lots of colleges near the Friendship Hotel with lots of exchange students, including many Africans and Arabs. They were expected to be at the event, as were the foreign experts – even the ones scheduled to work at night.

That night in my office, the English language section of the International Department, there were only two people on, me and a married woman named Wu Jiahui. She's not my boss, but I asked her permission to leave early, and she said it was fine. Fortunately, like most nights, it was slow. Jiahui even did some of her household laundry in a plastic tub. (Yes, odd.)

At 11 p.m. as planned, a Brit named Xavier Edwards, known as Exy, who works in domestic news and is the best Chinese speaker among all us foreign workers, called for an early car. That's how we get to and from work. They drive us. A minivan during the day, a car at night. Me, Exy, and two others returned to the hotel in a black Mercedes with one hour left for the party.

Outside the Foreign Experts Club, on the cascading museum-like steps, we immediately noticed trouble. You see this kind of shit in America — bar fights — but generally not in China. But the Chinese weren't fighting. It was an African and an Arab, each with his own supporters huddled around. Word is there are frequent fights between Africans and Arabs at the local universities, and also between French-speaking Africans and English-speaking Africans. I feel sorry for these poor guys. The Chinese government gives them scholarships, but they only have a few months to learn Chinese before classes begin. Can you imagine taking a course in physics or medicine and the instructor is speaking a language totally unlike your own? For them, the worst part of being here is the average Chinese person doesn't much like Africans. Most Chinese women will not date them and there are virtually no African women here. (don't know why) On the street they are treated poorly. A story circulated about an African trying to buy beer in a hotel. He was refused, and a fight broke out. He was beaten by about eight or 10 of the hotel's service people. Had to be hospitalized. The China Daily later published a front-page apology.

The Chinese look at the world with simple eyes and rate the white race high because of European and American success in commerce, industry, and war. They rate Asians second, and because of the unenviable state of Africa, rate the black race last. If you talk to Africans, they blame the whites, not themselves, for their difficulties in nation building. "The whites came and formed colonies with no respect for tribal boundaries," one told me. "Then they set the tribes against each other. Then they took all our natural resources. Then they left."

Back to the fight. The only real belligerent was a small Moroccan who removed his shirt and shoes and was wielding his belt like a weapon. Yes, he's from Africa but we will call him the Arab. He was at the bottom of the club's steps. His target was an almost 7-foot-tall Nigerian at the top of the steps who was surrounded by other Africans holding broken beer bottles as weapons. So much shouting and yelling. It sounded like a riot but it wasn't. The Moroccan, drunk of course, charged the 7-foot-tall Nigerian. He was repulsed with a kick to the chest and retreated to the bottom of the steps. He attacked again and was punched in the face. Retreated, then attacked. The other Africans now dropped their broken bottles and tried escorting him away. The Moroccan broke free and attacked. Chinese police, watching with mild amusement, latched on to him. He broke free and charged up the steps. The drunken Moroccan, exhausted, finally was apprehended and removed from the Friendship Hotel grounds. Me and my Xinhua mates looked at each other with wide eyes then went into the club for a beer. That was our eventful entrance.

Wall-to-wall people. The band was on fire. It sounded like home. They were playing an original number inspired by their time in China. It was called *Tomato-Ta Ma Da*. We all know what a tomato is. Ta Ma Da is a Chinese phrase that sounds like tomato. It means Go Fuck Your Mother. Crude but clever. Very punk. A contingent of young girls from an assortment of western countries danced near the stage and looked upon the band members as idols. A Peruvian named Fabiana, who is maybe 17 and dressed all in black, was among them. Quite drunk, she was, and I wondered if she carried on like that back in South America. Something about China turns people into not what they were but what they really are.

Me and four others made for a table in the back. Then I was grabbed by Jennifer Bascomb, a woman with charm, intelligence and looks, a confirmed ex-patriot who travels from country to country, doing this job or that, looking for something she has yet to find. "Dance with me," she said, and whipped me around. "Yuri has been after me all night. Can you keep him away?"

Jennifer, a native of Chicago, works for the Communist Party, polishing the English translations of major policy statements from the Central Committee. She sees these documents several weeks before they are released to the public. For this reason, and no doubt others, Yuri, whom everyone thinks is a Russian spy, pursues Jennifer. There's an interesting story going around about Yuri. When China was preparing to celebrate the 35th anniversary of Communist rule, Tiananmen Square was spruced up and painted. A portrait of Mao high on a wall was removed during this process, causing speculation that it wouldn't go back up, that the days of Mao worship were over. Yuri, the story goes, used high-powered binoculars to look at the spot where the painting once hung. He surmised that if the hooks holding the painting also were removed, the painting would stay down. If the hooks were in place, it would go back up. Yuri was able to see the hooks and determined that Mao would continue to be held in high regard. Such is spying in the 20th century.

Jennifer is a good dancer and we really moved around the floor. She led. When Yuri retreated, so did she. I went and sat with my friends. Talk. Jokes. Beer. During a band break, one Irishman sang a sea shanty. Then came closing time.

"After-party at Frank and Helen's," someone yelled. Frank Baxter is a fellow Xinhua worker from Iowa who reminds me of a portly Johnny Carson. He is married to the very pleasant Helen. Five of us got up from the table. Slip Myers, who works at the English-language China Daily and represents a kind of California cool, asked me to go with him on a beer run. "Can't go empty handed, man," he said. Slip is a bit of a stoner. Always introduces himself as Slip and says he got the name because everyone thinks he's about to fall but he never does. He could have left that nickname back home in Malibu, but I guess he likes it. Slip, around 32, is dating a slightly older Japanese woman named Kazuko. She's a teacher who, like so many foreigners here, speaks her native language, English and Chinese. She describes herself as the kind of woman no Japanese man would marry. There is no one thing exceptional about Kazuko. Everything put together makes her exceptional. I'm friends with her, too. She's high-born and from a wealthy family. She's full of jokes and sarcasm, although some people can't tell. I was in a bar with her once. I have a beard now and an Arab guy came up to me smiling and asked, "Are you Muslim?" Foreigners here are always looking for ways to connect with each other. I told him I was not Muslim and asked where he was from. "Palestine," he said. Then Kazuko cut in with, "I've never heard of that country. Are you sure it's a country?" I cringed. She smiled an evil smile. The guy knew she was kidding and, with a laugh, insisted Palestine is a country and always will be. This letter is long and getting longer but I've got to add one more thing about the Arab. The month-long celebration of Ramadan was coming up and I asked him if it was difficult fasting from sunup to sundown for 30 days. "No," he said. "We sleep all day and party all night. It's great."

And one more thing about Kazuko. I said she was older. She remembers the post-war occupation of Japan, how there was no milk, but the U.S. army distributed a powdered substitute to all children. She said it tasted awful, and to this day will not drink milk of any kind. As we left the Beijing bar that night, me with a person whose country launched a surprise attack on my country, she with a person whose country dropped two atomic bombs on hers, both of us breathing the air of a nation that her country once occupied and my country considered red and dangerous, I thought: Why couldn't history have just jumped ahead from 1937 to now, skipping all that death and destruction? Why did all those people have to die so me and Kazuko could walk as friends, unthreatened and unharmed, down this particular street together in this particular country at this particular time?

Deep, huh?

Slip and I made the beer run, on foot of course. We hit a couple of places where they normally sell beer. Closed. We went to Building No. 1, which stays open. There was one young man at the desk. Skinny, like most service workers. We asked him about beer. "Closed," he said, "but wait." He reached into a drawer grabbed a key, and walked off. He returned with 10 quart-size bottles and said, "You have a problem, I fix. Remember me. Problem solver." We paid for the beer and tipped him 10 yuan, less than $2 but about 20 percent of his monthly salary.

Slip and I arrived at the party while it was in full swing. The room was crowded, and we passed the beer around to cheering consumers. A few steps later, our eyes were immediately drawn to two Chinese women sitting on a couch. The only Chinese in the room. OK, they were beautiful. They were dressed in knockout fashion from 1930s Shanghai, those slim, tight-fitting, highly decorated dresses with a long slit up the side. They had on floppy hats with 8-inch brims. Deep red lipstick, heavy makeup and short hair fixed nicely with curls on each side. They were puffing cigarettes and doing these exotic French inhales, where smoke is drawn in with the mouth, then released and inhaled through the nose, giving the impression of a reverse waterfall, then exhaled through the mouth. They did this with great style and flair, as if they were on camera. Such a contrast to most women in Beijing, who look like they just left a ball bearing factory.

"That's not tobacco," my stoner friend said. Indeed, there are places around Beijing where marijuana grows like the weed it is. Mostly it's ignored. I guess not by these two women, who Slip and I learned are like something out of a movie, literally. The man sitting next to them was a German businessman who sells heavy earth-moving equipment to the Chinese. He stumbled upon these two women one day, looking normal but with great marketing potential. He dressed them up, made them up, and taught them to walk around bulldozers in a way that makes you want to buy a bulldozer. He filmed them in ads that now runs regularly on Chinese TV.

The night moved on. When the two Chinese women realized it was 3 a.m., they suddenly lost their cool sophistication and went into a panic, telling the German they had to get home and he needed to call a taxi. There are hardly any taxis in Beijing at rush hour, so there certainly aren't many at three in the morning. The two women began to scream. The German called a couple of hotels. Nothing. More screaming. More panic. The party's energy drained. I stepped in and said, "Come with me."

I brought the German and the two women to Building No. 1 and the skinny kid who said he can fix problems. "Give him 10 yuan and tell him what you want," I said. Then I left and began the short walk to my building and sleep. I didn't make it. Ten yards in front of me, Fabiana, the 17-year-old Peruvian groupie, was coming home from God knows where on her bike. Her state of inebriation was what the British call legless. She wobbled, then crashed into a pole, cut her knee and face, then vomited on the side of the road. I picked her up. She protested, but I took her to her apartment after parking the bike at the nearest building. "My father will kill me," she said. Too bad. I just hoped he didn't blame me.

He didn't. There was anger and frustration but he did not make a scene. That was for Fabiana's mother, who took the girl into a bedroom for patching up and a scolding. "It's almost time for breakfast," said the father, who looked like a good sport. "Do you want some Peruvian coffee?" I told him I did. I had never met him, although I knew his name was Cristiano. As he brewed the coffee, I asked what brought him to China.

"The Shining Path," he said, and laughed.

The Shining Path is a Maoist-inspired revolutionary group founded in Peru by a former philosophy professor after he visited China. It launched a revolt in 1980 and in 1983 knocked out several electrical transmission towers in Lima. At the time, Cristiano was the managing editor at a Lima newspaper. In an editorial, his boss condemned the attack, but said pressure from The Shining Path movement should encourage government reform. The next day the boss went missing and his son was found murdered. The Chinese embassy, no doubt in communications with The Shining Path, contacted Cristiano and offered his family asylum. He took it.

As Cristiano and I sat drinking his strong Peruvian coffee, I could see both nostalgia and contentment on his face. His daughter, crying loudly in the next room, was wild. He knew that. She was drunk. He knew that. She was hurt. But she was not dead, and while in China, with its protection and support, he can write whatever he wants and it will not put his family in jeopardy. He had not seen home in years, since home was a death sentence, but he was happy. And he was forever in debt to an unusual country that could have ignored or overlooked his dilemma, but instead went to considerable extremes to rescue him. Exactly why was a mystery he could live with, savor, and enjoy.

That's the end of this overwritten letter. I tell you all these things for one reason. I want you aware of the fact that there's an abundance of crazy shit going on in the world that Americans know nothing about. Got it? That little piece of wisdom is my gift to you.

Now I need a gift in return. Exy, the Brit, managed to find an old Polish-built oven from the '50s. He's the only person in Beijing with an oven. I told him to throw a party and I'd bake pizza, which I learned how to make when I worked at Sal's – our hangout -- during high school. I've got the cheese, the sauce, and the flour. If you send me two sticks of pepperoni, the party is on. Thanks.

Say hi to everyone for me.

Your brother, China Duke

10. Song Mei Gets Rich

Manhattan and elsewhere, 1988 thru the 1990s

Song Mei stood on Broadway in Midtown Manhattan with a small electronic bullhorn, speaking to five eager men surrounding her.

"Today we will see the Empire State Building, the Statue of Liberty, the Museum of Modern Art, Columbia University, the World Trade Towers, and Wall Street," she said.

The smallest man in the group asked, in Chinese, "Can we see Wall Street first?"

In China, there is something called "gray money." If you head a large agency, bureaucracy, department, or a government-owned business, you control and can perhaps use (for your own benefit) funds on deposit with that agency or business. That's gray money. These five unassuming men with Song Mei were caretakers of several fortunes in gray money. Song Mei, at the request of her ex-husband, Xu Gang, was going to help them invest it. Sometimes the money was returned to the government, as if it were a loan. Sometimes not. Gray money and its availability soared with the Chinese economy and helped advance it. By 2003, five decades after Mao's proletariat revolution, China would surpass the United States as the world's largest trading nation. Over 800 million people would be pulled from poverty. Decrepit cities would be rebuilt, as modern as modern could be. Trains, highways, bridges, and airports were constructed in places once considered backward and remote. Across the Huangpu River in old Shanghai, a breathtaking commercial district equal to or greater than Manhattan was constructed on swampy, undeveloped land. While it took 300 years to build Manhattan, the Chinese built Pudong in 30. Indeed, a proud new place in the world would be found for a country that, even in its darkest times, never doubted its worth or its ability.

"Yes, we can see Wall Street first," she said.

A subway ride downtown took Song Mei and her guests to the Financial District.

"What's that?" The group ran over to a massive bronze bull, 7,000 pounds in weight and 11 feet high. It was sitting right there, in a place called Bowling Green, and looked angry and dangerous. Cameras came out.

"They call this the Charging Bull," said Song Mei, who had done her homework. "The bull is symbolic of rising stock prices, or what's called a Bull Market." The men pointed their thumbs upward.

"Where is the stock exchange?" one asked.

"Let's go there next," said another.

"Can we buy stocks inside?"

Song Mei found their enthusiasm amusing.

"You can't buy stocks directly," she said. "On the floor of the stock exchange you'll see professional traders. You must work through them. They buy stocks for you and take a commission. You'll see them on the floor, crowds of them, running around, shouting, looking at prices on The Big Board, waving their hands with signals to buy and sell. The traders look like mindless children, but they are doing something very important."

Inside the New York Stock Exchange, the Chinese visitors were nearly overcome with awe, as if watching deities conduct holy rituals. As they gazed up at The Big Board, there was someone gazing at them. He was Harrison Oakleaf Banks, manager of the $5 billion Oakleaf Hedge Fund. Banks was known for his razor-sharp instincts, and something was telling him to befriend this group of foreigners. After more than an hour, the group left the stock exchange and Banks followed them out the door.

"Excuse me," he said to Song Mei, who looked like the leader. "May I recommend a visit to the Federal Reserve Bank? It's the size of an entire block and has a huge vault filled with gold. I can take you there."

"That's very nice of you," Song Mei said. Banks was encouraged by her command of English. "Do you work on Wall Street?" she asked. He said he did and introduced himself.

"Am I correct that this group is from China? What do you do there?"

The visitors spoke only rudimentary English but were happy to engage Banks.

"My job with China National Petroleum Corporation."

"Operate steel mill. Very large."

"Army commander."

"Governor. Special Economic Zone."

"Export import. Central Committee."

Harrison Oakleaf Banks, about 45, was in good shape, fit, and with a strong heart. Had his heart been any weaker, the sudden euphoria he experienced might have harmed him. Artfully, he contained himself, as if this were just another day.

"And you?" he said to Song Mei?"

"My name is Emily Song. I'm a student at Penn. A friend asked that I help these gentlemen out."

They toured The Fed. They saw Trinity Church, where Alexander Hamilton – arguably the father of American capitalism – was buried. They went to the Statue of Liberty. On the boat out, the five Chinese men leaned over the deck railing, trying to get closer to something they didn't fully understand. The wind mussed their hair as their eyes fixed on the green patina of the welcoming lady with her torch of truth and light.

"I don't really need to be free," the steel mill operator said in Chinese to his colleagues. "It's my money that needs to be free. My money needs to be in America."

Harrison Oakleaf Banks, the hedge fund manager, sat down with Song Mei in the ship's interior.

"Tell me a little about yourself and your mission today," he said. "Are you married?"

How to answer? she thought.

"My husband was a Philadelphia policeman. After I bought a 40-pound bag of rice from the Asian supermarket, he said I was too

Chinese, that I needed to become more American. He took me to an American football game, the Eagles, and we ate hot dogs. I was surprised at how many people were drinking, how many people were drunk. One man spilled his beer on another man. They began fighting, punching each other in the face. My husband went over to stop the fighting. That's his job. The two men both attacked him. They took his gun … and …."

Banks regretted prying. "I'm sorry," he said. "So sorry. That's just terrible. People come here to improve their lives and these horrible things happen."

They sat in silence for a time. "What do you do in New York?" Song Mei asked.

"I'm in finance," Banks said. "I'm what they call a hedge fund manager. Wealthy people give me large sums of money to invest. I've hired lots of smart people who find ways to make lots of money for our clients. When investing, there is always risk. But we handle risk in special ways that protect people's money. As a hedge fund, we are allowed to do things regular stockbrokers aren't permitted to do. Our clients are all important people, like your friends."

"This trip," Song Mei said, "was organized to get them familiar with American investing, to learn about some of the possibilities for investing here. China is changing and people are getting rich. Everyone worries this is temporary, that the government will change again. They want to protect their money in case that happens."

"Well, I can help them," Banks said.

"Can you really?" Song Mei asked.

"Of course. That's my business. I invest people's money for them."

"What do you invest in? Stocks?"

"All kind of things. Wherever we see a potential profit. We will even bet against a stock, or commodity, or currency. That means if it goes down, we make money, usually a lot. For example, if we think the weather in Florida is going to be exceptionally cold next year, and that the price of oranges will go up because there won't be many left after crop damage, we can make money off our guess. Do you understand?"

"A little," Song Mei said. "You do seem to be the type of person these men are looking for."

"That's wonderful," Banks said. "Will you be bringing more people to New York?"

"It's not really me. It's an old friend in China who organized this trip. Since I'm Chinese and I'm here, he uses me. I'm very busy with school but I know he's going to ask me to do this again … and probably again. When I was young, he helped me, so I cannot turn him down."

"That's excellent," he said. "Here is my card. Let's bring your guests to my office after seeing the Statue of Liberty. On the next trip, make my office your first stop. I'll take good care of your friends. And Emily, I'll also take care of you."

"Thank you. What do you mean?"

"The hedge fund will pay you a commission for getting investments under our management."

"Oh, no," Song Mei said. "I do this for friendship."

"Of course," Banks said. "So do I. But the hedge fund makes money for everyone, for me, my employees, and the investors you bring to us. It would not be fair to exclude you."

"I can't."

"You must."

"How does it work?"

"For investing money, my fund charges an annual fee of two percent on all assets. If your friends invest a million dollars, the fund collects twenty thousand. There is also a commission paid on money earned. It's twenty percent. Say the one million dollars earns one hundred and fifty thousand, or fifteen percent. If that happens, the fund collects thirty thousand. Our total then for the year is fifty thousand. Of that fifty thousand, we'd pay you a twenty percent commission, or ten thousand dollars. If you brought ten million to our firm, you'd be paid one hundred thousand dollars for the year."

Song Mei thought this might be a joke or a trick. "That's too much," she said.

"That's Wall Street," he said. "That's the American way."

As the boat pulled up to Liberty Island in New York Harbor, the oil company president lifted his hands to the sky and shouted to the colossal statue, "Na wo de qian (take my money)," and his colleagues all laughed.

Xu Gang, Song Mei's first husband and one of the new young tigers of the Chinese military, soon began scheduling two investor trips a week to New York, with Song Mei and Harrison Oakleaf Banks hosting. When Song Mei was properly licensed and registered, when her assets under management reached $100 million and her annual income $5 million, she dropped out of Penn and bought condos in Manhattan, Beijing, and Shanghai. She purchased a few small companies in the U.S. As China's economic reforms expanded, opportunities there grew. Harrison Oakleaf Banks told Song Mei her home country had the potential for the biggest upside investment in the history of finance.

In 1989, Song Mei did a reversal and began recruiting Americans looking to invest in China. Meanwhile, Xu Gang found backers and swarms of gray money in China. Together they formed a company called Phoenix Development. Its first big project was a military dormitory outside Beijing, a contract secured by Xu Gang, then a Beijing military commander. There were some bumps and missteps, and investors barely broke even on the dorm. It was, however, a learning process that would ensure future profits. With the government encouraging private home ownership, and the real estate market hot, Phoenix Development began building residential towers in third-tier Chinese cities. Then it moved to second-tier cities, with occasional projects in Beijing and Shanghai. The toughest part was getting permits from local officials eager to extract fortunes and favors in exchange for their approval. Song Mei spent the good part of 1998 taking bureaucrats to lunch every day, always bringing gifts for their wives.

Phoenix Development would borrow and build, borrow and build. Its subsidiaries owned a few tech companies that did well and supplied liquidity. Partnering with others, Song Mei and Xu Gang acquired landmark properties in the U.S. and set up multiple holding companies. They began building in North America. In all her dealing and all her travels, Song Mei stumbled upon a small American company named Ningxia Enterprises that was manufacturing in China. Its CEO, she learned, was a former journalist named Duke Amici. This bit of news lightened her, transported her to another place, made her realize she still resided somewhere in his mind, that she had not been discarded. She pulled out pen and paper and began writing a poem about a man who, each day at work, day after week, month after year, sees the haunting name of his old girlfriend's hometown on signs, trucks, and letterhead. Then the phone rang. It was a Central Committee member dissatisfied with her use of a certain subcontractor and not his brother. Song Mei crossed off the first two lines of her poem and began taking notes on the party member's complaints, assuring him they would be addressed. The poem was discarded.

Xu Gang, based now in the U.S. after falling into political trouble at home, was briefed on the complaint by Song Mei. "Never forget," he advised her. "In China, power is everything. Wealth alone amounts to nothing. Power shifts, then wealth shifts. Be prepared to shift with it. Be prepared to be hunted like a beast in the woods. Be prepared to turn and bite."

Eating dinner alone that night, something she threw together on the stove, Song Mei, AKA Emily Song, soon to be the third-richest woman in China, returned to the unwritten poem. She wrote a few words and no more. Instead, she sat and wondered if Duke Amici knew what she was doing, knew what she had become, knew if at this very moment she was thinking of him. She weighed the statistical possibility that she'd see him again. Maybe she'd buy Ningxia Enterprises. Maybe she'd push herself into his life. She laughed at the thought, watched a tape of a Chinese soap opera, then went to bed and fell asleep on pink silk sheets she didn't even like.

11. The Proletariat Scion

Beijing, 1984

This was the World Stage and Duke Amici had a place in the viewing stands.

It was the most monumental display of nationalism and pageantry he had ever witnessed, rivaling perhaps anything put on by Alexander the Great or Julius Caesar or some Egyptian pharaoh. He considered it almost beyond the limits of human logistics, coordination, and organization.

How do you get all these people together to do all those things? As he looked down on Tiananmen Square, the largest city square in the world, he imagined the existence of some hidden force or mystical layer of knowledge that was beyond his understanding.

It was an all-day event, with thousands marching smartly, knowing their parts, wearing their costumes and uniforms, showing pride, composure, and determination. A never-ending well of celebrants.

When a giant portrait of Mao Zedong passed, Duke turned to his companion, a native New Yorker wearing the drab blue clothes of a Chinese worker, and asked, "Are you a communist?"

Ainsley Acker, 32, hardly over 5 feet and lacking all attempts at visual self-improvement, looked back at him as he returned his gaze to the parade. "You're being ridiculous," she said. "Don't be ridiculous."

Unlike Ainsley's other friends in China, Duke alone knew she was incredibly wealthy, that her great-grandfather had been a business partner of John D. Rockefeller, perhaps the richest man ever to have lived.

The year was 1984. She and Duke sat in the bleachers among the special guests. They were there for the celebration of China's 35th anniversary of Communist rule. As expatriates, they held mid-level jobs working for the Chinese government. He as a copy editor for the Xinhua News Agency; she as an English teacher at the Foreign Languages Institute. That was enough to get them an invitation and choice seats to an event that had been in the planning stages for several years.

"A communist? How could I be?" she said.

"Well, you look like one. And you often act like one. Talk like one, too."

"I'm trying to respect what's being done here," she said. "That's all. I remain what I am. Being rich is not about what you wear. It's bred into you. It can't be removed or diminished. It stays forever, even if you take the money away; even if you leave the States and go to China to teach English to the sons and daughters of party members."

During a period when China was still closed to most outsiders, the country welcomed people from all over the world to work as so-called foreign experts. Ainsley Acker came for escape, which was not uncommon. Duke came for adventure and to meet women. He also came to see if the reds had anything to offer. He figured if they did, no one in the U.S. would bother to tell him.

Duke worked in the English language section of Xinhua, a five-language service whose name translates as New China. Pay was modest for such workers, but in China it was plenty to live on.

"Seems you're running from your money," Duke said.

"Well, you can run from money but you can't run from what it has done to you."

Ainsley liked these discussions. It allowed her to provoke, confront, show disdain, and jokingly mock.

In her youth, working as a paralegal back in the states, she encountered a '60s militant who called himself Will Forceful. Will, 6 feet 4 and wearing a dashiki and a black beret, presented Ainsley with a list of tenant grievances he wanted filed. When he angrily slammed his fist on the table in front of her, the sound reverberated throughout the room.

"The peoples are tired!" he said, adding an "s" to a word that was already plural.

Ainsley, a do-gooder who was nevertheless a patrician, stared at him for a long five seconds.

"For Christ sakes, Will, the correct usage is 'the people are tired.' Not peoples. If you're going to be a spokesman for the revolution, learn some fucking grammar."

The barb drew a strong, slightly embarrassed belly laugh from Will Forceful.

Now, Ainsley was preparing to send a few barbs in Duke's direction.

"I'm running from money? How would you possibly know? You wouldn't recognize real money if your own face were on the bills. You've never seen real money; never even been close to it. You've got a mark on your forehead that only people like me can see. It says: NO MONEY."

Duke thought this reasonably funny but ignored most of it.

"What has money done to you that you can't run from?" he asked confidently, as a man without means in a place where it didn't matter. In Beijing, Ainsley's money meant nothing. It was a wheel without an axle. It got her nowhere. She was without privilege. Duke discovered he liked this kind of equality.

"For one, money made me a better person, a better person, for example, than you." She wasn't being mean. It was a joust. "Money has made me something that you can't possibly be. We call it breeding."

"Like a horse?"

"A horse you will never ride," she said. "A horse too fast for you."

God, he thought. What does that suggest?

Duke kept his eye on the spectacle in front of him, aware that what he was seeing – this unity, this resolution, this ambition, this capability – might, in the long run, cause him and his country some harm. But it was a thought that quickly passed.

"I'm not in a race," he told Ainsley.

"No, you're not, and it's good you don't bother. Look, we're sitting here next to each other. We are watching the same show. We are chatting amicably. For all practical purposes, we are equals. You're even better dressed than I am and probably have more money on you than I have. But in my heart and in reality, we just cannot compare. What I know, who I know, what I've done, where I've been – it all puts me on another plain."

With that she stood up to applaud a tightly choreographed dance performed exquisitely by a couple thousand young women dressed in colorful traditional costumes. They were followed by soldiers and sailors and tanks and missiles. Deng Xiaoping, the supreme leader and chairman of the Central Military Commission, greeted the 10,000 soldiers, saying, "Comrades, you are working hard!" They responded in unison, "We serve the people!"

"Would your great-grandfather approve of you being here?" Duke asked.

"He wouldn't understand, but my father would," she said.

In World War II, Ainsley's father, an enormously wealthy Quaker who opposed war under any pretense, was a volunteer ambulance driver in Italy. That's where he met Ainsley's mother, Raffaella, a refined Italian with a strong appreciation for art, history, and culture. She lived outside Florence in the town of Vicchio. Her family's 600-year-old ancestral villa was not far from the home where Giotto, the great Renaissance painter, was born.

Before falling in love with his future wife, W. Emerson Acker saved her life. During a British bombing, Raffaella was hit by shrapnel and Acker rushed her in his ambulance to an overcrowded hospital. He convinced doctors to take her immediately and thereby averted danger. They married after the war, bought a Florentine estate with a 45-room house, staffed it with six to eight servants and raised a family of four children – Ainsley included -- until returning to America in the 1950s to run a breakoff piece of Rockefeller's Standard Oil empire.

Raffaella, whose name means, "God has healed," used to laughingly tell her children, "All I had to do in those days was come up with the menu for our meals. Nothing else. No cleaning. No cooking. Nothing at all."

W. Emerson Acker had it pretty easy, too, but he still carried a burden.

"The history of John D. Rockefeller and Standard Oil weighed heavily on my father." Ainsley told Duke. "He was a man trapped in business; a man who spoke four languages, a party-thrower and raconteur. And while he was trying to be this bon vivant, there was never-ending pressure from stockholders. They saw him as the living remains of a fabulously successful trust that never failed to make gobs and gobs of money for its investors."

Duke broke in. "Some would say the way they made money was criminal, or at least immoral."

"Now who's the communist? You can think what you want. I don't care. I've heard it all."

Ainsley had more explaining to do.

"So meanwhile, as investors demanded higher returns from my father, there was this equal and opposite force impelling him to give money away."

"I guess the idea is there's enough to go around," Duke said. "You know, if you don't take so much out, you don't have to give it back."

"You don't 'take it out,' Ainsley said. "You use your ingenuity and hard work to build wealth that helps all of society. Rockefeller endowed the University of Chicago, and Lincoln Center, and Spelman College, and the Museum of Modern Art, and the USO during the war, and helped eradicate hookworm disease in the U.S and funded research that developed vaccines for meningitis and yellow fever. There is only one Rockefeller and there will never be another Standard Oil."

"Let's hope not," Duke said. "When he wasn't giving away money, he was quite the son-of-a-bitch. I'm not sure if those he helped outnumber those he harmed."

"My father couldn't be like Rockefeller, didn't want to be like Rockefeller, and neither do I. It's stupid to even try duplicating something like that."

Ainsley didn't say so, but it was clear to her that Duke had no one to live up to, no name to preserve, that his heritage was humble, that his grandfather probably came over in steerage, and that he could just coast through life and still do better than his father. The past applied no pressure. She saw this as true freedom, whereas she felt enslaved.

Duke's attention had drifted from her and was on the goose-stepping soldiers who held rifles at the ready. He suddenly got this image of the Germans marching into Paris.

"Why are they goose stepping?" he asked. "Do you think those guns are loaded?"

"The Chinese are too smart for that," she said.

The show had gone on so long that the foreign workers in their special section, almost directly under the main gate of Tiananmen, were shifting about and getting restless. Too much of a good thing.

Duke turned back to Ainsley.

"I have no reason to, but I understand you," he said.

Ainsley knew he did and liked him for it, but she would never say so.

"Even with all his philanthropy, Rockefeller today is reviled. But my grandfather knew him and used to tell me that John D.'s innovations, his ability to find efficiencies, his idea to control absolutely all aspects of everything that affected or influenced his business — he made his own oil barrels, you know -- were for that time superhuman, godlike. He brought something important, something major, to civilization and all we remember is that the government found Standard Oil so reprehensible they broke it into tiny pieces, some of which I own."

The friendship of Ainsley and Duke, like many between the foreign workers, was both close and distant. They often saw each daily, usually in the dining hall. More important, there was a natural bond between people from the West who lived in the East, and it focused on similarities, not differences, at least not the deep, dark, hidden differences. But the common approach was not to share a lot of personal background. What Duke learned of Ainsley at the parade was an unusual disclosure.

Like everyone else, Ainsley came to China as a blank slate. When you arrive, you are without history and context. There is no person or thing, save yourself, that will expose your true nature, your flaws, prejudices, or interests. You are without possessions such as a car or home that allow people to read you. If you choose, you can create yourself anew. It's as if you are reborn or given a second chance at life.

People talk about themselves, but probing questions are impolite. If they come, they come after time. It took a year before Duke learned that four members of an Indonesian family at the Friendship Hotel were political refugees, that they would have been killed by a new regime in their home country had China not gotten them out. A guy Duke sometimes sat next to on the minibus to work seemed like a dullard but turned out to be one of South America's most influential writers.

At the Friendship Hotel, only Duke knew of Ainsley's connection to the Rockefeller legacy, and she told him only because he had accidentally seen evidence of it. She wasn't reluctant to discuss it but otherwise never would have mentioned it.

It happened after Duke was bedridden with a bad strain of Chinese flu. While he was sick, Ainsley, who lived next door, brought him food. She carried it over in food tins, the standard Chinese lunch box. When Duke got better, he went by to return the tins. On entering her apartment, Duke noticed reams of legal documents spread about on a coffee table.

"That stuff looks threatening," he said.

"Quite," she said, picking up some of the British affectation heard so often around the Friendship Hotel. "I ignore it all until I absolutely have to deal with it."

"What is it?"

She considering saying "oh nothing," but instead blew off a little steam and answered. "I'm being sued, along with some other members of my family," she said. "I've always been sued. Sued, sued, sued. Nothing involving money is ever really settled."

The lawsuit was a dispute over rightful ownership of the stock in several family companies.

"Some of this goes back to the 19th century. I have no time for it. Let's have tea," she said.

Ainsley cleared the table by swooping up the documents and tossing them into a corner, where they scattered.

Then she told Duke an abbreviated story of her life but skipped over the part about the person she often referred to as "the boy." With the help of a Chinese nanny, an ai yi, Ainsley was raising a child, her child. There was no husband in sight, or even a boyfriend. The 3-year-old, named Adam, seemed wholly Caucasian. She cared for him well but was burdened by him.

"I can't today. I've got to get the boy medicine."

"It's so cold this winter and I can't find the boy a proper coat."

"The boy is going to need an English tutor if he is ever to go back to the states. He learns more from the ai yi than from me. I speak to him in English and he answers in Chinese."

Out on the grandstand, Duke looked closer at Ainsley, outfitted in the most beat up of proletariat drapery, and wondered how she would come off if dressed like a socialite.

"Things are changing now," he said. "Are you going to get new clothes?"

"I'm not. You still see lots of people dressed like me, even at China's best universities. This is how college professors dress."

"It's a defense mechanism, to show they are red, to keep themselves out of jail if the radical left rises up again."

Ainsley brushed some of the dirt off her pants. "I won't disagree," she said.

"How much longer can this go on?" Duke asked, referring to the parade.

"At least another couple hours," Ainsley said. "Are you bored?"

The celebration was so breathtaking, so incredible, and so long that it became numbing. During the most dramatic fireworks display that either Duke or Ainsley had ever seen, the two decided not to wait for the finale and the arranged bus ride home. Instead, they left early to walk back to the Friendship Hotel.

On the way, Duke made a suggestion.

"Have you been to that new western hotel? Let's go there for a drink or maybe some western food," he said. "Boy, I could go for a steak."

"I don't go to those places," Ainsley said. "They're abominations. They remind me of the time when all the European powers carved up their own little pieces of China."

As China modernized, Ainsley found more and more to dislike.

"They knocked down a traditional hutong neighborhood to build that hotel, just so western businessmen can feel at home. You know the hutongs, don't you? Old residential communities with ancient walls, beautiful tile roofs, stone courtyards, and an oval gate. They're knocking them down all over the city."

China was traveling at breakneck speed to catch up with the west. Casualties were necessary. Old city walls came down to make room for apartment buildings and highways. The leaders knew there was something tragic about this, but it was necessary. Once, New York neighborhoods were destroyed in the same way.

Duke and Ainsley walked by a vendor selling soft drinks, mostly Chinese-made orange soda but also American cola.

"How about a Coke?" Duke asked. "Would that offend you?"

"I'll never drink a Coke in China," Ainsley said. "Besides, those things are warm. I'm adaptable to most things Chinese, but I can't stand warm soda."

"Yeah, I saw your apartment. You've got a . . ."

". . . refrigerator. A small one. I had it shipped in from Hong Kong. There's the boy to think about."

The soda salesman tried to keep the soda cold, but it wasn't working. He'd lay five or six bottles on top of a large block of ice, but they sold too fast to even get a chill.

"OK, forget the soda. How about something to eat?"

"There's a famous noodle place right over there," she said. "Let's go."

It didn't look famous. It looked exactly like one of those beat up places that Duke's Chinese coworkers told him to avoid. They told him that if he must go, he should bring his own chopsticks – to avoid hepatitis.

"That place?"

"Yes. You'll like it," Ainsley said, and they walked in, passing a peasant out front who sold fresh cucumbers to people going in.

The storefront had peeling paint and not even a sign, or at least Duke didn't see one. Inside, the floors and tables were dirty. Patrons sat on small wooden benches. Behind the service counter you could see a basin of cloudy water that dishes and chopsticks were dumped into and pulled out after a quick swish. Duke and Ainsley were the only non-Chinese in the place.

"What do we get?" Duke asked?

"They only have one thing. Cold spicy noodles."

"Why is everyone eating a cucumber with their noodles? They got them outside. Didn't they?"

"Cools the mouth. Get ready for some pretty spicy noodles," Ainsley said.

Duke looked around to study the various slurping techniques. One man created a hefty vacuum and easily pulled in a half-pound of noodles.

"See that?" he said to Ainsley.

"I saw it and I heard it. It's a lower-class art form."

"There are no classes here," Duke said. "The difference between rich and poor is the difference between a two-room apartment and a one-room apartment."

"Class isn't about money. It's about mind."

The cold spicy noodles arrived in chipped bowls. The chopsticks looked like they had been around for the 1949 liberation.

"The people from the hutongs must eat here," he said.

"Let me tell you something about those hutongs," Ainsley said eagerly, almost in a shift of personality. "In the next decade or two, those old hutongs will be rebuilt by Chinese entrepreneurs. They'll be right near a Chinese Disneyland of some sort and have western toilets – not squatters -- and central air. Tourists will pay $500 a night to stay there. All the comforts of home in a faux exotic setting. You watch. Count the number of cranes set up around town. It's all a precursor. I'll bet there are top Communist officials right now studying the life of Rockefeller.   Speaking of ideology, Deng Xiaoping said it doesn't matter whether a cat is black or white as long as it catches mice. Soon, a lot of mice around here are going to be caught by capitalists."

"I don't get you," he said to Ainsley. "You don't want them to sell Coke but you want them to build a Disneyland."

"It's not what I want. It's what they will do."

Ainsley noticed Duke's eyes were tearing up from the killer noodles.

"Do you want a cucumber?" she asked.

With his mouth full, he shook his head no.

"When that restaurant owner wises up, and he will," Ainsley said, "he'll start selling cucumbers with his noodles."

After eating, Duke and Ainsley paid their bill and did not – by custom – leave a tip. On the street, they tried catching a cab, an impossibility at this location. As they walked home, they smelled the residue from the lingering fireworks. Only slowly did the smoke dissipate from the Beijing sky.

The next day, as a joke, Duke went to the special store for foreigners and bought Ainsley a women's business suit, which he left outside her door. The card said, "For an heir to the Rockefellers." She opened the box without much interest, then tossed the clothes into the same corner where the legal documents sat. It was Sunday and the Chinese nanny was off. Her son woke from a nap and she made him a sandwich for lunch. Looking outside her widow, she counted. One, two, three …five cranes on the horizon; five major projects going up just in her neighborhood, just within her sight.

"Do you want anything else?" she asked the boy in English.

"I'd rather have rice," he answered in Chinese.

She patted him gently on the head and made a mental note: Starting Monday, regular English lessons for this child. Also, write home and have someone send a VCR and tapes of Disney movies, plus popcorn. Maybe the Dr. Seuss collection and a cowboy hat.

12. An Old Friend Visits

Florida, 1989

Huang Defu, on a break from his studies at the University of Missouri, fulfilled his promise and did indeed visit Duke Amici when Duke was living and working in Florida. On a hot August day in Jacksonville, after a beachside breakfast, the two men walked onto a quarter mile-long fishing pier that, to Huang, stretched forever into an ocean of freedom and opportunity. The fresh, clean air, unavailable in large Chinese cities, was abundant and inexhaustible. Huang noticed people on the pier, on the beach, in the water, at the shops. They all were doing exactly what they wanted to do, some of it routine, some of it odd and strange.

"You can't imagine what this means to me," Huang said to Duke. "Thank you for granting me this extraordinary experience."

"It's just an average day at the beach," Duke said. "Is that a tear in your eye?"

"I'm happy. I've wanted this my whole life."

"To stand on a fishing pier?"

"It's not something you can understand," said Huang, who went by the American name Daniel. "It's only something I can feel. And I cannot explain it. This is so different from my home."

"Well, take in as much as you want. There's no charge."

Breathing deep and rubbing the rough wood of the pier with one hand, Daniel said, "And tomorrow we go to Disney World?"

"Yes. The home of Mickey Mouse. Now, that's America."

Daniel watched as a man 15 feet away reeled in a flounder. His 3-year-old child played with a doll and ate a soft pretzel. "Do you know what I'm thinking about right now?"

"Getting yourself a pole and throwing in your line?"

Daniel laughed. "No. I'm thinking about a man named Fang Lizhi, a man of great courage and conviction. Do you know the name?"

"Don't know it."

"Now that I'm in America, seeing what I've seen, learning what I've learned, I could become like Fang Lizhi. I could go home with my new degree and lead China in an entirely new direction, a better, freer direction. The alternative is to follow my father, to choose his style of patriotism, to help lead China in whatever direction the party wants to take it. You know, my father is on the Central Committee. Sons often inherit the positions of their fathers, and that could be a possibility for me. In my life, my father and his Red Army legacy, that secret radio room, has colored everything I have ever done. I've religiously followed the party line. It made me choose not to do the things I really wanted to do."

"The Central Committee? You never told me that," Duke said.

"Of course, with the recent events at Tiananmen Square and your government's generous offer of protection to the Chinese who are here now, a third option is to not go home at all, to stay and just enjoy this kind of living, being a quiet, happy nobody. Never thinking or caring about a political party or a political line."

"Who is Fang Lizhi?"

Daniel launched into the story of the man whose teachings inspired a Chinese insurrection.

Fang Lizhi was once the vice president of China's University of Science and Technology. In the mid-'80s, he was invited to teach at Princeton. He returned to China a different man. Lizhi began touring college campuses and lecturing on human rights, freedom, and the rule of law. Market reforms were taking hold around this time. People were getting rich, but the money mostly went to high party officials and their relatives. Fixed prices, in place for years, were removed and inflation set in. The average person was worried about feeding his family, while party insiders were buying commodities at low prices and selling them at high prices. To promote efficiency, large companies were laying off workers, threatening the coveted "iron rice bowl" of a guaranteed job, medical benefits, and heavily subsidized housing.

In this environment, Fang Lizhi's words got attention. They triggered action, most notably a student movement calling for reforms. In various cities, there were protests and demonstrations. Young people argued that economic reforms should not be limited to the few, and that freedom should follow prosperity. In agreement with them, shockingly so, was none other than Hu Yaobang, the general secretary of the Communist Party. He and his faction pushed the students to continue their fight. But even the general secretary of the Communist Party can push too far. On Jan. 16, 1987, Hu was denounced by the opposition and forced to resign. This firmed up the students' resolve. They made these demands:

Acknowledge Hu Yaobang's views on democracy and freedom as correct.

Admit that the campaigns against spiritual pollution and bourgeois liberalization had been wrong.

Publish information on the income of state leaders and their family members.

Allow privately run newspapers and stop press censorship.

Increase funding for education and raise intellectuals' pay.

End restrictions on demonstrations in Beijing.

Provide objective coverage of students in official media.

.   Hu Yaobang died of a heart attack on April 15, 1989. Students thought the worst. They thought he was murdered. On the night of April 17, more than 3,000 protesters from Beijing University marched to Tiananmen Square. Others joined them. On April 22, the day of Hu's funeral, there were 100,000 people in the square. By May 13 there were 300,000. Martial law was declared, and 250,000 troops and tanks moved in. For a time, protesters blocked their entry into the capital. The students lectured the soldiers, telling them the Peoples Liberation Army was supposed to protect the people. Residents from the neighborhoods threw rocks and sticks at the troops. "Join us," the students yelled, and gave the soldiers food and water. Many soldiers were confused, ambivalent, morally confused, and compromised. Especially sympathetic to the protesters were the Beijing-based troops and their commanders. One local commander, Xu Gang, the ex-husband of Song Mei, ordered his units not to fire on civilians. Others did the same. The heaviest burden then fell on troops from the provinces.

The protests spread to 400 cities.

At 4:30 p.m. on June 3, a final edict was issued to troops:

The operation to quell the counterrevolutionary riot begins at 9 p.m.

Military units should converge on the square by 1 a.m. on June 4, and the square must be cleared by 6 a.m.

No delays would be tolerated.

No person may impede the advance of the troops enforcing martial law. The troops may act in self-defense and use any means to clear impediments.

At 4 a.m. on June 4, the lights in Tiananmen were turned off and a loudspeaker announced, "Clearance of the square begins now." By then, there were 1 million people to clear. No one knows for sure how many died. The government says several hundred. Outside estimates go as high as 10,000. Either way, the conservative wing of the Chinese Communist Party, in all its horror, had prevailed.

Less than a footnote to this story are Xu Gang and Song Mei, who was in Beijing on business during the June 4 incident. For ordering his troops not to fire on the crowd, Xu Gang was stripped of his military post, had his personal assets seized and served six months in prison. Song Mei was in Tiananmen among the protesters. In the chaos, she ran and fell. Others landed on top of her. They were shot. Their dead bodies shielded her from bullets. Song Mei lay under the dead for at least an hour, maybe two, before crawling out, bloody, and escaping down a side street.

"Where is Fang Lizhi now?" Duke asked Daniel.

"After the massacre he took refuge in the American embassy, got out of China, taught at Cambridge and Princeton, lectured, received the Robert F. Kennedy Human Rights Award. He died in Tucson, Arizona, of natural causes."

Duke said, "What he did certainly beats working at Xinhua in the cold of winter, when they turn off the heat to conserve fuel and you have to wear gloves to edit."

Daniel looked out over the calm Atlantic. A 20-foot, 250 horsepower Bayliner zipped by with a man and woman wearing bright orange bathing suits. "Do you have a boat?" he asked Duke.

"No. They say the happiest day in a Floridian's life is when he buys a boat. The second happiest is when he sells it."

"Can regular people afford them?"

"They're expensive. You take out a loan."

"If I stay, I'm getting a boat," Daniel said. "Nobody can touch you out there."

With coaxing, Duke convinced Daniel to leave the pier. The two men drove to a back street in the San Marco section of town and entered the little storefront Duke and his friend Jimmie the inventor were renting. Jimmie was inside, fussing over a 3-foot-high machine.

"Jimmie, I want you to meet Huang Defu. You can call him Daniel."

The two shook hands.

"Jimmie is working on a prototype of a machine that he invented and designed," Duke said. "I financed it and take care of the business side of a corporation we formed. We're going to sell this thing. Exciting, huh?"

"No more journalism? What does it do?"

"It draws water from the air," Jimmie said. "Drinking water. People in places without clean water can use it to save day-long trips to get fresh water."

"But you don't need this in America, do you?" Daniel asked.

"Some might," said Jimmie, who, like always, had a four-day beard and hadn't combed his hair. "We'd mainly sell it in the developing world."

Duke, now the excited one, said, "Next week I'll take it to a trade show. Big companies can check it out and maybe decide to license it. They can market it and distribute it, maybe even manufacture it. We'll get a licensing fee for each machine they sell."

Daniel was unaccustomed to the smell of oil and grease that hung heavy in the air at the little shop. The clutter of spare parts and tools was outside his realm, whatever that realm might be.

"Are you giving up journalism?" he asked Duke. "You came all the way to China because you were a journalist. I thought it was in your blood."

Duke opened some blinds to cast more light onto the machine.

"I'm still at the paper here," he said. "But sooner or later, most journalists realize their lives are spent writing about the things other people do, and that maybe it's time to do something yourself, to make a mark. In China, because of an odd turn of events, I came into some money. With this shop and this machine and with Jimmie's help, I'm putting that money to good use."

"I know a little about the 'odd turn of events,'" Daniel said.

"What do you know?"

"About the trash, and the Russians, all that."

"Christ," Duke said. "Did everyone know?"

"No, just a few. My father told me. I knew about it when I asked you to play chess on that boat. You weren't aware, but the Xinhua leadership held you in high regard."

"High regard. I damn near got myself jailed."

"That never would have happened," Daniel said. "You know, that girl you helped. I hear she invests money in the American stock market for Chinese big shots. She's here, in the states. Do you see her?"

Duke regretted the change in topics.

"Song Mei is a student at Penn," he said. "But we haven't kept in touch. After all, I'm married."

"You have no children?"

"No," Duke said. "We're keeping it simple. It's one of those marriages where both parties know there's a shelf life."

"Shelf life?"

"That the marriage could end soon. We don't fight. We are civil. After a time, whatever connected us disappeared. I'm not sure what it was, but it's gone. She hates this shop, this machine. She can't stand Jimmie."

Daniel looked at Jimmie and understood why.

"I love Jimmie," Duke said. "He's a lost soul whose brilliance was undiscovered, buried deep under his weaknesses. I helped him discover himself."

"He's still the writer," Jimmie, the former addict, said while turning a screw. "Everything's a story to him, even me."

"Is Francine coming with us to Disney World?" Daniel asked.

"No, she's flying to Philadelphia. She's on the board of the Philadelphia Museum of Art. They have a big fundraiser, a formal affair that she needs to attend."

"You're not going with her?"

"To the fundraiser? I used to go to those things. No more, especially not while I'm here. She has lots of friends in Philly. At this stage in our lives, it's clear she'd prefer to go alone. That's fine. She also has a job as the museum's chief development officer and spends most of her time in Philadelphia. She has an apartment there. She visits Florida, but not this weekend. We'll have more fun in Orlando without her."

The following morning Duke and Daniel left Jacksonville at 7 a.m. in Duke's 1987 Toyota Camry, heading south for the three-hour trip to Orlando. They stopped briefly in St. Augustine so Daniel, quite the tourist, could see the Castillo de San Marcos, the oldest masonry fort in the oldest continuously inhabited European settlement in the continental United States.

"Americans living in the Northeast think of American history as English, with the first real settlement at Jamestown, Virginia, in 1606," Duke said. "Then you move to Florida and realize the English were latecomers. The Spanish had been here since 1565."

"That's your start, 1565 AD," Daniel said. "China is so old we don't even know how old we are. The earliest recorded mention of a dynasty is around 2,000 BC."

"Sorry, I realize our history is modern times to you."

Up close at the Castillo de San Marcos, Daniel inspected the walls and listened to the ocean waves bouncing off them. "What is this material?"

"It's called coquina, a kind of limestone formed from broken seashells," Duke said. "The British would attack by sea and pound the fort with cannon fire. The walls always held."

"From the beginning, they were fighting over this land?" Daniel asked.

"Of course," Duke said. "Wasn't China also born of war?"

"It was."

Back on the Interstate 95, Daniel read the messages on billboards. Is that supposed to be funny? So many theme parks. Is it really all you can eat? What's a vasectomy?

Daniel's infatuation with Disney World was immediate. Wide roads at the entrance and good design and management kept the heavy traffic flowing. Each section of the parking lot is identified by a Disney character. From there, you are picked up by a tram.

"Our car is in 'Goofy.' Remember that so we can find it on the way out," Duke said.

"Goofy. The funny-looking dog."

"That's the one."

Once inside, it was non-stop. Daniel wanted to see everything and was in an exhaustive hurry to do so. Duke could hardly keep up. Daniel said the roller coaster drop at Space Mountain made him feel like he was dying. He rode it three times. Daniel couldn't believe his eyes at The Haunted Mansion, as a ghost suddenly appeared next to him. He was stunned by The Hall of Presidents, seeing every American president come to life and hearing the Gettysburg Address delivered dramatically by an almost-human Abraham Lincoln.

"China should do this with Mao," he told Duke. "It would be much better than his waxy corpse in that see-through coffin."

Pirates of the Caribbean. Tomorrowland. It's a Small World. On the Jungle Cruise, Daniel jumped out of his seat when the guide shot – loudly – at a raging hippo.

After the Magic Kingdom they went to EPCOT for a more educational experience. At the Chinese exhibit, Daniel thought Disney did a good job with the story of his country. "Pretty accurate." They ate a Chinese dinner in the park and continued the hectic pace. At 9 p.m., after enjoying the parks for 10 hours, Duke said, "There's a fireworks display soon. If we skip it, we can beat the traffic."

"Skip it? No. No. Please let's stay."

The two men watched the nearly endless sky show. Daniel, born in the country that invented fireworks, was mesmerized. "This is the best day of my life," he told Duke. When the display ended, the two men walked with the crowd to the exit.

"Goofy," Daniel said.

"Goofy," Duke said.

Halfway home, Duke asked Daniel if he was hungry, and if he liked hamburgers.

"I love hamburgers."

They stopped at a diner-like place. Daniel used almost a whole bottle of ketchup on his fries. Duke picked up the check. He had covered expenses for the entire day. Back in the car, Daniel fell into a deep sleep. At 2:30 a.m., the Camry pulled into Duke's driveway and Daniel opened his eyes.

"You are a friend like no other," he said. "I can't thank you enough."

"My pleasure. Next time we'll go Universal Studios," Duke said, knowing a next time was unlikely.

"I made my decision," Daniel said. "About staying or returning home. My decision is I will go home and over time work to bring everything I saw today, everything I felt, to China. I'll honor Fang Lizhi. And I want you to know that whatever I achieve, if I achieve anything, it will be a result of this day and you."

"Doubtful."

Then Daniel urged Duke to visit him in China.

"Believe me. If you come, I will make sure you are treated like a king."

Duke wasn't counting, but this was the second time he had been offered a position of royalty in a country where no such thing existed. Daniel's comment triggered the memory of Song Mei's long-ago plea: "Stay with me and I will make you the king of Ningxia."

"You're goofy," he said to Daniel.

"Yes, I am. Aren't I? Let's see where that goofiness takes me."

Duke liked Daniel a lot and appreciated his frankness, his willingness to express a forbidden affinity for the fresh air of freedom. But he knew that once Daniel was home again, the scent of America would leave him and the security of conformity would comfort him. Huang Defu would, once again, give up individuality for self-sacrifice. He would take the route of his father, the proven path to progress. Duke favored the American system, had confidence and faith in it, but readily acknowledged it could not operate with the speed, scope, and effectiveness of the Chinese system. Huang Defu didn't have to acknowledge this. To him, it was intrinsic. As for the wonders of Disney, he had no doubt that soon China, too, would have its own Magic Kingdom.

13. Song Mei's Letter to Duke

Philadelphia, 1987

Dear Duke,

I did something in America this week that I never did with you. I went on an American date with an American man. The man was nice. Well, not really so nice. But overall, it was a good time. We had dinner at an expensive restaurant called Bookbinders, which has a gigantic tank filled with live lobsters. Then we saw the Philadelphia Orchestra perform at The Academy of Music, a magnificent old theater that suggests things once were better in the U.S. than they are now. Have you been there? Of course you have. Everything was perfect until the end of the date, when the man, a medical student – I want to make a joke here – tried to, well, examine me. He got mad when I said I wasn't his patient.

I like the University of Pennsylvania. It has everything, and I'm doing well. People are smart and high cultured but dress informally and use foul, street language in regular discussions. As a city, Philadelphia is just so-so. Some parts are nice. Some parts are horrible. Why doesn't the government fix up those broken-down houses on Broad Street, the main entrance into town? You'd think it would want to put on a good face there. In China, people want to live in the city.

The lucky ones do. In America, I think people prefer to live outside the city. This I don't understand.

So far, I've seen Independence Hall and the Liberty Bell. I learned about your revolution, which was a little like China's but not quite. An American girlfriend took me to South Street. I can't say that was good or bad but it was fun. Such a bizarre place. There were regular people but mostly weird people with many body piercings and hair colored red and green, even purple. There were the strangest shops I've ever seen, some selling awful things in a bold and bright way, displayed in the store-front window, like a girl in leather underwear with a whip and a mask. I felt evil just looking at them. One store was called Zipperhead. That made no sense to me. There were restaurants of all kinds, including Indian, Greek, Arabic and Chinese. Music came out of some of the shops. My girlfriend said someone once wrote a song about South Street, calling it the hippest street in town, and that it was a hit record on the radio. Do you know that song? At least now I know what "hip" means. No one in China is hip.

I dream of going on an American date with you some day, of you holding my hand and calling me Mei-Mei, like you once did. This, of course, is probably impossible. I know that. Since you have a car, I don't see why it is so difficult to drive here from Florida and visit me. You could also visit your family. I could show you all the wonderful things about Penn. Sitting in the Academy of Music with you would be a different experience than sitting there with that medical student. By the time you come, if you ever do, I will probably know this city better than you. I know we were close, now we are apart. And I know why we are apart. That will be explained at the end of this letter. I knew our fate even when I begged you to come with me to Ningxia, where I'd make you king. How foolish of me to say that. I was a stupid romantic trying to live inside a Jane Austin novel. Being in the United States has given me clearer vision. For example, I can see that our first real date alone in China must have been painful and uncomfortable for you, and that you must have found me and my situation laughable.

Do you remember that date? It was dinner and a movie at my college. Dinner was, of course, nothing like Bookbinders. The dining hall where we ate was like a bunker, with dirty concrete floors and hard benches to sit on, not even chairs. I now know there are no benches in American restaurants. We had to bring our own bowls and chopsticks. Such a poor country, you must have thought. The Chinese movie shown in the college auditorium was boring. Called Two Women, it was about two love affairs. There was no kissing in it or hugging or touching, certainly no sex. You said the best part was when the man and women were in a restaurant slowly eating creamy cake with their hands and fingers and smearing it around their mouths while looking into each other's eyes. You said it was cinematically suggestive. I said it was rubbish.

Then I brought you to my dorm room. The hallway was poorly lit and you had to duck down so as not to hit the clotheslines strung with women's laundry, mostly underwear. I didn't think anything of it at the time. Now I'm embarrassed and ashamed. (We have a laundry at Penn) It's all so clear to me. Like it was yesterday. I remember as we entered the tiny dorm room with six wooden bunks and hard peasant mattresses that you noticed the orange peels on the floor. My five roommates and the two of us barely had space to stand. I introduced you and we all talked. There were nets over each bunk, and you asked if there was a mosquito problem. One girl said the nets were for privacy, and you, an American with everything, knew nothing in that room could ever be private. I had some walnuts for an after-movie snack, and you thought I was clever but barbarian when I put them in the hinge side of the door jam and shut the door to crack them. That's just how we did it. Then I kicked the shells into the hallway. The real tragedy of the night came when I offered you a pear. This is what set our destinies.

I'm certain you remember this. I gave you the pear. There was a knife nearby. You cut the pear in half. I screamed. My five roommates screamed. But it was done, and it is why you are there and I am here. We are apart because you cut that pear. You must be laughing now at our Chinese superstition. You laughed then, when I explained that pear in Chinese is li and to cut it is feng and that the second meaning of feng li or cut pear is for people to separate, and that two people who share a pear will no longer see each other. That is what we believe. Well, it happened. I knew it would.

There was an ice storm that night. I walked you to the gate of the college and worried that on your way home your bike would slip, and you would fall and hurt yourself. I worried about a man who would eventually leave me.

Maybe I'll write you again. Maybe I won't. Maybe you'll write back, and maybe you won't. So I'll tell you now. I enjoyed every minute of our time together, and that what you did for my father, getting him that medicine, is something I never will forget. It will bond us eternally. Remember that bond every time you cut a pear.

Emily Song

PS   Thanks for the $50 gift certificate to the White Dog Café. At least you remembered my address.

14. Under a Chinese Crepe Shop

Beijing, 2006

Standing outside the gates of a modern, almost gleaming Chinese factory, Duke Amici fumed. Song Mei, his business partner, tried explaining.

"It's common," she said. "Every factory does this. China doesn't play by your rules, doesn't have your morality or sense of fairness. It's business. Always business. A customer asks. It provides."

"Did you translate everything I said?" Duke asked.

"I tried being polite, but I think the sales rep understood English," Song Mei said. "And the way you came across, I don't think words were necessary."

"I'm sorry, but it's outrageous," Duke said. "We pay them to manufacture a unique product – our product. We give them all the specifications, then someone else says, 'Make it for me, too,' and they do. We're taking our business elsewhere."

"That's fine," Song Mei said. "I probably can get you a better price and quicker delivery, but I can't guarantee they won't make the machine for another entrepreneur."

"Meanwhile, we still have to contend with those thieving bastards at Menlo," Duke said. "Can you imagine? Using the factory we use to manufacture the machine we invented. We need to sic the lawyers on them again."

"We can fix Menlo," Song Mei said. "Tell the factory you want to update the product. Give them a faulty part, or a piece designed to fail in a month or two. Don't order any of the new machines. Menlo will do that. As their machines fail, we'll take our machines, without the flawed design, somewhere else. Okay? By the way, and it's not important and you shouldn't care, but the factory sales rep called you a da bizi, a big nose. You call us slanty eyes. We define you by your comparatively large noses. Now let's get something to eat," she said. "I know a place. I know the owner."

"My nose isn't even that big," Duke said as they walked away.

After China became the World's Factory, businesspeople in the U.S were advised: Invent here, manufacture there. But as things progressed, American entrepreneurs no longer needed to invent anywhere. If they saw a product they liked – a designer shirt, a fancy pair of sneakers endorsed by an NBA star, a machine that performs EKGs or a machine that makes drinkable water from the air – the Chinese would gladly build an exact copy for you. For entrepreneurs, it became: Steal there, manufacture there, do very little here.

With the preponderance of so-called American products being manufactured in China, and subject to knockoffs, participation in the world economy broadened. In the overall picture, the knockoffs were almost inconsequential. What needed attention and study, understanding and reevaluation, were the causes and consequences of the cataclysmic shift that scooped up American industrial power and plopped it down in China.

What caused such a shift? One thing? Two things? An array of things? Ignorance? Complicity? Greed? The elevation of profit over patriotism? Some proposed that the genesis of it was the end of the Cold War and the elimination of communism as a threat to American capitalism. Without communism breathing down the necks of American industry, horizons broadened and the wagons of commerce were un-circled.

There was a time in American history when large corporations feared and believed that unhappy workers had a realistic alternative to top-down capitalism. Expansive, in-your-face communism was right there, almost on the doorstep, with a party in every large city. Consider General Motors in 1936. Inside its factories, 100,000 people who normally assemble automobiles decided to sit down for 44 days and do nothing. They didn't picket or march. They just sat down when they should have been building 280,000 cars. That strike by the United Auto Workers was a startling display of raw power. It was no surprise then that in subsequent years, GM wages rose, doubled, and tripled. Benefits increased. Formerly dissatisfied employees started calling their company "Generous Motors." This became the pattern throughout industrial America, a country that unified, grew stronger, and defeated the Red Menace.

When the Soviet Union lost its punch, when the West outspent it and forced it into bankruptcy, it was then that American corporations felt less pressure to keep wages high. This was around the time of stockholder primacy, when big companies were under great pressure to slash costs to boost profit and stock prices. The hunt began for cheap labor overseas. Domestic workers wouldn't go commie now, and new laws weakened unions, so who cared if people were put out of work? Japan was first to offer a viable work force at low cost. When an agreement allowed it to devalue its currency, those costs went even lower. Then Nixon went to China – and so did corporate heads looking to manufacture products at an even lower cost. China followed the Japanese model and moved far past it. The benefit of manufacturing in China went beyond cheap labor and a devalued currency. China lacked the costly rules, regulations, standards, and oversight that made American manufacturing expensive. Labor was not only cheap (2 percent of U.S. costs), it was also docile. If a company needed to fill a large order fast, Chinese workers were ordered to pull double and triple shifts, maybe sleep in dormitories, and stay on the job until the order was filled, all impossible in the U.S. Plus, when China built new factories for all its new business, it made them more modern, more efficient, and more competitive than most factories in the West. China ultimately became the world's largest user of industrial robots. Sure, products had to be shipped 10,000 miles back home, but in comparison to the savings, that cost and inconvenience was minor.

First it was textiles, then electronics. Research and development eventually moved to China. The Chinese labor force soon became more skilled and better educated than America's. For these reasons and more, Duke Amici decided to manufacture in China, which had 128 million jobs in manufacturing compared to 16 million in the States.

Still angry but hungry, Duke and Song Mei walked away from the factory that made his machine and toward Wangfujing street, a crowded pedestrian thoroughfare of shops and restaurants, not far from Tiananmen Square. "Do you know what jian bing guozi is?" she asked him.

"Like a French crepe," Duke said.

"It's not French," she said. "It's Chinese. Do you want one?"

"Sure."

They took a side street and entered a tiny store front. Song Mei order ordered two jian bing guozi and chatted with the cook in a lively fashion, apparently a lao pengyou (old friend). While the cook talked, he poured batter onto a grill to make thin pancakes. He brushed them with egg, then added a sauce, cilantro, ham, green onions, and a sort of fried cracker. When done, it was rolled and wrapped and handed to the customers, who ate standing up, with some drips falling to the ground.

"Good?"

"Good."

Between bites, Song Mei spoke to Duke in a manner more formal than conversational. "I think we have firmly reestablished our friendship," she said. "I think we owe each other loyalty and consideration and trust. From all we have done, now and then, I think there is a bond. Do you agree?"

Duke wiped his chin with an old handkerchief. "So serious. Why bring that up now?"

"Because it's time," she said, and stopped eating. "It's pleasant being with you back in Beijing, almost like the years in between didn't happen. Our relationship is very different from what it once was. Yet it is something."

"I know what you mean," Duke said. "We've changed. This city has changed – I can't believe these buildings, the newness, the activity – and the country has changed. Yet something hasn't. You don't have to be a poet to know that."

"A former poet," she said. "I need to ask you something."

Duke finished his Chinese crepe and sensed a solemnity in his business partner. "Ask," he said.

"If one day I go missing, I want you to come here and look for me."

Duke was puzzled.

"I don't know what you mean. Why would you go missing?"

"The why is not important," she said. "If I go missing, I want you to use whatever power you have, your knowledge of China and your instincts and intelligence, and come looking for me. Maybe even use your government. Can you promise to do that? A firm, real promise?"

He wanted to chuckle but didn't. "It's a hell of a big city, but, yes, I'll come looking for you. Where, I don't know. But I'll look. I promise."

"Okay. That makes me feel safe in showing you something." She tossed the remaining bit of her jian bing guozi into a can and spoke again to the shop owner, who nodded in agreement. The cook, a man with few teeth and little hair, opened a back door to his tiny restaurant. It was a cracked and broken wooden door, barely on its hinges. Inside was a small storage room. On the ground was a trap door. The cook lifted the plank, turned on the light from a hanging bulb and motioned for the couple to descend a rusty ladder. There was the smell of mold and dampness.

"What is this?" Duke asked. "You want me to go down there? Why?"

"I'll go first," she said. "You follow. It's part of an old bomb shelter. And believe it or not, I helped build it."

The description "bomb shelter" was hardly descriptive enough. The tunnel into which Song Mei and Duke Amici were descending was part of an 85-square-kilometer underground city. It was built between 1969 and 1976 on orders from Mao Zedong, at the height of tension between China and the Soviet Union, when the Soviets claimed the border island of Zhenbao and a nuclear attack on China was considered realistic (it's why Mao reached out to Nixon). The underground city was sometimes called The Underground Great Wall because it was built as a military defense. It was dug by 300,000 citizens, including volunteers and students, Song Mei among them. A true city capable of protecting 6 million people, it had restaurants, clinics, factories, theaters, schools, a roller-skating rink, warehouses, a mushroom farm, complex ventilation, and access to water wells. The shelter had about 90 entrances hidden in shops along city streets. When the Soviet threat diminished, most of the entrances were closed off or sealed. Tourists were allowed to visit certain parts and some of the shops stayed open. The entrance at the crepe shop went down to a small, extended tunnel far from the main section of the shelter. It had been closed but then reopened by the shop owner.

"This is truly eerie," said Duke, who at times was claustrophobic.

"I want to show you something," Song Mei said, and she led him to a large, leather, mildewed chest, which was padlocked. "Look and remember." On the dirt floor, under a rock, she picked up a key and opened the lock. Dust rose as she lifted the lid to show a top wooden drawer. Inside were old papers, photographs, and a manuscript written in Chinese.

"This is my novel," she said. "It's all about the Cultural Revolution, what happened to me, what happened to others. All the insanity that nearly destroyed my country. A publisher told me to hide it, to keep it unpublished until great change had occurred in China. I'm not sure if that change has come, but when it does the novel is here waiting. If I ever leave China for good, which is unlikely, maybe I'll translate it and take it to America. Either way, I want you to know it's here."

Duke didn't like being in the tunnel. He didn't like learning Song Mei's secrets. He didn't like being pulled into something odd and strange. Being involved in intrigue and espionage as a young man was exciting. As an older man, intrigue and espionage were not as appealing.

"The trunk is big," Duke said. "What else is in there? Is that a false bottom?"

With a pause, Song Mei answered, "My family treasure is in there."

Duke, slightly dizzy, wanted to say, "Okay. Can we leave?" Instead, he looked inside as Song Mei revealed the hidden contents wrapped in paper and cushioned on peanut shells and straw. Golden hair pins, bejeweled bracelets, carved jade spoons, cloisonne cooking pots, ornate wooden boxes, statuettes, toy soldiers, blue-and-white porcelain, vases, gems.

Astounded, Duke said, "When you wanted to make me King of Ningxia, did that mean you were the queen?"

"You know there aren't any queens," she said. "Not today. But there were. Once. Long ago. Not in Ningxia, but right here in Beijing, in the Forbidden City, which still stands. In that palace, when the Ming Dynasty ruled, my ancestors were part of the court."

"How much is all this worth?" asked Duke, who had forgotten about his claustrophobia.

"Impossible to say. As a whole? Maybe priceless. These are museum pieces, more than 500 years old. That vase alone could sell for 20 million American dollars."

"Can I touch it?"

"Go ahead and touch. Just don't drop it."

Instead, Duke picked up a 5-inch golden hair pin fashioned to look like a raging flame. Alternating along its edges were six sapphires and six rubies, with a larger ruby in the center.

"You were rich before you got rich," Duke said. "Does the cook know?"

"Only about the novel, and I told him there were other writings here. He doesn't know about the key, about the treasure. But now you do."

Duke returned the hair pin to the chest, afraid to handle anything else.

"How did you get this? How did you move it? How do you keep it? What if they find it?"

"My ancestors were advisers and high civil servants in the Ming dynasty, which was strong and powerful but after several hundred years grew weak," Song Mei said. "There was money trouble. The army wasn't getting paid and couldn't be relied on. There was chaos. People were frightened and Manchu invaders from the north were poised to attack. The Manchus approached the Great Wall, which the Mings built. A Chinese general, a traitor, opened the gates for the Manchus, who marched into Beijing and took over. The emperor hanged himself, but some people kept their heads. The story I've been told is that, as everyone was running for their lives, my ancestors packed up the things you see here, dressed as peasants, and escaped into the countryside. The treasure was buried and my ancestors went on to live simple lives, generation after generation, never revealing themselves, until they once again became educated and joined the intellectual class. With the civil war, then world war, then revolution, the treasure had its own little journey, but was mostly kept intact. My family had a hu tong, a courtyard house, and it was buried under a patio. When they sent my father to Ningxia and the government decided to knock down the hu tong and build a high-rise, I slowly, gradually, moved the treasure here."

Duke belched up some cilantro from the jian bing guozi. "I'm flabbergasted," he said. "I can hardly speak."

"Flabbergasted means you can hardly speak?"

"It means I don't know what to say and I don't know what to think, that I'm astonished and amazed by you, your family, China, and its history. I saw nothing of this in that poor little poet."

"Do you see it now?" she asked.

"I probably began seeing it back at the Waldorf Astoria, but now it's clear," he said. "I feel pretty small standing near you, standing near this, standing in this dank place with you smelling of sweet roses."

"Fate is all it is," she said. "That and a $300 bottle of perfume."

"Why did you tell me this?"

"I need you to know. One day it will be important that you know. Now let's get out of here."

They climbed back up the rusty ladder to the light of the dim bulb. Song Mei said her goodbyes to her friend the shop owner, adding, "Ji zhu ta de mian zi. Da bizi."

"What was that?" Duke asked.

"I told him you'll be back, and to remember your face, especially the big nose."

15. The Big Belt

Chongqing, 1985; Omaha, 2011

Stand near the heart of a raging steel mill and you'll feel a sense of dread. A slight move in the wrong direction means disaster. Duke Amici thought exactly that while touring a Chinese mill, but there was even more to think about. What would become of all this steel, this power, this potential?

Was this pocket of hell just a factory or an omen?

Amici and a few other foreign workers, still rare in China during the '80s, were led around the plant by a young tour guide named Yuan Chen. The noise, the heat, and the danger didn't at all bother Yuan Chen. Rather, it fueled his excitement. His job was to show the future to those who doubted or questioned China's role in it. In his mind, that future would commence with steel.

Steel had allowed America, both an enemy and a model for China, to build an unrivaled military and a fleet of ships that patrolled, policed, and intimidated the world. But America was producing less and less steel. China's fleet of ships was insignificant when compared to America's, yet China was turning out more and more steel. Someday, these two lines on a graph would cross and the world would change.

Then what? That's what occupied Duke as he walked carefully through the mill, a dramatic contrast to the clumsy, backyard furnaces where peasants – at the urging of Mao – once made small quantities of bad steel by torching their farm implements. In the process, they neglected their crops and caused one of history's greatest famines.

Duke had been in China for a year. In that time, he had witnessed remarkable change and dreamlike growth. There was a long way to go, but the progress was relentless and frightfully exponential.

In an information session after the tour, over tea while sitting in covered chairs, Duke chuckled at the belt worn by Yuan Chen. It was a long belt and Yuan Chen was a thin man. Most men in China were thin, some exceptionally thin, like Americans in the 20s, yet they all wore these long belts. After the buckle, a six-to-eight-inch piece of leather would just hang down. It was almost as if the belt owners were expecting to put on a lot of weight.

Perhaps, he thought, belts came in only one size to make manufacturing easier, sort of like the time zones in China. The country is about 3,200 miles from coast to coast but by design has only a single time zone. They say it's to simplify train schedules. But if there was only one belt size and most Chinese were thin, why didn't they make the one size smaller?

During a critical phase of the Chinese Revolution, big belts played a part in keeping the Red Army from starving, or so it's been said. As with any revolution, there are overspun stories of glory and success that enlarge the truth and become a sacred part of history. A lot of mythology is association with China's Long March, which began in 1934 as a westward retreat by the Communist forces after being encircled back east by the Nationalists. It was rushed, desperate, and without a plan. But as the group passed aimlessly through the hinterlands, they preached revolution and picked up support. They engaged in skirmishes with the enemy and learned that the only smart way to fight was with guerrilla tactics.

Over a year, they traveled 4,000 miles, crossing 24 rivers and 18 mountain ranges, and fought their enemy effectively. The march ended in Yanan in Shaanxi province. The Communists established a strong, expanding base there. During World War II they fought the Japanese. After the war, they chased the Nationalists to Taiwan. By 1949, they created what they called New China.

On the march, food often was scarce. In the worst of times, the revolutionaries – many of them young farm boys – did something even the hungriest American wouldn't consider.

They boiled their leather belts to make soup.

Duke Amici could picture young Yuan Chen as a member of the Red Army boiling that long belt during that Long March. Comically, he wondered if the Chinese – whose ways, logic, and reason always befuddled foreigners – could have designed the big belts as an emergency food supply.

Impossible.

Duke left Asia a few years after he toured the mill. By 2011, China was the world's largest producer of steel. Yuan Chen was in America then, with a Green Card, a Wharton MBA, and a small chain of Chinese restaurants based in Omaha, Nebraska. He also did some importing and counseled other Chinese on investments.

If you went to one of his restaurants on a night when he played host, you would see the same enthusiasm he exhibited at the mill. What you would not see is six to eight inches of leather dangling past his belt buckle. His belt, a $395 Ferragamo, now fits him well. It's no smaller than the one he wore in 1985, but over time and with a changing lifestyle and a new place in the world, he has filled it out nicely.

16. Buying a Song Mei Condo

Vancouver, Canada, 2010

In the city of Vancouver, in the Canadian province of British Columbia, many college students from the Peoples Republic of China own multi-million-dollar homes. Henry Wan, a relative newcomer, was not a college student, but he owned three such homes. He rented them all, saving only one small bedroom for himself. Soon, he'd have four condos, then six. All were built by a company called Phoenix Development, controlled by a woman named Emily Song, aka Song Mei, a former poet.

At his old job in China, Henry Wan, a stage performer, was always in motion. Now, as a security guard at a Vancouver casino with a mostly Chinese clientele, he moved very little. Stood mostly, doing nothing. As a performer in China, he was The Monkey King, perhaps the most physically demanding role in all of theater. The character comes from a 16th century epic Chinese novel called *Journey to the West*. The Monkey King is a magical, man-like creature with 72 powers. He can transform himself into other animals, make copies of himself, fix people in place, even change the weather. On stage, for at least a couple hours, he primarily fights, using incomparable martial arts skills with and without weapons. He is quick as a blinking eye and does non-stop mind-blowing acrobatics, leaps and turns and spins and somersaults.

Henry Wan began training for the role when he was 10. His father was a Monkey King. His grandfather was a Monkey King. His great-grandfather, and so on. In 1990, at age 32, he left all that behind when a friend sponsored his immigration to Canada.

Still, when he looks out the floor-to-ceiling glass window of his Vancouver high-rise, he feels a little like the king he once was. So do all those rich college students who don't even have jobs.

Vancouver is home to 500,000 Chinese, representing about 20 percent of the population. In the beginning, Henry's friend guided him in western ways, but mistakes were unavoidable. He was cheated when buying a $2,000 car. He was swindled when investing in a small start-up company. Yet he ultimately prevailed in Vancouver, often called The Most Asian City Outside Asia. It is also called The City With Too Much Money. And that money is Chinese.

As a casino security guard, Henry Wan saw a lot of that money – stared right at it. He saw it on the tables, for sure, but also in duffle bags, suitcases, and small trunks. It was routine for patrons at The River Rapids Casino and Resort to unload, say, $250,000 in bricks of 20s and purchase chips. Maybe they'd play, maybe they wouldn't. Then the $250,000 in chips would be cashed in, effectively laundering the money and allowing it to be used without question anywhere in Canada. It was the same routine at four other casinos in the city. There were regulations designed to account for large cash sums, perhaps the profits of illegal activities, but in Vancouver they were largely ignored. Much of the laundered money came from Chinese elites who would buy Vancouver real estate. Describing that market as "hot" would be the grossest of understatements.

In the beginning, Henry didn't exactly buy real estate. He'd buy the right to purchase a piece of real estate, usually a condo in a high-rise that the builder promised to build. At this stage, there were fancy brochures and a location but no actual construction. These were pre-sales. Following the pattern of nearly all his friends, Henry purchased the right to buy a condo for $10,000 and a month later sold it for $20,000. He'd take the 20 and do it again. Eventually, he purchased an actual condo, which he'd sell when the price doubled. He'd buy more, always renting them to newly arrived Chinese – the spoiled, fun-seeking sons and daughter of big shots -- and taking only a single room for himself. The single room was adequate because he purposely worked double shifts, weekends, and holidays at the Rapid River Casino and Resort.

In almost every case, Henry Wan was doing business with Emily Song and Phoenix Development. Building after building after building. Emily Song once invested other people's money in existing real estate. Now she was constructing buildings that others would invest in, a much more lucrative play.

With Vancouver being a magnet for Chinese nationals and their money – much of it gray and ill-gotten, stolen or borrowed from state-owned companies or government agencies – Emily Song and even Henry Wan could not fail. Chinese came to Vancouver because immigration policies were welcoming and immigrants were treated fairly and with respect, plus Vancouver, unlike New York or Chicago, was a relatively quick hop across the Pacific. Also, you go where your friends go. In the modern era, the Chinese first came to Vancouver from Hong Kong, then Taiwan, then the mainland. The regular flight to Vancouver from Hong Kong was Flight 888 –the luckiest and most auspicious number in Chinese culture, representing triple fortune. That alone said volumes. What didn't need to be said was that Vancouver's laws and regulations cared little about transparency and accountability, not just at the casinos but with real estate and business. A person could own whatever they wanted and remain anonymous, like all those student owners of multi-million-dollar homes, the ones whose parents back home were running China. In the end, about $800 billion in Chinese capital landed in Vancouver, flooding into real estate, into dealerships for Lamborghini, Ferrari, Rolls-Royce, and Aston Martin, and making an easy sale of $800,000 luxury car condos (garages).

Of course, things changed when regular Canadians, increasingly priced out of the housing market, began complaining. Regulations stiffened, laws designed to cool speculation were enacted, and a special 15 percent surcharge was placed on foreigners purchasing real estate. By then Emily Song and Phoenix Development had made their money. In fact, Emily lost interest in housing construction and took herself out of the day-to-day operations of Phoenix. Instead, she focused on a small tech company she owned, one that facilitated purchases by cell phone. Its use was exploding all over China and other parts of Asia. She made money with every cell phone purchase, but the real profit was in the collection and marketing of data from people using the service. The one little wrinkle was the governing party of China took serious exception and leveled a vengeful eye at anyone or anything gathering more information than it did.

As for Henry Wan, rich by some standards, he went back to China for a visit. In a search that lasted only two weeks, he found himself a bride and brought her to Canada. Finally, he took an entire condo for himself. Over the course of a year, his new wife purchased a five-carat diamond, religiously ate steak or crab twice a week, spent a minimum of $1,000 a month on clothes, then divorced Henry Wan and took three of his six condos, valued at a little more than 3 million Canadian dollars.

With China's economic ascension, many things had changed for Chinese people both in and outside the country. This included romance, which unlike bank accounts and the quality of life, was not a victor but rather a victim. Love and marriage, for so many couples, were no longer connected. In time, Henry Wan found a new woman, a Chinese woman, who readily married him for his money. He knew it and accepted it. After two years, he was ready to divorce her but not so ready to lose more assets.

One day she found an old photo of him, costumed and made up as the celebrated Monkey King, posing to strike one of his many foes, looking regal and powerful.

"Is this really you?" she asked the man known to her only as a security guard.

"I was something back then," he said.

"But not rich. Now you're rich."

Henry Wan said no more and walked out the door, heading to the casino to cover a night shift where he'd watch over the unloading of suitcases filled with money and wonder if, at a moment's notice, he could do a convincing back flip and with a quick one-two punch knock out an opponent twice his size.

17. The Tea Party

Beijing, 2007

He didn't want to go. She insisted. Since she owned 51 percent of his company, Ningxia Enterprises, he really had no choice. Duke Amici had been working well with Song Mei, the one-time poet and his one-time girlfriend. As partners, they were productive, amicable, and profitable. His business was only a tiny bit of hers, and this planned trip to Beijing was about a real estate deal unrelated to him. So why did he need to go? It's not like they spent much time together socially. They didn't. Then Song Mei explained.

"In the 1980s, when we were in China together," she said, "I was often embarrassed by my own country. You, from rich America, had to see donkey carts in the streets of the capital, had to see our worn and faded clothes – which we wore on purpose so as not to look bourgeois. You had to see the peasants come in from the countryside with their cabbages and watermelons, sell them on the street, and when the sun went down to sleep on that same street until morning, when they would begin selling again. You mocked our lack of technology. You saw people with bad teeth who didn't wash regularly or comb their hair. In our stores you saw poorly made merchandize that no American would want. And the new concrete buildings we were so proud of, you considered them boring, featureless, and apt to fall over one day. Well, in anticipation of the 2008 Olympics, there's been a great deal of building. I want you to see it, and I want to be there when you do, to personally represent all that the Chinese people have accomplished and to have you directly associate it with me. Aside from that, there's one meeting I want you in on. Just sit there. You don't have to say anything."

They arrived on a Monday, on an unusually clear spring day. The Beijing sky was about as blue as it ever gets. Duke wore jeans, a polo shirt and worn sneakers. The most expensive item on him was his Ray Ban sunglasses. Song Mei, who would remain in China for three months tending to her empire, was dressed in a cashmere jumpsuit from Bergdorf Goodman and comfortable Italian shoes. She deposited Duke at the Shangri-La China World Hotel, which houses the China World Mall, one of the largest in Beijing. The city was in full view from his spacious suite. She stayed at a condo she owned. After resting the first day, Duke walked the city he last visited in 2006. He rode the subway and noticed a feature not used in American subways: a transparent safety wall between the platform and the train tracks. In a call home to his wife he said, "Americans think the Chinese are not good to their people. But they built the Great Wall to protect them from invaders. They built the Grand Canal to link the economies of the north and south. And they spent extra money to prevent transit riders from falling or being pushed to their death in the subways. I wonder when we'll do that."

On Thursday, the two partners had a scheduled meeting with a company called Wide Horizon, a major developer of Chinese real estate. Wide Horizon wanted Song Mei's organization to invest in one of its planned projects. Prior to that, Duke and Song Mei checked in with each other each day and ate several meals together. They went to a movie. One night they stayed in Duke's room and watched TV, an episodic Chinese soap opera everyone was talking about. When one of her meetings was cancelled, she shopped with him at the China World Mall and convinced him to buy new sneakers. On Wednesday, they took a cab and she showed off Beijing's signature buildings, her purpose in bringing him here.

"They call this 'big pants,' because it looks like a giant pair of pants," Song Mei said, referring to the 51-story headquarters of China Central Television, which cost $900 million to build. Duke said it looked like the bottom half of a walking robot. The gleaming legs were two leaning towers with a connecting piece, like a lower torso, 246 feet above ground.

"This one resembles a giant egg, doesn't it?" Song Mei said. It was the National Centre for the Performing Arts, a titanium and glass ellipsoid containing a concert hall, an opera house, and a theater. The entrance is underwater. It cost $400 million.

They drove toward the airport.

"Those look like three interconnected mountains," Duke said. "But very futuristic."

"That's the Wangjing SOHO, an office and retail center," Song Mei said. "The three buildings look different depending on where you stand. Either interconnected, or not connected. They change as you change. They seem to shift."

"Everything is so shiny," Duke said.

Each building on Song Mei's tour was more visually shocking than the last. The eccentric designs defied the idea that such concoctions of steel and glass and God knows what else could even exist. Who in their right mind would have the courage to propose such things, let alone build them? The interiors were swirling lines of architecture that made you dizzy and extended the definition of modern. This was all about compensating for a slow start in the 20th century. Limits were pushed and pushed again, until they bordered on the ridiculous. In 2014, President Xi Jinping was so bothered by this unprecedented flamboyance that he called for an end to "strange and weird" architecture.

"Thank you for showing me the sites," Duke said. "It made an impact on me."

"Thank you for agreeing to come on this trip."

They were always polite to each other.

"Are you sure you need me tomorrow at the meeting with Wide Horizon?"

"I don't need you. I want you."

"What's going to happen? Will you invest?" he asked.

"No," she said. "I'm meeting with them just to see their proposal, to help me better understand the competition."

"You still could invest. It might be a good project."

"Five years ago, they asked me for a loan," Song Mei said. "A substantial amount. For part of the collateral, they put up a warehouse full of copper. A year later I sent an agent to check on the warehouse. It was mostly empty. No copper. No collateral."

"Credit's a loose game in this country," Duke said. "One day it's all going to bust. You watch. There's been too much too fast. Don't fall into that trap. OK?"

She looked at him like a teacher just corrected by her worst student.

The next morning the two business partners went to the hyper-modern headquarters of Wide Horizon. They were welcomed by the CEO and CFO and led to a lavish room for entertaining.

"Would you like some tea?" the CEO asked in Chinese. He was tall, athletic, and handsome, wearing a Hong Kong suit.

"Yes," Song Mei said. "That would be nice."

A small cherry wood tray table was brought out. On it were two ceramic teapots no bigger than tennis balls. One was for brewing, the other for pouring. There were four miniature teacups, more like tiny saucers than cups. Each held about one sip. From his breast pocket the CEO pulled a 2-by-1-inch foil packet of tea.

The CEO spoke and Song Mei translated for Duke.

"This, my friends, is Dahongpao tea from Mount Wuyi in Fujian Province. There are only three trees that produce it, and each is 350 years old. Twenty grams of this tea were recently auctioned off. My company was lucky enough to get the winning bid, which amounted to 5.2 million yuan per kilogram."

Duke struggled with the conversion math in his head, changing kilos to pounds and yuan to dollars. His conclusion: Dahongpao tea costs $1.7 million per pound. Could that be right? He waved his hand toward the CEO, suggesting a thimble of the tea was too rich a gift.

"I insist," the CEO said.

He opened the packet and with his fingers pulled out a small amount of tea. He stuffed that into the tiny brew pot.

"You brew this very briefly, maybe eight to 10 seconds. No more," the CEO said.

Then he filled the teapot with water from a hot water dispenser. After 10 seconds, the CEO poured the tea into the second pot, which had no lid, and then used it to fill the four little cups. A toast was offered. All four participants drank. To Duke, the tea was mild and no different from the cheap tea he drank at Xinhua in 1984.

He expected to be served only once. Instead, more hot water was put into the brewing pot, and the cups were refilled, again and again, until fresh, million-dollar tea had to be put into the brew pot. The business discussion, with visuals, did commence, but the CEO never stopped making and pouring tea. He also encouraged everyone to eat from a tray of sweet Chinese snacks.

Duke likened the Chinese CEO to the French king who discovered a popular new drink – coffee – and happily brewed it like a servant for his honored guests. Duke then wondered how many thousands of dollars he soon would be pissing out.

After an hour, business was concluded in a positive fashion but without a commitment from Song Mei, whose network of connections, her guan xi, was needed for a hotel-casino resort planned for China's tropical Hainan Island. The CEO was getting resistance from an old rival, a deputy mayor. He required Song Mei's party contacts to neutralize him. Years ago, not long out of college, the CEO and the deputy mayor competed during the Asian Games in the 5,000 meters. The deputy mayor claims he lost to the CEO because of an illegal shove not called by the judges. The grudge was never forgotten.

In addition to Song Mei's contacts, the CEO also wanted her money, which was of secondary importance.

There were handshakes and a cordial goodbye.

In the taxi back to his hotel, Duke asked Song Mei, "Was that tea for real?"

She said something to the driver, then pointed out a little shop that had been at the same location since before liberation in 1949.

"Like everything in China," she said, "the tea is an expanded dream, a hope or vision, an expectation, a partial fantasy, a story more than a reality, a method."

"You should go back to writing poetry," Duke said.

She opened her purse, which carried a fancy logo Duke did not recognize.

"He gave me this before we left. I had to accept it or I would have appeared ungrateful," Song Mei said. She placed a packet of Dahongpao tea into the palm of Duke's hand. "Invite some friends over and tell them what this tea sells for. Tell them the story of the tea ceremony with a powerful, incredibly rich Chinese CEO. Brew it carefully, then pour them some. They will never look at you the same again."

Duke studied the decorative packet and tried making out the Chinese characters, only recognizing cha, or tea.

"After this trip, I don't think I'll ever look at you the same again," Duke said.

"Then my mission has been accomplished," Song Mei said. "You leave tomorrow at 8 a.m. Get some rest tonight. Traveling this far again so soon can destroy you."

18. Song Mei Goes Missing

Washington, D.C. 2015

Being unexpectedly summoned to the State Department was intimidating, not as intimidating as being summoned to the worn and weary office of an emotionless woman dressed in revolutionary attire who knew you were a spy, but intimidating nonetheless.

In 1985, when Feng Yaohua, Duke's Xinhua boss, put him on the hot seat, she had been informed he was working for the Russians, if that's what you call trash stealing. But what did this State Department guy know or want, this undersecretary in an off-the-rack dark blue suit? Duke Amici couldn't begin to guess.

In a way, the State Department building in Washington presented an image not unlike the Xinhua building in Beijing. Both were imposing and rectangular. The difference was a strong wind might knock over the old Xinhua building while the stone-like State Department was rooted, firm, immovable. Or so it seemed to Duke as he walked into State, wondering what awaited him. He had been told nothing. Just told to come.

Undersecretary Bromwell Clingman was a nice enough man. He offered Duke coffee.

"Thank you for coming, Mr. Amici," Clingman said. "The State Department has a situation that you may be able to help us with."

Good start.

"Please call me Duke. What kind of situation?"

"I'll get right to the point. An American student studying international affairs in China was befriended by a Chinese classmate at Fudan University. This classmate was, shall we say, the opposite of risk aversive. He was a thrill seeker and a rule-breaker. He decided he wanted to go to North Korea, just to see it. He asked the American student, Jason Benchman, to go with him. Benchman agreed. North Korea, of course, is a strong ally of China but an enemy of the United States. Somehow, they snuck across the border. Then they got caught. The two were extradited back to China. The Chinese student drew a slight reprimand. The American student was imprisoned. There were back-channel negotiations with the State Department, and it was agreed that Benchman's case would be handled by a three-person panel, one person chosen by China, one by the U.S. and a neutral party agreed to by both. Oddly, the Chinese have submitted the name of an American as the neutral party. They chose you."

"This must be a mix up," Duke said.

A former journalist of no significant stature who was a small businessman of no significant accomplishment was somehow being pulled into a significant conflict between nations with a significant history of animosity. How could this happen?

"How could this happen?" Duke asked Clingman.

"That's what we want you to tell us."

"I'm at a loss," Duke said. "I've got to think this through."

"Go ahead," said the undersecretary, who leaned back in his chair, took a sip of his coffee, and shuffled a few papers, giving close inspection to one that Duke felt was about him.

"You know I worked in China for a couple years … for a government news organization?"

"We know that."

"I made some friends. They were nothing then. Maybe they're big shots now. Maybe they submitted my name."

"That could be. But there must be more," Clingman said. "This isn't a casual thing. Why would they trust you to be neutral … or might they even have reason to believe you'd side with them?"

"Why would I side with them over an imprisoned American kid?" Duke asked.

"We don't know."

"Did they say anything about me? Did they give you a hint?"

"They said you are a businessman, that a wealthy Chinese national is your partner, that you manufacture a machine in China, and that the Chinese government buys that machine and distributes it in Africa."

"All true. Sounds like reason enough."

"It's not enough," Clingman said. "You started your business when you returned home from China. May I ask, where did you get the seed money?"

He knows.

"Well, I've been a journalist most of my life. In China, I wrote freelance articles for the New York Times, the Wall Street Journal, some magazines, things like that. And I saved it all."

"I hadn't realized freelance writing was so lucrative. Anything else?"

Oh, what the hell.

"Yes," Duke said. "I spied for the Russians and then became a double agent for China."

Clingman went back to his coffee, then calmly said, "That seems like reason enough."

Duke went on to tell how he met Song Mei. He explained how her father needed heart medicine and how he was able to get it by spying. He talked comically about stealing the trash, and how Feng Yaohua turned him, how he then was paid real money instead of just medicine. Clingman, in subtle terms, asked if he had slept with Song Mei.

Duke blushed and stuttered. "Let's just say we dated. Can we leave it at that? We were mostly friends. Now we are strictly business partners."

The undersecretary didn't smile, although his face communicated gratitude.

"I want you to know we are delighted to have the third member of the panel, the so-called neutral party, as an American," Clingman said. The two shook on it.

Arrangements were made for a series of briefings. A strategy session, a session on what to expect and how to act, details on similar arbitration panels and the results, standard Chinese tactics. In short, Duke Amici received a quick course on how to be a State Department employee while outwardly appearing neutral and ultimately repatriating an imprisoned American thrill seeker. It was like spy time again.

"Thank you so very much for your cooperation in this matter," Clingman said. "You'll probably be leaving for China in two weeks. The State Department will handle all the arrangements. You'll fly over with a delegation on Air Force Two, which the vice president and the State Department both use. And one more thing. Unrelated. Your girlfriend, sorry, your business partner, has gone missing and is believed to be held in Chinese custody."

Outside the State Department, Duke called Song Mei. No service. Back at his hotel, before flying home to Florida, Duke telephoned Xu Gang, Song Mei's ex-husband who was living in the states after being imprisoned for his conduct during the Tiananmen incident. The former military commander was doing well running several businesses. No, he hadn't heard from her.

"My guess is they are holding her at Zhongnanhai," he said, referring to the large compound northwest of the Forbidden City in Beijing, the seat of both government and party power. Zhongnanhai simply means Central South Lake, but to the Chinese it reads like White House, or Kremlin, or No. 10 Downing Street. Officials not only work there, some live there.

Duke had known about Xu Gang since those early days back in Beijing with Song Mei. On their third date she gave Duke the particulars of her life. Song Mei cried telling the story of her divorce yet insisted Xu Gang remained important to her. She attributed the beatings he gave her to Cultural Revolution psychosis. It drove people past the limits of decency, she said. Xu Gang could be trusted, Song Mei told Duke, and so Duke now would trust him.

"I won't get into the specifics, but by some miracle I'm going to be in Beijing in two weeks," Duke told Xu. "I'll be meeting with some top people, probably at Zhongnanhai. I guess I can go around opening doors until I find her."

"Somehow I suspect it won't be that simple," Xu said. "And once you find her, then what?"

"I'll improvise," Duke said. "Why do you think this happened?"

"In China, you owe your good fortune to the powerful," he said. "They allow you to get rich. To do anything important in business, layers upon layers of approval are necessary. You need a patron of great importance to get you through this process. In exchange, you must make them rich. Many gifts and acts of kindness, but also a piece of the profits. If the person or persons you made rich fall from power, so do you. The game ends. The riches end. This is what happened to Song Mei. Also, having been married to me was no help."

"Can you tell me who it was that fell from power, and the person responsible for pushing him out?" Duke asked Xu.

"There were many people along the way who helped, but the key person was Deputy Premier Yu Xiaodan," Xu said. "The person who brought him down is chief administrator of Beijing, who wants to become deputy premier and is good friends with the general secretary. His name is Peng Guo."

"Thanks. That's a start. I want you to know I'm not totally without help. I have an old friend who climbed up the party ranks. I'm counting on him to guide me. I'll find Song Mei. At the very least, I've got to try. She saw this coming and made me promise."

Song Mei met Yu Xiaodan on one of the Wall Street tours organized by Xu Gang. More than others, Yu showed a special interest in her. With Song Mei investing his money, Yu Xiaodan saw returns as high as 40 percent in some years. More than money, she gave him stature by purchasing for him North Jersey real estate within one of the nation's best school districts, a school system that is 38 percent Asian and routinely sends 10 percent of its graduates to Ivy League colleges. Yu Xiaodan's family, friends, and important contacts took turns using those properties, allowing their children to attend those fine schools. Song Mei did not go unrewarded. When Phoenix Development started building high-rises in Beijing, Yu Xiaodan ensured approval at all levels of government. Once, while seeking permission for a hotel-business complex, Song Mei took a dozen local officials to lunch at a 5-star restaurant. Sitting alone at a nearby table, so all 12 officials could see him, was Deputy Premier Yu Xiaodan, who occasionally waved and smiled and gave a thumbs up. Yu Xiaodan's cut of this project and all others was 30 percent, with stock usually going to close relatives, even toddlers.

Real estate development was good to both Song Mei and Yu Xiaodan, but the floodgates of profit opened wide with Ge-GePay, the phone app. Song Mei (and therefore Yu Xiaodan) bought the tech startup just as smart phones took hold in China. Ge-GePay allowed smart phone users to pay for goods and services on their phones. In a flash, everyone in China was paying for everything with their phones. Ge-GePay expanded and offered credit to users. It allowed customers to pay their utility bills with Ge-GePay. It sold insurance and train tickets. Perhaps most important in the age of high technology, it gathered important data on its users, tracking them as they made purchases, following them as they walked around town, looking over their shoulders as they used other apps and added contacts to their phone. In the modern age of marketing, this data carried tremendous value. It was as good as currency.

As Peng Guo uncomfortably watched the rise of Yu Xiaodan, he formulated a plan to move against him. The momentum was already there. The party was entering yet another of its ideological purity campaigns after realizing so many of its members – the cream at the top – were gorging themselves on the free marketplace and making the party look bad. A campaign was needed, and a few examples made. Peng Guo realized one of those examples could be Yu Xiaodan.

In that campaign, party publications warned members against "being disoriented and losing themselves." The Central Commission for Discipline Inspection ramped up. With Peng Guo's direction, investigative reporters at the People's Daily looked closely at Yu Xiaodan's holdings and the intricate web of family members who became rich. It was all revealed. A total of $8 billion in holdings, or approximately one-third of Song Mei's $24 billion fortune.

Yu Xiaodan was arrested, charged with corruption and taking bribes, and stripped of his position. Song Mei was not arrested. She just disappeared.

"Tell me about this Peng Guo guy," Duke said to Xu Gang.

"He's both ambitious and insecure," Xu Gang said. "That's what makes him dangerous."

"What about his personal life? His family. What does he like to do?"

"He has a daughter, about 12 years old. And son in his late 20s. The son is a modern artist. It once was dangerous to paint like he paints. With the changing times and the influence of his father, he's been quite successful and considered a young pioneer."

"What kind of things does Peng enjoy?" Duke asked.

"He likes history, Chinese history," Xu Gang said. "He's a collector. He collects artifacts from the Ming Dynasty. Some of these things you are not allowed to have. They should be owned by the state. He has them. People know it but say nothing."

Duke's immediate thought: Damn, Song Mei is smart. This is going to be easier than I expected. The trip to the Chinese crepe shop now made sense. He'll go back to the shop, get a piece of Ming jewelry, bribe Peng Guo, and get Song Mei released.

"If I were going to look for Song Mei in Zhongnanhai, where would I begin?"

"On that I cannot help," Xu Gang said, and the two men ended the conversation.

Duke Amici went home to Florida and, two weeks in advance, began packing his bags for the trip to Beijing.

19. Socialist Realism

Beijing, 1985

It was Saturday at the Xinhua News Agency, which means a half day for the foreign experts. Five of them planned a lunch excursion to a place they called Alister's Restaurant. This was not the actual name of the restaurant. None of them knew the actual name. They called it Alister's Restaurant because it was "discovered" by a foreign worker some years ago and his name was Alister. He was long gone from China, but word of the restaurant was passed down to waves of incoming westerners and his name was always attached to it.

The notable thing about Alister's Restaurant was it served Indian food, a rarity in Beijing. To get there, you took the battered 109 bus from the Xinhua complex, traveled through the Xidan shopping district, got off right before the National Art Gallery, then walked a block or two. The group consisted of American Duke Amici, the down-to-earth British elitist Xavier Edwards, working-class pub-crawler Eric Davies, light-hearted Canadian college professor Larry Altman, and Frank Baxter, the calm Midwesterner who organized the outing. Standing on the crowded bus, they got closer to each other than they wished, but such is expected in a city of almost 10 million. Outside the restaurant, only the fluent Xavier, whom everyone called Exy, could read the sign: Savory and Tasty Food From the West. Frank led the party and took his friends inside. It was a cold January day and a layer of quilted insulation hung on the door frame of the restaurant. Inside was the smell of unfamiliar spices, as if China had fused with India. A coal stove burned in the center of the unadorned, mostly unsanitary eatery that the foreigners classified as a "masses restaurant," the kind educated people avoid, the kind where it is advisable to bring your own (clean) chopsticks. The five Xinhua workers were the only non-Chinese in the place.

A friendly woman in dirty kitchen clothes, probably the proprietor, approached the table. She made no particular fuss over the foreigners, which was appreciated. Frank told Exy what to order and he translated. The proprietor gave them a thumbs up and went back to the kitchen.

"Did I see you sitting with those two Hong Kong girls at lunch yesterday in the dining hall?" Larry asked Duke.

"They're women, and yes, you did. They always sit alone. No one ever goes over to their table. So I did."

"So brave. And?"

"Very friendly, almost flirty," Duke said.

"It's funny. They're Chinese but they look and act so different from the Chinese here," Larry said.

"What's flirty?" Eric asked.

"They were informal and at ease," Duke said. "We told each other our stories. Both are single. Ivy and Rose. They work for a Taiwanese computer company and get paid double for being posted here, plus free housing and a per diem. But they don't like it. They consider the people here simple and unsophisticated. Ivy said she would never date a man from the mainland."

"Unlike you, all intelligence, charm and wit," Larry said. "How'd they like your boring life story?"

"I explained my situation and out of nowhere Ivy said, 'You sure must like Chinese women.' I asked what she meant, and she said, 'Well, if you've come all the way from the United States, you must really like the women here. It's got to be the women because there's nothing else to like.'"

"She got that right," Eric said.

Frank wondered what he would do about or with Chinese women if he were single. He fastened the top button of his jacket to protect himself from the cold, inhaled a strong whiff of garlic and changed the subject.

"You know, they're taking our Chinese coworkers up there near Mongolia to plant trees as a way to stop the desert dust from blowing into the city," he said. "Me and a few other foreigners wanted to go. Thought it would be cool. But the bosses consider it demeaning for 'mental workers' to labor like that. They didn't want to embarrass us and told us we couldn't go. Their people, of course, are the exception. The party doesn't mind putting shovels in the hands of their own mental workers."

"You can't fight them," Exy said. "Don't even try."

"I'd go," Duke said.

"Me, too," Larry said.

"Well, it won't happen," Exy said.

"Have you seen my son lately?" Eric asked. His son was Donnie, a bright and cheery lad who was aggressive and independent. He attended fifth grade at a Chinese school.

"At the Friendship Hotel, I see him all over the grounds," Exy said. "He's everywhere, hustling, washing bikes for people and filling tires with air. Donnie's giving lessons to the Chinese in capitalism."

"Have you noticed what he's wearing?" Eric asked.

No one did.

"He's wearing a red bandana around his neck," Eric said. "He won't take it off. Wears it everywhere … like, you know ... the Young Pioneers."

"A young commie, is he?" said Larry, a semi-socialist who two years before worked in Russia. His tone was complimentary.

"What's that about?" Duke asked.

"My kid doesn't like to be bettered," Eric said. "But at school, no matter what, he can't be the overall best. He can't be among those the teachers give favor to, the ones with special status, the ones being groomed for bigger things. Only the Young Pioneers get that. They earn their positions through dedication and hard work, by showing selflessness, setting an example, and preaching the teachings of Chairman Mao. For them to stand out, to show what they've accomplished, they are given a red bandana. Donnie was so envious of that damn bandana, that badge of honor. He told the teacher he wanted one and would do whatever it took to get it. Politely, she told him as a foreigner he didn't qualify for the Young Pioneers. Not willing to accept that, my kid found a store that sells the bandanas and bought one. Now he won't take it off."

"That's exceptional," Duke said.

"That's embarrassing," Eric replied.

"He's a good kid," Exy said. "Don't worry about him. Donnie wants to succeed. There's nothing wrong with that. So, who beside Frank has eaten here?"

"I have," Larry said. "I came with a group that included an Australian woman who just finished teaching in Papua New Guinea. Do you know where that is?"

"We're all internationalists, Larry. We know our onions," Exy said. "Skip the geography lesson and get on with it."

"I asked her what language they speak there, and do you know what she said?"

"Yiddish."

"Pig Latin."

"Broken English."

"She said they speak more than 800 languages," Larry said. "People can't communicate with each other. Get this, when you go to the hospital and the doctor explains what's wrong with you, he often needs a chain of seven or eight translators before his language can be turned into the patient's language."

"What the hell is dating like?" Eric asked.

"Bunch of faff," Exy said.

"All right boys," Frank said. "Here comes the food."

There were several bowls of what looked like rice, brown meat, and curry. There was something like eggrolls, and triangular shaped tarts filled with spicy meat. Lastly was a plate of muttonskewers covered with a hot red sauce.

The five men dug in quickly, forcefully, and unashamed. This vigorous consumption was interrupted by a young Chinese man who approached their table. He wore a black fedora, a white silk scarf, and a black cape. In his hand was a fancy walking stick. There was something theatrical, charismatic, and agreeable about him, and he spoke with a uniquely controlled excitement. It was clear he was among those rare individuals who simply enjoy living. He couldn't have been older than 25.

"Good day, gentlemen," he said with a wave of his hand. "They call me Didi." His acceptable English had an edge of Beijing twang. "Welcome to China. Are you staying at the Youyi Bing Guan – the Friendship Hotel? If you are, I have a proposition for you."

Before the group could say anything, Didi reached into a breast pocket and pulled out a handful of theater tickets. "In your countries I'm what is known as an impresario," he said while adjusting both his cape and hat. "I put on shows and concerts. I entertain people. The new China needs more entertainment and I'm going to provide it. These are tickets to see The Monkey King, a fantastic show with lots of wu shu – you know, fighting, martial arts. Please accept them as a gift."

"In exchange for what?" Duke asked.

"Are you American?" Didi asked. "I love Americans. The tickets are in exchange for friendship, and for you giving my card (which he produced) to the manager at the Friendship Hotel. Please tell him I'd like to hold a dance there and ask him to call me. Very simple."

Three of the foreigners looked at each other. Frank kept eating.

"I think we can do that, Didi," Duke said. "We'll be happy to do that."

Western-style dances, once considered spiritual pollution, were coming to China. Under the leadership of Deng Xiaoping, much was being tried, much was being experimented with. Beginnings were always slow and cautious. New ideas were first discussed at party meetings in small towns and big cities to gauge public reaction. It was Chinese-style democracy. Then the ideas were tested. When China awoke to the necessity of capitalism, it first set up a single special economic zone in the southeastern city of Shen Zhen, across the water from British Hong Kong, already a hotbed of commerce and industry. Small steps. See if it works. And that's what happened with dancing.

Xinhua, the news agency, was involved in the process. It didn't write about dances. Rather, it held one – prior to official party approval. A date was set, a hall (on Xinhua grounds) was secured, and a band (of Xinhua workers) was enlisted. Months prior, in anticipation of the dance, a group of Xinhua journalists (Chinese) received lessons in waltz, tango, foxtrot, and quickstep. They would be the show pieces of the event. Tickets were printed and all foreign workers invited.

"Please do not give these tickets to anyone else," a Xinhua official advised. "These are just for you. Not transferrable." The night of the dance, all varieties of thugs and hoodlums stood outside the hall, pushing and shoving and trying to get in, but they were denied. This was a controlled experiment.

Duke and nearly all his colleagues eagerly attended, although at the outset they acted like wallflowers – the Great Wall Flowers of China. First, it was all too weird for them. Dancing in China? Second, they were intimidated by the sleek moves of the trained Chinese dancers, who, as it turned out, were much better dancers than the westerners they were trying to imitate. After the first hour, the band sat and recorded disco music played. That's when the place broke loose. Everyone danced, even the foreigners. The Chinese journalists were like animals sprung from cages. All over the floor, they were, waving every appendage, gyrating every torso, with not even an attempt to dance with an actual partner. As the dervishes whirled, Feng Yaohua, Duke's boss in the international section, said, "You see, this is very healthy exercise. It is not decadent."

Not long after, this item about another such event appeared in the official English language newspaper, China Daily:

". . . workers at the Beijing Mass Recreation Center gathered in a shabby hall and there were many worried faces. They were holding the first ever city-wide dance competition but were not sure about the official response. When a man wearing a worker's hat entered the hall, the organizers and participants relaxed immediately. He was Beijing Mayor Chen Xitong, and he was there to give his official blessing."

At the Savory and Tasty Food from the West Restaurant, also known as Alister's Restaurant, the tickets-for-introduction deal was sealed with handshakes. Then Didi, soon to capitalize on Mayor Chen's blessing, said something none of the five foreigners had ever heard a Chinese person say: "Thank you, my friends. And now, I bid you adieu. With a flourish of his cape and cane, Didi the impresario was out the door and gone.

"Some dude, eh?" Canadian Larry said.

Frank, in his even-keeled midwestern accent, said, "We should have asked for more tickets."

Eric, for no good reason, stomped his foot on the restaurant floor and created a large puff of dust.

"You hear about the new Xinhua high rise?" Eric asked.

"The apartment building for senior workers?" Frank said. They're fighting to get in there. It's considered choice."

"I'm not sure about that," Eric said. "A balcony on the 11th floor collapsed. It killed a worker on the ground, a peasant laborer from the countryside who had been in the city one day."

"For real? Poor bastard."

"China is a house of cards," Eric said. "The whole bloody country will all fall down soon. I give them credit for trying, but the West – and Japan – just has them outmatched."

The last morsel of Indian food was scraped from the dishes and the group got up to leave.

"I don't want to ride that bus again," Exy said. "Let's see if we can get a cab."

"You guys go on ahead," Duke said. "I'm going to hang around."

The others seemed puzzled.

"Why?"

"I'm going to the new show at the National Art Gallery, just down the road," Duke said. "I'm meeting someone."

"Meeting someone?"

"That Chinese girl people say you're dating?"

"Not really dating. She helps me understand things."

"I'll bet she does."

"Piss off," Duke said, and his four friends did just that.

Song Mei, a poet and student at the Foreign Languages Institute, arrived on time. She and Duke met on the gallery's front steps.

"Thanks for coming," he said.

"My pleasure," she said.

"What have you been doing since we last saw each other?"

"Studying, of course. And writing. But last night we saw a new movie, a Russian movie called *Moscow Does Not Believe in Tears*. Have you seen it?"

"I've never heard of it," Duke said.

"It's about the lives of three young women and their lovers," Song Mei said. "It's so romantic, and tragic. We all cried."

While domestic movies in China are without sex, or even kissing, this Russian film did not hold back.

"The girls from my dormitory really like the way the characters lived their lives, the freedom they had to do what they want, with whomever they want, whenever they want. The freedom to love without constraint or judgment," Song Mei said. "We envied those characters and want to be like them – of course, in theory only."

"Yes," Duke said. "In theory only."

The cold of January bit into Duke's bones. Like all foreigners, he didn't dress properly for winter because he was too used to heated buildings. He looked at Song Mei, in her padded jacket of faded blue, with two sweaters, two shirts and probably two layers of cotton long johns and one of wool. You dress that way when your dorm has virtually no heat. Everyone in Beijing dresses that way in winter. Her appearance wasn't important to Duke, but he eagerly anticipated summer and seeing her in a thin gingham dress and maybe stockings. She'd look nice, even without makeup or styled hair, unless all that suddenly became popular and accepted, like dancing. If you did see a fancy woman in Beijing, you'd assume she's from Hong Kong then be shocked if you discovered she's a local. Such women were on the fringe, stubborn, single-minded, independent, like social outlaws. There were men like that, too, but their concern was business and making money and finding holes in the system, not glamor and fashion, although Didi did dress well.

Duke and Song Mei went inside the gallery.

The show was billed as "The Sixth National Exhibition of the Best Art Works of China," with 919 paintings on display, both professional and amateur. All work was done in the style known as Socialist Realism. There was nothing abstract or modern. As Duke walked through the gallery with Song Mei, he saw in the paintings all the things he had witnessed since his arrival: Worn clothing and shoes, the lunch tins used by everyone, the baskets and scales of the street vendors, those tiny desks in school rooms, the mountains and streams he had visited on vacation, workers tending to all that needed tending to, soldiers protecting and defending all that needed protecting and defending. It was all there. Technically, the paintings were good. Somehow, each contained the indefinable quality of optimism. Faces smiled or showed concentration and determination. Light was used in a way to show China bathed in truth and success. And sprinkled throughout the many elements of a life were subtle, symbolic peeks into a more progressive future, like a much-coveted cassette player or a color TV, just sitting there, incongruous and irrelevant to the painting's overall content. Symbols, no doubt.

The painting Duke liked best was of three female construction workers on a lunch break. One sits in the dirt wearing a hardhat and reading a newspaper. A second rests on her lap, taking the traditional xiu xi, the noon nap. A third rests on the second. They are in the foreground. In the background, right behind them, is a monstrous tire from a huge piece of mostly unseen construction equipment. Clearly, something important was accomplished here, and the respite is well deserved.

"Do you like these paintings?" Duke asked.

"Yes, very much," Song Mei said. "They are quite good."

"There's no one in any of these that speaks to your kind of person or what you do." Duke said.

"Every one of these women is me," she said. "We are Chinese people building a country."

"All I see are workers, peasants, and soldiers. No scientists. No teachers. No poets. Not even a painter."

Song Mei motioned to several of the paintings, started speaking and then stopped.

"Do you see what I mean?" Duke said.

"There was a time, and it is ending, when there were only three respected careers: worker, peasant, soldier," she said. "That era is gone, and a new one is coming. It takes time for the artists to catch up."

"Do you think everyone wants the new era?" Duke asked. "There was a letter in the China Daily recently complaining that intellectuals are taking over the country. They added sarcastically that perhaps the sickle and hammer should be replaced with the spectacles and pencil."

"Nonsense. In China we all want change," Song Mei said. "That letter probably was written by a foreigner who wants China to stay backwards, not to modernize. I have an American professor who complained for 30 minutes about Coca-Cola coming to China. What's the harm in that? I tasted it. It's not even good."

"It grows on you," Duke said.

"Grows on you? Like a plant? A fungus on your skin?"

"No, no, no," Duke said. "It's an expression. It means the more you drink it, the more you like it."

"It grows on you. I understand," Song Mei said. She turned away from Duke and walked toward a sculpture, mumbling, "You grows on me."

They toured the entire exhibit, snacked on sunflower seeds, then took the bus back to the Friendship Hotel. Duke had a new bottle of heart medicine for Song Mei's father. At the hotel gate, as they entered, Song Mei got the usual dirty looks from the guards.

"It's always exciting to come here," she said. "Anything can happen in this place."

In his two-room apartment, Duke went into a desk drawer, pulled out the medicine and gave it to Song Mei, a ritual he'd been performing now for several months. She was especially attentive this day, and looked at him with the dreamy, seeking eyes of a second-rate actor. Duke suspected she had that Russian movie in mind, and perhaps not only in theory. Song Mei was no ingenue. He knew this. He knew she had been married, divorced, and like Duke, was in her 30s. OK, she was from a country where most women did not have sex until marriage, and where men expected virgin brides, but Song Mei, her cultural modesty aside, was from a different realm. The problem was Duke had just given her something of value. As she warmed up to him, he did not want it to appear as if he were taking advantage of his gift. Nothing at all romantic about that, he thought. Worse, perhaps, was the anti-erotic, physical gymnastics required to remove layer upon layer upon layer of clothing. Maybe some would find this exciting. Duke did not. Song Mei had assumed he left the medicine back in his room as an excuse to get her there, which he did. Then the change of mind came.

"You know I give you this medicine to help your father and to free you from one less worry. The gift is heartfelt," he said.

"I know that," Song Mei said. "I know what this gift means."

"Exactly. And I don't want you to think it means anything else. Can I talk about language for a minute?"

"Language?"

"I want to explain something," Duke said. "Let's sit down. It probably won't come out right, but I'm going to try. Do you know the expression 'quid pro quo'?"

"No." Song Mei was puzzled, and not just by the Latin.

"It's Latin," Duke said. "But we use it all the time in America, like it's English. The simple meaning is 'this for that.' The deeper meaning is negative. The deeper meaning is that you won't give something without getting something in return."

Song Mei didn't like this talk, didn't like the sudden mood change and the lesson is Latin.

"That's not you and me. We are not quid pro quo," she said. "Not us. I hope not us. It's not me. Never me."

"And it's not me, either," Duke said. "In America we have something called appearance. Things can look bad even if they aren't bad, they just appear bad."

"To whom? It's just us."

"I'm having a difficult time making my point, and it's not your fault. I guess what I'm saying is we can be close, but at another time. Another time soon. Just not this time."

"Because you think it's deng jia jiao huan. That's my translation of quid pro quo."

"I don't think that's what it is. I know that's not what it is. Even so, I don't want either of us to have the smallest doubt."

Duke studied Song Mei's face as she considered what had just transpired, what its genuine purpose might be, and if the two of them had a future together. She believed Duke a decent man and assumed this was all part of that.

"I understand," she said softly.

"Wonderful," Duke said. "After today, you'll never hear me say quid pro quo again. It's out of my system. In fact, when spring comes, I'm going to buy you an expensive dress from Hong Kong or New York. You'll wear it and we'll go out and have a great time." With some difficulty, he visually took in her entirety and pictured it in such a dress. "Makeup, too."

"I don't want those things," she said. "You mentioned spring. In a few weeks it will be Spring Festival, the Chinese New Year, our biggest celebration. We spend it with our families. I'll be going home to Ningxia. Will you come with me?"

This was not expected. He had just pushed away and now was being pulled back. As much as he wanted to treat Song Mei like any woman in the States, to just enjoy her and live in the moment, forgetting about the possibility of cultural misunderstandings and wide gaps in perception, this situation felt uncomfortable. He fumbled for words then said, "Xinhua has travel plans for all the foreign workers over Spring Festival. We're going to visit five or six cities. Go to Guilin and Sichuan. I've already signed up. I'm sorry."

Song Mei composed herself and, on the outside, casually dismissed his rejection. A sudden cloud burst brought heavy rain against the hotel window, startling the couple.

Pointing to the window, Song Mei said, "Ren bu liu ke, tian liu ke."

"What does that mean?" Duke asked.

"You don't want the guest to stay, but the sky does."

Duke got up from his chair. "Let's have some tea," he said.

As they talked about the best colleges near Duke's suburban Philadelphia home – Penn, Princeton, Swarthmore – the rain stopped.

"I should be getting back to campus for dinner," Song Mei said. "I'm walking so I should leave now."

Duke convinced her to take his bike. He could get it back later. They left his apartment and braced for the cold. The bike was pulled from the overfilled rack and the couple walked it along a path inside the walled compound and toward the gate. "The tire is flat," Song Mei said. Almost immediately, out of nowhere, young Donnie Davies, wearing his red bandana, appeared with a pump.

"I can help you," he said, all chipper and cheery.

"That's very kind of you," Song Mei said. "Are you a Young Pioneer?"

"Sort of," Donnie said, "but not really. I can do anything they can, so it doesn't matter."

"Yeah. How much," Duke asked.

"Yi kuai," he said. "One Chinese dollar."

"That's a lot for air," a surprised Song Mei said.

"It's a lot out there, but not in here," Donnie explained.

Duke paid him, the tire was filled, and Duke and Song Mei went through the gate and out into the street.

"I hope I didn't confuse you with all my stupid talk and hesitancy," Duke said. He kissed her lightly on the cheek, and she was off.

Moscow may not believe in tears, but on this frigid evening, Beijing did. Song Mei could feel the cold dampness drip down her face, and she quickly wiped it away, fearing it would turn to ice. She wiped and pedaled, faster and faster, riding a borrowed bike that she now realized belonged to a borrowed man.

20. The Rescue

Beijing, Beidaihe, 2015

"Larry, it's me. Duke Amici. From the Friendship Hotel. 1984. Do you remember?"

"The Trash Stealer?" Larry asked.

"You knew?"

"Knew what? I didn't know a thing. I didn't know you stole a gas stove. I didn't know you snuck at least one Chinese girl up to your room. I didn't know you told The Portuguese she had an ass for blue jeans."

"I never told her that. And you helped me steal that gas stove. You're back in Beijing?"

"I'm back in Beijing. A bigshot journalism professor training future Xinhua reporters," Larry said. "They have a school now."

"You left in '87," Duke said. "We last spoken, when? Like, 1990? I knew you went back. I saw your post."

"Right. I went back to Canada and taught at my old university. Several years later I took another leave and went to live in Vietnam. Then there was something in South America. Two years ago, I was Beijing bound. The place has changed."

"So I've heard."

"Where are you?"

"You won't believe this, but I'm in Beijing for a couple weeks working on a secret mission with the State Department."

"Sure Mr. Kissinger. And you need my help, obviously."

"I need your help, yes. I need you to help me steal something."

"Like old times. Get me a black knit cap and a hoodie. I'll be there."

The two met outside the little Chinese crepe shop run by a man whose name Duke had forgotten or never learned. Duke and Larry hugged, talked about old times, told each other how bad the other looked.

"How's your Chinese?" Duke asked Larry.

"Pretty good."

"No doubt better than mine. Do you know how to say, 'bomb shelter'?

"No."

"Well look it up on your phone. You're going to tell this crepe guy that the big nose friend of Song Mei wants to go down into the bomb shelter."

"Who is Song Mei?"

"The woman I snuck up to my room in 1984."

"I see. Long-term relationship. Is there anything else you need to tell me? Did the State Department really send you? What are we stealing?"

"A trunk," Duke said. "It's down in the bomb shelter."

Larry talked to the old cook, who appeared to remember Mr. Big Nose. But the cook shook his head and waved his hand, as if something was wrong. He took the two men to the back of the shop. The old wooden door had been replaced with a locked steel door. Solid and secure.

"Ask him if he has the key," Duke told Larry.

The key, they learned, was in the hands of city administrators.

"What now?" Larry asked.

"We've got to get down there another way," Duke said. "Through one of the main entrances, I guess. But then how do we find our way back into the bowels of this underground city and the small tunnel under the crepe shop? We've got to regroup."

"Yes," Larry said. "Regroup. Can we buy a crepe?"

The two men ate crepes and proposed and rejected at least a half dozen ridiculous ideas. Duke developed a headache. Larry asked him about his wife."

"I live in Florida. She took a job in Philadelphia and moved there. That should tell you enough."

"What kind of job?"

"Head of development for the Philadelphia Museum of Art," Duke said. "She raises money. She's tied into Philadelphia society and its league of rich philanthropists, of which she is one. How is Shelly?"

"Prenup?"

"None of your business."

"That means yes. Shelly? She's here with me, making sure I don't run into the arms of some young Chinese woman who wants to come to North America."

"Are you physically capable of handling something like that?"

"On good days, maybe. After coffee and a lot of vitamins."

Then the idea came.

"You have an iPhone, don't you?" Duke asked Larry.

"A new one. Made right here in China."

"Give it to me."

Duke allowed Larry's phone to track his own, then left his phone at the base of the steel door in the crepe shop.

"I'm still hungry," Duke said. "Let's get some ice cream."

In a short time, Duke and Larry were in the still-open mall section of the bomb shelter, at the ice cream shop they both visited years ago.

"How many scoops?" Larry asked.

"No time for that. Is your phone working down here?"

"You know the Chinese. They think of everything. When people began paying for everything by phone, they installed special antennae boosters down here," Larry said, looking at his device. "It's working."

Using the "find phone" feature and the phone's compass, they headed off into the approximate direction of the crepe shop. Deeper and deeper into the underground city they went. "Is that the roller rink?" Larry asked. The corridors got smaller and smaller as the tunnels fanned out into a complex network. A door and a warning sign – Do Not Enter -- blocked their way. Larry jiggled the door. He turned and pulled on the knob. The door opened. There were no more shops, and scant lighting. Duke and Larry could hear rats, and a few brushed against their feet. Water dripped on them from above. One section of ceiling was damaged. The intruders had to step over a large pile of dirt. Duke's claustrophobia visited but he contained it. They kept walking, following the phone-tracker and using the compass but unsure if they were approaching their target. Occasionally, the signal cut out. It was August, and the tunnel grew hot.

"Call my phone," Duke said to Larry. "If the crepe shop owner picks up, tell him it's the Big Nose and ask him to bang on the steel door."

Larry did this, and the old cook answered. Then, at a not unreasonable distance away, they heard clanging. They followed. There was the trunk.

"I was worried that whoever put the door on took the trunk," Duke said. "We're damn lucky," and he picked up the key still hidden under the rock.

"I still wish I knew what this was all about," Larry said. "Since I'm an accomplice."

"In the chest are seditious writings," Duke said. "Essays. Poems. Assorted papers and a novel. We are rescuing them."

"The author is your old girlfriend? Thirty years later you're doing this? That's too weird."

"We went into business together," Duke said.

"Even weirder. So this is not your State Department assignment? If you even have one, you bullshitter."

"Not this. I've got that tomorrow. This is a side job."

By the weight of the chest, Duke could tell its contents had been undisturbed. He and Larry carried it back the way they came. About 100 feet from the mall, still on the forbidden side of the unlocked door, they were confronted by a boyish security guard in clothes too big for him.

"Tingzhi (halt)," he shouted while raising a billy club. "What's in there? Where are you going?"

Larry stepped up.

"Ni hao. Ni hao (hello, hello). Do you live down here?"

"What's in there?" the guard asked. "Who are you? Why are you here?"

"This chest is filled with gold," Larry said. "It's Mao's gold. Years ago, he put it down here. He hid it from the Communist Party. They want it back and asked us to get it."

Duke flinched at the mention of gold.

"Ta shi fungqu de ren (He's a comedian)" Duke told the guard. Then to Larry, "Show him your Xinhua ID. Tell him you're picking up old papers for them." Larry did that and Duke opened the trunk to show the guard the papers on top of the false bottom. The guard grumbled and banged his stick against the palm of his hand, then let them pass, telling them never to come back.

Outside, they hailed a cab (much easier than in '84) and put Song Mei's treasures into its back seat. Larry was thanked, over and over, then dropped off at his downtown apartment. Duke retrieved his phone then went onto the American embassy. Before entering, he opened the chest, took out the papers, removed the false bottom, shuffled through the items and took out the gem-studded, gold hairpin that resembled a raging flame. It went into a pocket. Inside the embassy, he explained who he was, what he was doing for the State Department, and asked if he could leave the now-locked trunk there and have it shipped home with him on his return flight.

"What's in it?" he was asked.

"Papers and writings belong to a businesswoman named Song Mei, who after the arrest of Yu Xiaodan went missing. She contacted me and asked me to get them out."

"We are aware of the Song Mei case," the person said. "Are you her friend?"

"Business partner," Duke said. "I'm trying to find her."

"Be sure to let us know if you do."

The following day, Duke Amici left his room at the Hilton Beijing around 9 a.m. and arrived early for his arbitration session at Zhongnanhai. He entered through the southern gate and was greeted by signage espousing long life to the great Communist Party of China and lauding the invincible thought of Mao Zedong. He was afforded the luxury of walking around and tried to determine where the residences were located, assuming that's where Song Mei would be held, as opposed to a prison or jail. In the air was the smell of unfamiliar cleaning products. As he walked, he tried pushing that odor aside and sniffed around for the scent of Song Mei's expensive perfume, Jo Malone London, Rose & White Musk Absolu. He found none of that. Duke boldly opened a few doors and peered in before he was directed to the non-distinct meeting room where the case of the American student who wandered into North Korea would be discussed.

In Duke's pocket was the priceless Ming Dynasty hair pin. He asked an officious-looking person if Peng Guo was at Zhongnanhai, and if he might be attending the session. No, the newly appointed deputy premier was out of town. An unexpected setback.

Bromwell Clingman, the undersecretary of state, gave Duke a quick briefing. Then the meeting began. To Duke's surprise, it ended after only two hours and to the full agreement of all parties. The terms were these. Jason Benchman would:

Be expelled from Fudan University and denied all academic credits earned.
Return to his home country and be forever banned from China.
Be fined $10,000 (likely paid by the State Department).

The case was then turned over to the two state departments to work on the timetable and details. Duke exited the meeting room, hoping to further roam Zhongnanhai. Then his phone rang.

"This is Daniel," the voice said, with exuberance. "Huang Defu. The guy who visited you in Florida. I finally made it to the Central Committee."

"Daniel, old friend. Was it you who brought me here?" Duke said, suspecting some stratagem of unknown purpose. "Did you put me on this arbitration panel?"

"Forget that," Daniel said. "Let's go to the beach."

Duke pictured Daniel on the Jacksonville fishing pier, almost crying because he was so happy. Daniel, Duke assumed, wanted to return the favor and bring him to his beach. Daniel's tone on the phone evinced thoughtfulness and nostalgia.

"I'm sorry. It's impossible," Duke said. "I've got to keep searching for my friend."

Daniel laughed loudly. "Don't be such a goof. She's at the beach. That's why we're going. We leave tomorrow."

The beach referred to by Huang Defu is Beidaihe, about 186 miles east of Beijing on the Yellow Sea, a two-hour ride by bullet train. But it is not just a beach. It is a notorious summer retreat for China's political elite; a place where fresh deals, schemes and policies are hatched. It is China's equivalent to America's smoke-filled room.

Regular tourists, however, do go there as well. In fact, Duke and Song Mei went there for three days in the summer of 1985. They had separate accommodations in a musty rooming house. At that stage of undeveloped Chinese tourism, beachgoers did not bring bathing suits to Beidaihe. Rather, they rented them, choosing from an assortment (none of them attractive) hanging on clotheslines strung up on the beach. Duke remembered Song Mei looking all puffy and frumpy in her suit, which she wore shyly.

There are 20 bullet trains a day running from Beijing to Beidaihe. Duke and Daniel took an early one. In 1993, Chinese trains traveled at a speed of about 30 miles per hour. Then, in a single decade, China built a 40,000-kilometer (24,855 miles) network of high-speed trains running as fast as 220 mph. It takes travelers 4 hours to go from Beijing in the north to Shanghai in the south, about 1,200 miles, like going from Philadelphia to Miami.

The bullet trains are sleek and new; clean, unmarked and comfortable. Duke and Daniel rode in business class. The seats resemble individual capsules that operate like machines. With plenty of leg room, they recline completely, like a bed. At each seat are an assortment of free snacks.

Duke and Daniel sat up rather than reclined. Once they were on their way, Daniel produced a business card.

"See this," he said, handing the card to Duke."

"President and Editor-in-chief, Xinhua News Agency," Duke read. "Impressive. In winter, do you turn the heat on now?"

"We do turn on the heat," Daniel said. "Xinhua is now the largest news agency in the world. We have 170 bureaus abroad and 32 in China. When you worked there, I think we produced the news in five languages. Now we publish in 20."

"I saw your new North American headquarters in Midtown Manhattan."

"At 1540 Broadway. Top floor of a towering skyscraper. From our offices you can look down on the New York Times."

From the train's oversized windows, Duke watched the landscape whiz by, noticing that there were no more donkey carts pulling oversized loads.

"You seem satisfied with your decision to return to China, to be part of the system and to work within the system. You've gone a long way. Central Committee, right?"

"By virtue of my position at Xinhua, I'm on the party's Central Committee. It's almost hard to grasp the importance of this. I'm on speaking terms with the select group of people running China, with the architects of our economic miracle, with the people who pulled 800 million citizens out of poverty and made China a world power."

"And killed 10,000 in Tiananmen Square," Duke said.

Daniel was quiet.

"I apologize," Duke said. "I understand your enthusiasm. No American anywhere could have predicted China's rise. They would have considered it an impossibility. Of course, you've got to give some credit to the voracious consumers in the U.S. who buy all your stuff."

"God bless them," Daniel said.

"Down to business. You know all these powerful people. You've set a meeting with Peng Guo?"

"It's set," Daniel said. "We will have lunch with him and his family. After lunch, we go to his guest house and finalize the arrangement. I don't expect any problems. You have an acceptable, what should I call it, incentive?"

"Peng Guo collects Ming Dynasty artifacts, correct?"

"He's a fanatic about history, especially the Mings. What do you have? You couldn't? Could you?"

Duke reached into his pocket and pulled out a velvet bag.

"Put this under a magazine or something before you look at it," Duke said.

Daniel pulled it from the bag, said something in Chinese that Duke did not understand, then put the gold, gem-encrusted hair pin back into the bag.

"Astounding. I don't believe what I just saw." A pause, then, "You must love her."

"This is not about love," Duke said. "It's about keeping a promise. Someday, not today, I'll explain it all to you."

Then there was quiet.

Duke and Daniel checked into the Holiday Inn, a breathtaking high-rise a mere 11-minute walk to Golden Dream Beach and 18 minutes from Xin'ao Underwater World. With a few hours to spare before their meeting, they dressed in shorts and went down to the water. It was hot but not unbearable. The morning sea breeze was cooling. To Duke, the setting resembled New Jersey and towns like Ocean City and Wildwood. It smelled like those places: the salt air, that hint of dead aquatic life, the suntan lotion. He had to remind himself that what he saw was not the Atlantic, or even the Pacific, but a large, harbor-like sea.

"You like it here?" Duke asked his companion.

"It's quite pleasant," Daniel said. "But no, I don't have the same feeling as in Jacksonville. I still feel contained and restricted."

"But you're working on it, right? Being on the Central Committee, have you accomplished anything … anything that has changed China?"

Daniel grimaced as he and Duke walked the sands.

"I'm new," Daniel said. "Change takes time. There are 200 of us on the committee. I'm one person. The committee elects the party secretary, the members of the Politburo, and the Central Military Commission, so I get a say. We go through what you might call a democratic process, but in the end, when we finish, the public is told all votes are unanimous. What I've done outside this process is to encourage more people to speak honestly and candidly, to treat the party like any fallible group of people. I've made progress with that, slow progress. What I've also done is speak out against retribution, vendettas, and purges – like the one against your partner's friend, Yu Xiaodan."

Daniel reached into the surf to pick up some shells.

"I like to bring these home," he said.

"You're a good man, Daniel. I appreciate what you are doing for me, and I'm thankful for what you are doing for China. If I haven't stressed that, let me do it now." Duke patted his friend on the back. The sun was almost overhead. "Time to go back."

As they headed off the beach, they noticed a commotion between a white woman, perhaps an American, and a vendor renting beach umbrellas. The woman spoke fluent Chinese and was yelling, something about using her umbrella for only two hours and being charged for three. The vendor was trying to back off from the hysterical woman, who thrashed at him with her verbal assault.

"That's very Chinese," Daniel said. "The insane screaming to get your way, we call that da ma. Literally it is 'big mother,' but it means what you see. She must live here. She must have learned it from the locals."

When Duke and Daniel were within a few feet of the fracas, Duke said, "I think I know that woman."

She was dressed in a sleeveless yellow cotton shirt and three-quarter-length Capri pants. On her head was a New York Yankees hat. Underneath, her hair was short and formless. It was Ainsley Acker, from the Friendship Hotel. In her early 50s now, like Duke.

Taking a 20-yuan bill from his wallet, Duke approached the shaken vendor and put the money in his pocket. In Chinese, he said, "She's mean, but not a bad person."

Ainsley Acker turned to direct her rage at this interloper. Nothing came out of her mouth. Her eyes squinted in the sun as she looked up and down.

"Shorts don't become you," she said. "I hope you know that."

"Is that you, Ainsley? I'm Duke. Duke Amici. Do you remember?"

"I remember. I'm the one who led you around Beijing, trying to show you what was what, where this is and that is, how to act and what to say. I was like your mother, for God's sake."

"You always knew how to make a guy feel good. That hasn't changed." And they embraced.

"What are you doing here?" Ainsley said. "You look well. You didn't have to pay off that thieving umbrella man. I was handling it. You always were a considerate dear, even if bothersome."

"I've been here just a few days. On business in Beijing. This is a side trip."

"Business? Didn't you write little stories?"

"I wrote little stories and edited little stories. Then I went into business."

"Successful, I'm sure," she said.

"Not at first, but eventually. I've got this machine that makes water."

"Marvelous," Ainsley said. "Water is in great demand."

"The technology we employ has many applications. NASA is looking at it."

"When they go to Mars, maybe they'll take you."

"Serious for a moment, please. What have you been doing all this time? Did you never leave? Oh, this is my friend, Daniel, Huang Defu."

"Nice to meet you," Ainsley said. "I left for a short time. I returned to our family house in California. But the boy – you know I have a son – didn't like it. Beijing was his home. His Chinese was better than his English. He friends were in Beijing. He knew how to get around China. California was cool at first, but that didn't last. After Stanford, he wanted to come back. He's all I have, so I came back with him. He's an engineer. Works for a big company called Phoenix Development. Married a Chinese girl. We both have apartments in the same building. It's a wonderful building. Not like the Friendship Hotel. I returned to teaching. The students are so different. Like spoiled Americans."

"How are things at Phoenix Development?" Duke asked.

"Are you familiar with it?"

"I've heard of it."

"We're worried. The Chinese grabbed the owner, a woman named Song Mei, and hid her away. It's possible they might shut down the company. The boy worries he'll lose his job."

"Tell him not to worry. She'll pop back up."

"You're quite the optimist," Ainsley said.

The sun was getting hotter now as the day dragged on.

"Would you like to have dinner?" Ainsley asked.

"That would be sensational. I wish I could. We're not exactly here on pleasure. There are some important matters to take care of. Then we head back to Beijing and then I leave for the States. I guarantee that next time I'll look you up."

It was difficult for Duke to say no, but he needed to change clothes, get the golden hair pin, and meet Deputy Premier Peng Guo for lunch. Duke did something he never did in 1985 back at the

Friendship Hotel. He kissed Ainsley Acker on the cheek and wished her well.

The table was set for six in a private section of the over-decorated restaurant. Peng Guo introduced his wife and 12-year-old daughter to Daniel and Duke.

"I'm afraid my son cannot make it," Peng Guo said. "He's a modern artist and he decided to spend the entire day painting the sea. The problem is when he's finished, it doesn't look at all like the sea." The deputy premier laughed at his own joke. "Let me show you his work."

The pictures on the phone used multiple colors, some faint, some strong. There was considerable white space and an attractive geometry. Most were abstract. Some had a modicum of realism. A futuristic city rose from sharp strokes of color, zooming here and there, rising and bursting.

"Lovely," Duke said. "Quite good."

The group sat. Duke looked over his shoulder at an elaborately carved dragon.

"We are here today to express friendship," Peng Guo said. He was a less-than-handsome man, less-than-graceful, and less-than-convincing, but more-than-dangerous. His thick hair was dyed midnight black. Speaking to Duke, he said, "I hear that yesterday you served China by helping solve a diplomatic problem. You are a wise, kind, and worthy person. China is grateful to you."

Daniel gave a gift of expensive chocolates to Peng Guo's wife. Duke rose and said, "In the interest of friendship I'd like to give your daughter a gift."

He took the velvet bag from his pocket and set it on the table in front of Peng Guo, whose enormous expectations could not be hidden. He let the bag sit for a minute before opening it, touching only the velvet and feeling the shape inside. When he pulled out the treasure, he arranged it on the white tablecloth and put his hand to his mouth. His wife placed an arm around him as he cried. Peng Guo's daughter jumped out of her seat and approached the object, causing the father to hold her back with one arm.

Composing himself, Peng Guo said, "I have heard of such things. I have heard that certain people possessed them. I dreamed of owning something this rare and exquisite, knowing that would be the zenith of happiness. Yet I never imaged a relic this beautiful would ever be placed within my grasp."

With his index finger, Peng Guo counted the circle of 12 stones. He wiped away a small trace of beach sand. Rising, he went to Duke, placed the fist of his left hand into the palm of his right hand and bowed deeply.

"Our bond of friendship is everlasting," he said.

"May I?" asked Duke. He took the hair pin, showed it to the daughter, and placed it comfortably in her long hair. She giggled. Peng Guo took photos with his phone, then removed the hairpin. The daughter moaned and frowned and had to be calmed by her mother.

After an elaborate meal of 10 dishes consisting mostly of seafood, Daniel, Duke, and Peng Quo retired to a guest house. It was modern, well-equipped, with air conditioning and a new kitchen. Modest by American standards. Party officials, being communists, like comfort but try to avoid excess for the sake of image. Peng Guo laid out his terms.

Song Mei would:

Be released and have all her rights restored. She would be allowed to travel freely in and outside China.

Turn over to the state Yu Xiaodan's shares in all her businesses. She would keep her own shares.

Give user data from Ge-GePay to the government and return 20 percent of the profit on that data to customers.

Quick, simple, and straightforward. A deal.

"When can we see Song Mei?" Duke asked. "When can she leave?"

"I'll have someone take you to her," the deputy premier said. "She can leave whenever she likes. From now on, I am her friend. She will no longer associate with Yu Xiaodan. I'll be the one offering her help and patronage."

Duke contained his enthusiasm and marveled at his success. A promise fulfilled. How in God's name did he pull this off? Out of curiosity, he asked, "What will happen to Yu Xiaodan?"

Peng Guo answered, "Ta ma de."

In American parlance: "Screw Yu Xiaodan."

An aide led Duke and Daniel to where Song Mei was held. Outside the front door was a guard, large and threatening and unlike the punk in the bomb shelter. Daniel showed the guard his identification and said Song Mei was being released to him. The guard appeared to know the release was imminent and unlocked the door without question, saying something under his breath.

Duke, having heard the guard, asked Daniel, "What is xiao san zi?"

"Don't be offended," Daniel said.

"I won't be," Duke said.

"It means 'little third person,' or mistress. He thinks Song Mei is your mistress."

When they walked through the door, Duke noticed first that Song Mei was safe and looked well. Next, he noticed she was packing. She looked up, stunned to see Duke.

"You came. You found me," she said, and took a half step toward him.

In this situation, any other woman, friend, acquaintance – perhaps a stranger -- would have leapt forward and smothered the rescuer with affection and gratitude. Song Mei did not. She stood her ground.

"You found me. You looked for me, and you found me. I could have been anywhere in China. But I'm here, and so are you."

Duke was peppy and full of joy. He wanted Song Mei to smile.

"I promised you, didn't I?" he said. "You're packing. Did you know we were coming? Can word travel that fast?"

How to explain?

"What you have done, I can never, ever forget," Song Mei said. "You are the exceptional friend. Your loyalty is beyond the loyalty of a person for his country. My life, much of my entire adult life, has been influenced by you. I'm not sure if you are aware. It's true. Your shadow follows me. It guides me. Your mind communicates with my mind when you walk, when you talk, when you sleep, when you are near and when you are far. From this day forward, I am your servant. There is nothing I can do for you that is too much. You've got to know that. Please know that. But as the person I've become, with responsibility as wide as the largest ocean, I cannot rely on others. I had to find a way out myself. My dear friend, you were what Americans call a backup plan, my insurance. I hope this doesn't anger you."

"You mean you got out of this jam yourself? How."

"I called your wife."

"You called my wife?"

For Duke, it was as if the air in the room had changed. First, he was not the hero. Second, his at-a-distance wife had somehow gotten involved.

"Yesterday, Phoenix Development donated $5 million to the Philadelphia Museum of Art, in part to sponsor an exhibition by one of China's top new modern artists, who happens to be the son of one of our leaders, Peng Guo," Song Mei said. "It will premiere during a celebration of Chinese New Year, with fireworks and a festive parade up the art museum steps. It will be quite an affair."

Duke took the easy way out. He laughed. He laughed hard.

"That bastard! That bastard Peng. He double dipped. He got us both."

"What did you give him?" Song Mei asked.

Daniel grew uncomfortable. He turned and faced the door.

"The gold hairpin with the rubies and sapphires."

"I would have chosen the same."

Duke moved closer to Song Mei, pushed away the hair over her ear and whispered. "I've got the whole chest. It's at the American embassy. We're getting out of here and taking it with us."

Physically, this was the closest he had been to her in almost three decades. Song Mei could feel the heat of his mouth and lips.

"I couldn't have done that myself," she said, "so maybe you're not my backup. You're my partner."

When the 4 p.m. bullet train pulled out of Beidaihe for Beijing, Song Mei, Duke, and Daniel were on it. When they got off, Duke turned to Daniel and vowed that someday soon they'll be back in the U.S. together again. Maybe go to Niagara Falls or the Grand Canyon or both. Then Duke repeated one of the best know phrases in China, the words Mao Zedong supposedly spoke to his successor, Hua Guofeng: Ni ban shi, wo fang xin.

"With you in charge, I'm at ease."

Then he walked off with the former poet, and once, only once, and by accident, addressed her as Mei-Mei.

21. Duke and Song Mei Go Home

Beijing-Washington-Jacksonville, 2015

The debriefing at the U.S. Embassy took several hours. Surprisingly, the conversation dealt more with the missing-now-found Chinese businesswoman than with the kid caught in Korea.

"We consider the rescue of Emily Song by an American businessman a coup of sorts for human rights," said Undersecretary of State Bromwell Clingman. "The fact that the businessman was coincidentally in China on a State Department matter, and that the person rescued was an old and dear friend of the person who found her, well, I have to tell you, this is a story the news media will go big with. And it's something, frankly, the State Department will want its name on. Do you understand what I'm saying? There is going to be publicity. I hope you are ready and willing to deal with it in a positive, professional, and cooperative manner. Can you do that?"

Emily Song looked at Duke like a young Chinese girl hearing English for the first time.

"To begin with," Duke said. "It was not all that dramatic. There was no danger, no mystery, no cloak-and-dagger. I just asked around, gathered information, and did what any friend would do."

He looked at Emily and gave an insignificant nod that also asked a question. Emily raised her eyebrows. She raised her shoulders. She nodded yes.

"But yes, we can handle some publicity." Duke said. "We will do some interviews. I trust, however, the story in its entirety, the down-and-dirty details, can remain private. There can be nothing said that will risk Miss Song's return to China and her ability to do business there."

"Absolutely," the undersecretary said. "We will work together to craft a safe but convincing narrative. That can be done with our public affairs people on the plane ride home."

And so it was agreed.

"Incidentally, the ride home will be a treat," Clingman said.

There was one day's rest. Early the next morning, a shuttle took Duke, Emily, her trunk, and a large contingent of State Department officials out to the plane known as Air Force One, arguably the most luxurious aircraft in the world. Duke and the State Department contingent had arrived on the more modest Air Force Two, the vice president's plane also used for State Department business. It returned home without them. At the same time, Air Force One, the president's plane, was being outfitted with new electronics. The gear had to be tested (without the president) and did so successfully on a test flight to China. Consequently, it was available to ferry official passengers home just as Duke and Emily were leaving Beijing.

The customized Boeing 747-200B has 4,000 square feet of floor space on three levels. That's bigger than most homes. It has meeting rooms, bedrooms, office space, rooms for relaxing, a five-star kitchen, a medical facility, and some regular, although oversized and highly comfortable, seating.

"When you took me to that American Embassy party on the Fourth of July, I was disappointed," Emily told Duke as they prepared for takeoff. "That hurt you. I know. I expected it to be grander. Well, this is grand, and I'm no longer disappointed."

Everyone had a magnificent lunch and a magnificent dinner.

When it came time to sleep, Duke and Emily were offered beds. Unsure of the exact arrangement, they declined and chose to recline their seats, which were nearly as comfortable as beds.

Before retiring, Duke said to Emily, "We'll be well rested when we arrive in Washington around 9 a.m. I'd like to rent a car, load up the treasure chest and drive straight on to Florida. No way I'm going to put that chest on a commercial plane. I'd like you to stay in Florida with me, hide out at my home for a while. You can't risk having another commie thug grabbing you off the street and taking you away. Can't risk that."

Over the next 15 minutes, Emily Song refused the offer three times, then consented.

"I'll bet you can almost afford a plane like this," Duke said. "How much are you worth? Really. Maybe 20 billion?"

"Less than that," she said, "but close. What you and everyone else doesn't realize is that my so-called money is not sitting in a checking account waiting for me to write checks on it. It's working capital. It's invested. It's real estate and shares of companies. You cannot spend it."

"But it sure will get you a lot of credit," Duke said. "I cannot even remotely calculate what that kind of fortune can do. If you line up all the dollars, do they reach to the moon? To Saturn? To the next galaxy? For you, it's like money doesn't exist. You acquire whatever you want without financial consideration. That's how I view it."

"It's not entirely like that."

Feeling good, heading home, relieved of almost all anxiety, Duke decided to have some fun with Song Mei's fortune.

"With all I've done for you, running around China, poking my head into places where it didn't belong, sniffing for a scent of your perfume and hoping you weren't dead or behind bars, I'm going to ask you for a favor. For a brief moment in time, I want you to put me in a situation where I can feel as if money is as abundant as air."

"And how do I do that?"

"When we get to Washington, before we leave for Jacksonville, I want you to buy me a $10,000 suit. It's not about the cost. Or even the suit. I care about the feeling. I want to experience it just one time. The feeling of unlimited riches. Maybe it will help me better understand you."

"It won't. Can you buy a $10,000 suit in Washington?" Emily asked.

"The town is loaded with ambassadors and the most pompous, self-important people in the world. There has to be a place to buy a $10,000 suit."

After Emily shut her eyes, Duke checked to make sure he could get a car, preferably a Chrysler 300, at the airport when they arrived. He also made a morning reservation for a fitting at a place called Edmund & Perry, where you could indeed buy a $10,000 suit.

It was the quaintest of shops, like something out of Dickens, with a hand-painted shingle and nothing electric on the outside. When Duke and Emily walked up to the front door of the Brownstone, a large man with four Super Bowl rings walked out.

"Welcome to our little place of business," the mustachioed proprietor said. "You must be Mr. Amici. Would you like to start with espresso or champagne?" Since it was 10 a.m., they chose espresso and were directed toward croissants and caviar.

"What is your preferred music?" asked the proprietor, who was the Edmund of Edmund & Perry.

"Ah, Beethoven," Duke said, and soon after Fur Elise was playing.

"Please sit," said the proprietor, presenting two silk upholstered chairs and explaining the process at Edmund & Perry. "You will choose every single aspect of your suit, selecting from among 10,000 fabrics and deciding on the stitching, the number of pockets, the lining, the buttons, everything. If you want, we can monogram your name on the inside of your jacket. We will carefully and precisely take 32 measurements to ensure the most comfortable fit. Do you have an idea of what you are looking for?"

Duke did.

"I'm not fond of contemporary suits," he said. "The jackets are too short, too tight, and too shiny. I want something retro. I want to look like Cary Grant in 1936."

"You are a man of class," Edmund said. "I respect that. We have a number of styles that I'm sure will satisfy you. For the fabric, let's start with Vitale Barberis Canonico from the mills of Italy's Biella region."

Duke touched the wool. "Yes, this even feels like Cary Grant," he said.

"Is this one of your less-expensive or most-expensive fabrics?" Emily asked.

Edmund coughed. "They are all of the highest quality, but in terms of price this falls in about the middle."

"Show us your most expensive wool," Emily said.

Edmund looked at Duke with appreciation. "Your wife takes very good care of you."

"I'm not his wife," Emily said.

"My apologies," Edmund said, with no change in demeanor. "What I meant is you treat him like a king."

"We call him a king," Emily said. "We call him the King of Ningxia."

"Stop," Duke said.

"Ningxia. And where is that?" the proprietor asked.

After a sip of espresso, she answered, "Far away. Very far away."

There were many questions for Duke regarding his expected activity while wearing the suit, and, of course, the critical question related to the tailoring of fine trousers: "What side do you dress on?"

Duke was stumped.

Edmund nodded toward his crotch.

"The left," Duke said, and blushed.

With the suit business concluded, Duke and Emily grabbed two croissants for the road, walked out onto Fourth Street and bumped into the Swedish ambassador, who was coming in. The ambassador smiled, tipped his fedora, and proudly entered the womb-like comfort of Edmund & Perry. Duke and Emily got into their roomy Chrysler 300 with its multi-million-dollar cargo and headed south on Interstate 95.

Washington to Jacksonville is a 10-hour, 700-mile drive. During that drive, Duke and Emily ate at McDonald's, the Waffle House, and the Golden Lotus, where the Chinese food was horrible. They bought souvenirs at South of the Border and gas at places where the attendants used to say, "Yawl come back now, hear?" and still do if you buy boiled peanuts. They talked and they were silent. Some sentences were one word. There was music Emily Song did not like. And questions and requests from each side. Duke: Tell me about your second husband. Emily: Are American women prettier than Chinese? Duke: Did you really believe that stuff about the pear? Emily: How many girlfriends does an American man have before marriage? Duke: What was it like under those dead bodies at Tiananmen?

When they crossed the Georgia state line and entered Florida, a mere 40 minutes from their destination, the billionaire former poetess and the man recently fitted for a $10,000 suit stopped for free orange juice at the Florida welcome center. It was closed.

The Chrysler 300 pulled into Duke's neighborhood around 11 p.m. Under darkness, he and Emily brought the chest into his one-story, four-bedroom, Florida-style home in Jacksonville's Mandarin section, named that way, Duke thought, because oranges must have once grown there.

"I hope you have the key to the trunk," Emily said.

"Got the key," which Duke pulled from his pocket and gave to her.

Before opening the chest, Emily said, "Let's sit for a minute."

"In the Florida room," Duke said, and he turned on the lights there. An historic, black-and-white photo hung on the wall. Emily asked about it.

"That's beautiful," she said. "It's Manhattan, from above, correct? What year?"

"The year is 1949," Duke said. "That's a photo of the world's largest airliner flying over the world's tallest building. A Boeing 377 Stratocruiser nearly touching the tip of the Empire State Building. All representing power, glory, and triumph."

"Where's the tallest building now?" Emily asked.

"Dubai," Duke said. "What do you want to talk about?"

"Two things. First, I'm returning my shares of Ningxia Enterprises to you. I don't need them. I probably only took them for spite, and I apologize for that. I was being small. A kind of revenge. I've got more than enough to focus on without Ningxia. You deserve to run and control your own company. As of today, as of right now, consider yourself the real King of Ningxia. The queen resigns. I'll still help you with certain contracts, as will Peng Guo. You're doing fine and you'll continue to do fine." She extended her hand in an exaggerated, comical motion.

"Shake on it," Emily Song said, smiling a relaxed, natural, sincere smile for the first time in a long time.

Duke, not fanatical about money or control, liked having Emily as part of the company.

"Really, the suit was enough," he said. "We'll go into the office tomorrow and work on a couple of things that need our attention. Like partners. Things have been piling up."

"The suit was a gesture, a kiss on the cheek," Emily said. "This is neither a gesture nor a gift. It is rightfully yours. I was just an investor who saw an excellent return on my investment. Now I'm out."

Duke considered a real kiss on the cheek but instead sealed the deal with a manly handshake.

"What else did you want to talk about before opening the chest?"

Emily Song shifted in her chair, exhibiting discomfort.

"When I spoke to your wife, Francine, about the donation and the art exhibition for Peng Guo's son, she asked me to pass something along to you."

"Yes ..."

"She wanted me to tell you she filed for divorce."

History with a person, even when some of it is bad, occupies a place of importance inside one's consciousness. When that history's continuum abruptly ends, with every assurance it will never restart, the heart hurts.

"It was inevitable," Duke said. "Not a surprise. I knew the specter was there, crouching and ready to pounce. Now it pounced. Time to move ahead as a man with one less, what, one less sword hanging over one's neck. What else did she say?"

"That's all."

"I'll bet she said, 'Go ahead. Now you can have him.'"

"She didn't. Time to open the chest," Emily said.

In the living room, she put the key in the rusted lock and opened the lid, first taking out her papers and manuscript.

"Let's get that book translated and published," Duke said.

"Let's."

Emily removed the false bottom and inspected a few of the items. Cushioning peanut shells, real, not synthetic, fell to Duke's carpet.

"Everything is fine," she said. "It all survived the gentle ride on Air Force One and a bumpier trip down Interstate 95."

She pulled out a $20 million, 16th-century, Ming Dynasty, blue-and-white porcelain vase, inspected it, looked at Duke's $500, unadorned, Home Depot fireplace mantle and put it directly in the center. Emily stepped back, didn't like the symmetry, and moved the vase to the left.

"Temporary," Emily said. "Just temporary. I want to see what my treasure looks like in America."

"Make sure we lock the door tonight," Duke said. "We need rest now. What a day, huh? There's a guest room you can use. It has everything you'll need. I should tell you I have security cameras set up around the house. Like the ones at the Friendship Hotel. Remember? If you go wandering into someone else's room, the authorities will know."

Emily returned the lock to the chest. "In an American movie, I once heard a pretty girl with big hair tell a handsome man, 'Dream on.' What does that mean?"

Duke nodded with a thin smile that said "touche."

"You like movie quotes?" he said. "Here's one: 'Louie, I think this is the beginning of a beautiful friendship.'"

"I'm not Louie and this isn't the beginning," Song Mei said.

"I know. But it's a good movie. We'll watch it tomorrow after dinner."

The house now smelled of Jo Malone London, Rose & White Musk Absolu.

"Good night," Duke said.

For the first time ever, together yet separate, comfortable yet uncomfortable, Duke Amici and Song Mei, aka Emily Song, fell asleep safely in the Mandarin section of Jacksonville, Florida, under the wavering light of a protective, diffusive, capitalist moon. Neither was sure there would be a second night like this, but both were enjoying this one and the mere prospect that there could possibly be another.